The Genesis and Struggle *of the* Anya-Nya in Southern Sudan

Professor Storrs McCall
and Dr. Lam Akol

Africa World Books
Pty Ltd

A Note from the Publisher

The publisher wishes to acknowledge and thank Dr Douglas H. Johnson for his invaluable help and support for Africa World Books and its mission of preserving and promoting African cultural and literary traditions and history. Dr Johnson and fellow historians have been instrumental in ensuring that African people remain connected to their past and their identity. Africa World Books is proud to carry on this mission.

Design and typesetting by Africa World Books

Preface

The bulk of this book was a manuscript on the Anya-Nya written by Prof Storrs McCall, a Canadian who had developed great interest in the struggle of the Anya-Nya and was in close contact with its leadership up to 1972, when the Addis Ababa Agreement was signed. The information he used in writing the manuscript was provided by many of these leaders. It is therefore a very important contribution to the history of the first civil war in Sudan waged by the Anya-Nya.

I came across the manuscript in scanned form in early 2016. Some pages were missing and the author had indicated in the text that the veracity of some specific pieces of information needed to be checked. On 17 March 2016, I wrote an e-mail to the author attaching the scanned manuscript with a view that he can provide the missing pages so that it can be published in his name. In his reply he stated that he didn't have a copy of his manuscript but made an elaborate response as to how the manuscript should look like if it were to be published.

I undertook to fill the gaps in the manuscript trying to maintain the original text whenever possible. This was done by reading the relevant literature and through interviews with some of the Anya-Nya officers whose names were mentioned or those who took part in the military engagements covered. Most of the Anya-Nya/SSLM politicians are, unfortunately, no longer on this world. They could have corroborated the information they gave to the author or fill in what they did not. I had to revise some of the author's conclusions especially in chapters connected with the political events in the country. On the military side, the chapter on Upper Nile was extensively revised. Also other chapters, especially on Western Equatoria and Bahr El Ghazal were revisited in light of the information that became available since the manuscript was written.

To complete the picture, I introduced a chapter on the administration of Joseph Lagu. It will be recalled that it was Lagu who negotiated the Addis Ababa Agreement with the Government of Sudan in1972. The agreement itself is beyond the scope of this book.

The book is a useful contribution to the history of the Anya-Nya in Southern Sudan from eye-witnesses and actors in the struggle.

Contents

Acronyms

ADC	Assistant District Commissioner
ALF	Azania Liberation Front
ANAF	Anya-Nya National Armed Forces
CMS	Christian Missionary Society
DC	District Commissioner
HQ	Headquarters
KTI	Khartoum Technical Institute
MP	Member of Parliament
M.T.	Mulazim Thani (Second Lieutenant)
NCO	Non-Commissioned Officer
NUP	National Unionist Party
OAU	Organization for African Unity (replaced by African Union)
PDP	People's Democratic Party
PSE	Plebiscite Support Union in Ethiopia
SACDNU	Sudan African Closed Districts National Union
SALF	Sudan African Liberation Front
SANU	Sudan African National Union
SDF	Sudan Defence Force
SF	Southern Front
SSLM	Southern Sudan Liberation Movement
SSPG	Southern Sudan Provisional Government
UAR	United Arab Republic (currently, Arab Republic of Egypt)
UDI	Unilateral Declaration of Independence
TTC	Teachers Training College.

CHAPTER 1

Events Leading up to the 1955 Mutiny

IN MAY 1955, on the day of *Eid el Adhha* celebration, Prime Minister Ismail Al-azhari publicly announced that his government would abandon its policy of seeking to link the Sudan with Egypt, and instead would aim at complete independence.[1] Two months later Sir Alexander Knox Holmes took over as the Governor General replacing Sir Robert Howe who retired for reasons of ill-health. The Governor General embarked on enacting laws necessary to transfer the administration to the Sudanese as required by self-government. In the middle of June, the Liberal Party stated its intention of holding a second conference in Juba (the first having taken place in October 1954). To this conference were invited not only Liberals, but in addition the Southern NUP members of Parliament. The inclusion of this latter group apparently displeased the government, and they made efforts to frustrate the conference. In Yambio the D.C. and the A.D.C. obtained by false pretences the signature of 13

---

1   Makki Shibeika, The Independent Sudan, New York 1959, p. 491.

1

Azande chiefs to a telegram supporting the government and dissociating themselves from the aims of the Liberal Party. This telegram was widely publicized in the North.[2]

The Liberal Party convention took place in Juba on July 6-7, but according to one informant was poorly attended and weakened by a split between two wings of the party. These two wings were headed by Benjamin Lwoki and Stanislaus Paysama, respectively. The exact difference of opinion between them is not clear.

At about the same time as the Liberal conference there occurred another notorious telegram incident. This involved, an allegedly forged message from Azhari to government officials in the South which read as follows:

> To all my administrators in the three Southern Provinces:

> I have just signed a document for Self-Determination. Do not listen to the childish complaints of the Southerners. Persecute them, oppress them, ill-treat them according to my orders. Any administrator who fails to comply with my orders will be liable to prosecution. In three months' time all of you will come round and enjoy the work you have done.[3]

This telegram circulated widely among Southerners, and undoubtedly contributed to the outbreak of the Torit mutiny. Whether it was forged or genuine will probably never be completely determined, although its authenticity seems unlikely. The Report of the Commission of Inquiry holds it to be a forgery, presumably on the *a priori* grounds that the Prime Minister could never have written such a telegram. Those who argue for its authenticity claim that the telegram was in fact received, in cipher, in the Juba posts and telegraphs office while a Southern clerk was on duty. This man (Samuel? Reuben Yacobo?) stole the key to the cipher from the postmaster's drawer and thereby obtained the original Arabic version, which according to one informant was translated into English by a man called Fraser Ako. The message was then circulated through

---

2   Report of the Commission of Inquiry .into the Disturbances in the Southern Sudan during August, 1955, Khartoum 1956, p. 87. (Referred to henceforth as Report.)

3   Report, p. 82.

the South by the Juba secret committee of Marko Rume and Daniel Jumi. As against this view, it is surely unlikely that if Azhari had sent such a message to his Southern administrators, more private means than Posts and Telegraphs of conveying the message would not have been used.

Meanwhile, the affair of the earlier telegram signed by 13 chiefs was having repercussions in Zandeland. The Liberal MP. for that area was Elia Kuze, a man who for some time had been attacking the government and the Northern Sudanese in general.[4] (Kuze also supported the cause of unity with Egypt, and appears to have accepted and distributed money in this cause, but according to the Report this part of his platform was not well received by the people.) When he heard about the telegram, Kuze organized a public meeting at Yambio on July 7th (note that this was the date of the Liberal conference in Juba, which Kuze obviously did not attend). 300 – 500 people went to the meeting, and passed among others the following resolutions:[5]

1. That Sayed Elia Kuze MP., being duly elected by the people to represent them in parliament, is the only person to talk on their behalf, and he should have been consulted prior to sending the telegram by the A.D.C.
2. That all the chiefs who had signed the declaration should be removed from their offices.
3. That they do not wish to be ruled by Northerners.
4. That it is not fair that Northern Sudanese should be superior in both Houses of Parliament, and the administration. They were completely lost and dominated by their "false so-called Northern brothers."
5. That if the organizers of this meeting were put in jail, all other Azande would go to jail too, and that a lawyer brought free outside the Sudan should come to try them.
6. That the A.D.C., by calling and asking the chiefs to sign the declaration had himself interfered in politics, contrary to government regulations.

These resolutions indicate the strength of feeling against the Northerners at the time. Resolution (2), however, gave offense to the Avungara chiefs who had signed the telegram, and two of them instigated legal

---

4   Report, p. 91
5   Report, pp. 92-93

proceedings against Kuze and five others. The trial took place on July 25th, in Chiefs Court composed entirely of Avungara chiefs, with Chief Soro as president. The accused were found guilty, and sentenced to 2 years' imprisonment each. When the verdict was announced, a crowd of 700 staged a demonstration outside the court, which the police broke up with tear gas. The crowd dispersed into small groups, attacked some Northerners on the streets, and raided a shop belonging to a Northerner[6]. Although a re-trial was later ordered by the Chief Justice of the Sudan, it is obvious that the affair had seriously damaged North – South relations in Zandeland.

Worse was to follow, however. The next day, July 26th , workers at the Equatoria Projects Board cotton mill in Nzara rioted, and the crowd was eventually dispersed only by the army using a machine-gun. The affair seems to have originated as follows.[7]

The Zande scheme, which began in 1949, had grown into a flourishing industry by 1955, employing many thousands of Azande in the growing, spinning and weaving of cotton. Nowhere else in the South was a comparable level of industrialization achieved. A consequent widening of outlook soon arose on the part of the Azande people, through contact with foreign managers and employees, making them among the most "advanced" of the Southern peoples. By 1954 various forms of collective organization, including a trade union, had started among the textile workers. One of these organizations was the Anti-Imperialist Front, which although it owed its inspiration to a similarly named communist group in Northern Sudan, soon came to adopt a tone that was anti-North as well as anti-Imperialist. The following is an extract from one of its leaflets distributed at the end of December 1954.

> "Malakal, Wau and Juba should be states each having its own Parliament; but the central (Southern) Parliament should be at Juba, and from this Juba Central Southern Parliament members should be selected to represent us in the Khartoum Central Sudan Parliament. In this way we shall have our own Governors, District Commissioners etc, but as far as we are going to be ruled by Northerners as it has begun now there is no

---

6   Report, p. 96
7   Report, p. 97

difference for us with the time when the English were our rulers, and worse still it means very surely that we are to be only slaves"[8].

The tone of this pamphlet strongly indicates some link with the secret committee in Juba, although there has been no confirmation to this. Following the distribution of the leaflets, there were various signs of discontent and unrest among the cotton workers, but nothing serious until July 1955, when 300 Southern textile workers were dismissed for reasons of economy. As this came at a time Northern Sudanese were taking over administrative posts in the industry from foreigners, the impression was inevitably created that Sotherners were losing their jobs to Northerners. On the morning after the Kuze demonstration, demands for higher wages in the mill at Nzara were received, and Northern officials were abused and told to "go back to their own country". A mob formed which smashed windows and marched to the Nzara market area, where Northern shops were broken into. A telephone call to Yambio for help brought five policemen and 11 soldiers, the latter being armed with rifles, a bren gun and a sten gun. When the mob refused to disperse the army officer in charge, Mutassim Abdel Rahman, ordered his soldiers to open fire. Six people were officially reported to have been shot to death, and two others died in the resultant stampede of the crowd. In all probability the actual death count was a little higher: one authority (Samuel Abujohn) puts it at 14. The effect of the incident was to destroy any remaining confidence in the administration on the part of the people: the event was in fact "regarded by them as the beginning of a war"[9].

Thus by the end of July 1955 the stage was set for a full-scale rebellion on the part of the South, and the occurrence which triggered this off was the army mutiny at Torit on August 18th. Because of an event which took place on August 6th we are able to know something about the origins of this mutiny and the planning which preceded it. How far this planning went, however, and in particular how many Southern officials and politicians knew about it, remains in the realm of speculation.

On August 6th, at Torit, a Southern soldier named Saturlino Oboyo shot an arrow in the dark at a man near the post office whom he mistook

---

8   Report, p. 98.

9   Report, p. 102

for his Northern commanding officer. He was arrested, his house searched, and a number of documents discovered. The latter revealed that Oboyo, who styled himself "President of Southern Corps", was involved in a plot to murder all Northern officers in the South, that at least 24 other officers and men of the Equatoria Corps (whose names were listed) were also involved, including soldiers at Wau and Malakal, and that Oboyo had been in touch with the Liberal Party Committee in Juba and with a Southern army officer named Reynaldo Loleya. It appeared that Oboyo had already tried to get Loleya to lead an army uprising in Juba on August 4th, with the aim of capturing the ferry and the aerodrome, but that Loleya had urged him to be patient and to wait. Oboyo was of too impetuous a character for this, however, and took matters into his own hands with the shooting of the arrow.

Following the arrest of Oboyo, an emergency meeting was held at Juba and a request sent to Khartoum for the immediate dispatch of Northern troops to the South. Marko Rume and Daniel Jumi were arrested, although to avoid precipitating events none of the soldiers mentioned in Oboyo's lists were[10]. At that time the last of the British troops were due to leave Khartoum for England, and it was decided that the mutiny might be defused by transferring No. 2 Company of the Equatoria Corps[11] from Torit to Khartoum to take part in the farewell ceremonies. This stratagem failed, however, and in the end, it was the refusal of No. 2 Company to obey orders that set off the rebellion.

---

10   Lt. Emidio Taffeng, however, a former sergeant who had been promoted from the ranks and who was on Saturlino's list, was sent to Juba on duty as a precautionary measure. When the mutiny broke out he was imprisoned, spent 5 years in jail and was released in 1960. Lt Reynaldo Loleya was also placed under semi-arrest in Juba, but escaped at the outbreak of the mutiny.

11   The Equatoria Corps was composed of five companies, all Southereners except officers. Nos. 1, 2 and 5 companies were in Torit, No. 3 in Wau and No. 4 in Malakal (Poggo, p. 31).

The Mutiny of August 1955

On the morning of August 18th No. 2 Company of the Equatoria Corps was drawn up on the parade ground at Torit, preparatory to going to Juba and thence by steamer to Khartoum[12]. The troops were apprehensive, many of them being convinced that the move to Khartoum was part of a plot to murder them. When the command was given to enter the waiting Lorries No. 1 platoon disobeyed, and immediately afterward the whole company rushed to the arms and ammunition stores and broke into them. Five Northern officers and N.C.O.s were killed by the mutineers, who then rampaged through the town, killing Northerners and looting Northern shops. According to the Report, 78 Northerners died in Torit, as well as 55 Southerners who panicked at the initial shooting and were drowned in the Kinyeti river.

News of the uprising spread rapidly through the South, and Northerners were killed and property destroyed at Katri, Kapoeta, Terakeka, Tali Post, Yei, Loka, Lainya Corner, Maridi, Amadi, Ibba, Mundri, Yambio and Nzara. Those who took the initiative in these incidents were not only army

---

12 Report, p. 32.

personnel, but Southern police, prison warders and civilians.

For details see the Report. All these places are in Equatoria: events in Upper Nile and Bahr el Ghazal will be described later. The casualties of the mutiny, according to the Report totalled 261 Northerners and 75 Southerners[13]. It is significant that of the two alien groups living in the South at that time – Northerners and Europeans – there is not a single case of a European being molested. In fact the deepest wish of the mutineers seems to have been that the insurrection should bring about the return of the British administration to the South[14].

The mutiny, once started at Torit, suffered from an immediate and crippling lack of leadership. In fact, of all the problems of the southern liberation movement from 1955, to the present, the lack of leadership has been the most severe. Had there been a concerted plan of action in 1955, it is quite possible that the South would have achieved independence at that time. Instead, although Reynaldo Loleya escaped from Juba and assumed command in Torit, communication between him and his colleagues rapidly broke down and eventually ceased to exist.

The initial plan was this[15]. Reynaldo was to direct operations at Torit, while a concerted attack was to be made on Juba where the only Northern forces in the South were stationed. A force under Albino Tombe was to attack from the east, while Ali Gbatala[16] was to cross to the west bank of the Nile (on which Juba is situated) and collect various elements of the Equatoria Corps stationed in Yei and Yambio to attack from the west.[17] For the successful execution of this plan speed was essential, since the Northern garrison at Juba was daily being reinforced by troops airlifted from

---

13   Report, p. 80.

14   See the telegrams sent requesting help from British forces in East Africa in Report, pp. 44-45. These telegrams indicate not only the wish but the belief that such help would be forthcoming.

15   Report, p. 42.

16   Born in Maridi, a Mundu. Speaks Arabic but not English. Joined the Sudan Defence Force in 1932, fought in the Ethiopian campaign in the Second World War as a corporal and took part in the capture of the Italian garrison on the Boma Plateau. Did an officers' course and was promoted in 1953/4. At the time of the mutiny was one of 9 Southern officers with the rank of Mulazim Thani (second Lieutenant), the highest rank achieved by any Southerner since 1924. (At that time following the assassination of Sir Lee Stack, the British discontinued the policy of having Southern officers in the army, and did not resume until 1953).

17   See the distribution of the 1,770 officers and men of the Equatoria Corps on August 18th in Report, pp. 24-25.

Khartoum in RAF planes.[18] Gbatala and Tombe accordingly proceeded with 198 men to the junction of the Nimule and Juba – Torit roads, where they spent the night of August 19th. The next day Gbatala, David Dada, and 36 men crossed the Nile 4 miles above Juba by canoe, and Dada established himself with 18 men at Rejaf[19]. Meanwhile Albino Tombe decided that he didn't have enough ammunition to attack Juba, and returned to Torit to get some. But when he arrived, he found that the arms store had been emptied and the ammunition taken by individual soldiers into the bush. With ammunition disappeared any hope of capturing Juba.

Ali Gbatala took a car that David Dada had found and drove to Yei. But the soldiers there had heard reports of the events in Torit, had murdered their Northern officer and the District Commissioner, and had dispersed into the bush. Unable to reinforce David Dada, Paul Ali Gbtala returned to Lainya Corner, where on August 24th he spoke to Reynaldo on a radio telephone and learned that he was contemplating surrender. Paul Ali urged him not to surrender, but Reynaldo would give no assurance about this, and the two had no further communication from that time on. Paul Ali remained in the Yei area until hunted by Northern troops from Juba, when he eventually crossed into Congo and was given sanctuary by the Belgians. David Dada stayed a month or more around Juba and Belinian (his village), then crossed into Uganda.[20] Years later, both Gbatala and Dada returned from exile as freedom fighters.

Meanwhile, under strong pressure from Governor General Sir Knox Helm, Reynaldo surrendered on August 28th. Knox Helm was one of only a very small number of British officials left in the Sudan by 1955, and his time was shortly to run out, but nevertheless he was able to give Reynaldo firm assurances:

Mr. Azhari has given you his personal word about a full and fair investigation, and treatment as military prisoners if you surrender. Myself now give you the same assurance"[21]

---

18   See the series of articles by Eric Downton in the Daily Telegraph, Aug. 20, 23, 24, 26, 27, 29, 30, 31; September 1 and 2, 1955.

19   Information from an interview with Paul Ali Gbatala.

20   Gbtala claims that Dada fought an engagement with Northern troops who came in a lorry to Rejaf, but this is not confirmed.

21   Telegram from Knox Helm to Reynaldo, quoted in the Daily Telegraph, Aug. 26, 1955

On this basis, Reynaldo surrendered, although when Northern troops occupied Torit on August 31st· they actually found only Reynaldo and two or three others, the remaining mutineers having fled. With the help of Reynaldo many of them were rounded up in the following days, although many others went into exile or stayed in hiding. The surrender terms, however, were never kept. Over 200 of the mutineers were sentenced to death by specially appointed courts.[22] Albino Tombe was tortured in Torit and killed two weeks after the mutiny.[23] Even Reynaldo had no immunity, being summarily tried and shot early in 1956. In Yei 7 loyal police and prison warders were shot on September 22nd when they were drawn up on the parade ground to welcome the returning Northern troops[24]. The aftermath of the mutiny was far from a happy time in Equatoria Province, and did nothing to diminish Southern resentment and antipathy.

In Upper Nile and Bahr el Ghazal, the situation was quite different from that in Equatoria. The units of the No. 4 Company of the Equatoria Corps stationed in Malakal knew nothing of the outbreak of the mutiny, their one contact with the conspirators at Torit having been quietly transferred to Juba after his name had been found on Saturlino's list[25]. The army commander at Malakal took the precaution of disarming all the soldiers there, and put the ammunition in a secret place. Hence when the order suddenly arrived from Juba on the morning of August 18th to immediately embark all the soldiers on a steamer for Khartoum, the troops were surrounded by armed mounted police (mostly Nubas) and had no alternative but to obey. They left without apparently hearing of the events that day in Torit. However, there was shooting in Malakal later, on August 22nd, when Northern Paratroopers, who were transported by steamer from Khartoum, attacked the police and prison headquarters, and fighting with the Southern policemen and prison warders continued

---

22   The Daily Telegraph, Dec. 22, 1955. Oduho and Deng, The Problem of the Southern Sudan, London 1963, pp. 28,33, put the number at 300.

23   Information from a medical assistant who was in Torit at the time.

24   The Daily Telegraph, Oct. 22, 1955; The Times, Dec. 8, 1955. This information needs further checking.

25   Report, p. 66

for a day[26]. The Governor decided to disarm the Southern police there. Other minor incidents in Upper Nile are described in the Report[27].

In Bahr el Ghazal, the first news of the uprising was brought on August 19th by refugees from Yambio and Nzara, where earlier in the day Southern troops had killed their commanding officer. The body of this officer was brought in a car by M. T. (Lt.) Nimir to Wau. There was considerable excitement at the news among the Southern troops in Wau (about 1/5 of which were Dinkas and 2/3 from Equatoria) and among the police. Whether they also would mutiny hung on a thread for a day or two, but the situation was relieved by the sudden departure of the Governor of the province, Daud Abdel Latif, and all other high-ranking Northern officials and officers on the night of the 21st. They commandeered the steamer "Dal" and sailed down the river to Malakal[28]. This left all effective control at the province in the hands of Southerners, notably Louis Bei, an Assistant District Commissioner, Lt. Nyang Diu, a Southern officer who had been in Yambio at the start of the mutiny, and Gordon Muortat Mayen[29], the Chief Inspector of Police. These men prevented any violence in Bahr el Ghazal, and continued to run the province as a semi-autonomous state until the end of October when Northern troops entered Wau. If, on the other hand, Reynaldo had not surrendered when he did, it is quite possible that Bahr el Ghazal would have joined the mutiny. One authority[30] reports that when Reynaldo's capitulation was announced on the radio, the majority of soldiers in Wau were very disappointed. It seems that there was no communication at that time between

---

26 Poggo, p. 31 puts the date at 21 August; Stephen Ogut confirms the incident and mentions Cpl Thomas and Pvt Nyang Rundial to have been involved in the fight against the attackers and later joined the Anya-nya.

27 Report, p. 64 and p. 72

28 Report, p. 75

29 Born 1922 near Rumbek, Mourtat attended intermediate school at Loka. In 1946 he joined the police, graduated from the police college in Omdurman in 1952. He was transferred to the North after the muyiny and during the military regime changed to the civil service and became an A.D.C. In 1964 he joined the Southern Front, and was Minister of Works, April – June 1965. Mourtat left the Sudan for East Africa in 1967 and became Minister of Foreign Affairs in the Southern Sudan Provisional Government of Aggrey Jaden. In March 1969 he became President of the Nile Provisional Government.

30 Frederick Brian Maggott, who was in Rumbek and Wau.

Wau and Torit[31]. By October 1955, the Equatoria Corps was no longer in existence[32]

One final question concerning the mutiny – was it entirely planned by Saturlino's group within the army, or did the idea of it originate elsewhere, at a higher political level? There are three schools of thought on this matter.

1 The first is what might be called the Egyptian school, who see the figure of Maj. Salah Salim, the Egyptian Minister for National Guidance and Sudanese Affairs, behind the plot. It is certainly true that the Egyptians were extremely disappointed by the change in the thinking of Azhari and others away from union with Egypt toward complete independence. It is also true that they were distributing money freely in the South to support their cause, and that it was only in the South that they could expect to find support for their opposition to independence. But this being said, it is unlikely that the Egyptians would have gone as far as to encourage mutiny. For one thing, the success of such a mutiny would undoubtedly have resulted in what the Egyptians least wanted to happen, namely the return of the British to the Sudan. In fact, a much more plausible hypothesis is that it was the British themselves who conceived the idea of the mutiny.

2 The "British school" has this to be said for it: (a) there were a number of British administrators in the South who were known to be unalterably opposed to the idea of Southerners being administered by Northerners, (b) there was a clause in the transitional constitution prior to independence that if the administration of the country broke down, either for economic reasons or as a result of insurrection, then the British would remain in the Sudan until good government was restored. It is therefore conceivable that the idea of mutiny was planted in the minds of certain Southerners by certain British officials

---

31 An interesting sidelight on the mutiny is provided by the reaction to it of people in Darfur. Some of the enlightened Fur people apparently considered the mutiny ill-conceived in the sense that it had been insufficiently well prepared. If they had known about it they might have taken part, because they wer not happy with the government and felt they were being dominated by Khartoum. There was, for example, no secondary school in Darfur at that time. (Information from Aggrey Jaden, who was in El fashe at the time of the mutiny.)

32 Poggo, p. 31

before they left. No firm evidence is yet forthcoming on this matter. Note that the "British" theory is not entirely compatible with the third theory, namely;

3 The theory which holds the mutiny was largely conceived and planned by Southerners, with little or no outside influencing. Many Southern politicians in the Liberal Party, for example, must have watched with dismay as the country drifted closer and closer to independence, while at the same time the guarantees and safeguards which would have protected the Southern people against exploitation were progressively swept away, and the British in the civil service replaced almost entirely by Northerners. It would surely have occurred to some of them that the armed force of the Equatoria Corps could be used as a last resort. Moreover, such force might well be dissipated after independence, if the Southern army units were broken up and stationed in different parts of the country. Hence there was need for haste. This line of reasoning has a certain logic to it, and it is quite possible that the mutiny was planned by certain elements of the Liberal Party working in collaboration with Saturlino's group. On the other hand, if there had been full collaboration, and if the main weight of the Liberal Party organization throughout the South had been behind the plan, it is unlikely that the mutiny would have failed.

Chapter 3

The Declaration of Independence

The Anglo-Egyptian Agreement of 1953 laid down long and completed procedures for achieving self-determination. These procedures included the election of a Constituent Assembly, which would then decide the future of the Sudan and draft a constitution. But once the mutiny had been ended, Azhari's government were in too impatient a mood to follow these procedures. The Southern M.P.'s, on the other hand, were more unwilling than ever to be rushed into a state of independence that would perpetuate Northern control. They proposed either that a plebiscite be held in the South under the auspices of the United Nations, or that the International Committee of the Red Cross be sent to report on the situation[33]. Conditions were, however, still too unsettled for a plebiscite, and the idea of sending international observers to the South proved to be anathema to the British Government. The latter's position was stated by the Marquis of Reading:

---

33   Oduho and Deng, op.cit. p.32.

The dispatch of United Nations' observers would almost certainly revive and strengthen the movement for some sort of self-rule in the South, thus widening the gap between South and North and running counter to the declared intention of the Anglo-Egyptian Agreement that the future of the country should be decided as one integral whole. H.M. Government are strongly of the opinion that the future interests of the Sudan can be served only if the authority of the Sudanese Government is maintained and strengthened."[34]

The situation seemed to be stalemated, when on December 15th the departure of Sir Knox Helm to resume his leave, which had been inter-rupted by the mutiny, provided Azhari with a golden opportunity for a short-cut. The government tabled a resolution in parliament calling for immediate independence. The fact that the resolution violated the Anglo-Egyptian Agreement seemed to trouble no one:

It was promptly pointed out in Khartoum that such a declaration would be unconstitutional. The Sudanese Government has taken the law into its own hands by simply proclaiming Sudanese independence"[35].

Only one thing was lacking, and that was the agreement of the Southern M.P.'s. Although they numbered only 22 out of 97, an independence resolution which passed by 75 to 22 would not have provided a very encouraging start to the new state. To win them over, the independence motion was phrased in the following manner:

(1) That the house is of the opinion that the claims of the Southern members of Parliament for federal government in the three Southern provinces be given full consideration by the Constituent Assembly.

(2) That an address be presented to the Governor-General in the following terms: 'We, the members of the House of Representatives in Parliament assembled, declare in the name of the Sudanese people that the Sudan is to become[36] fully independent sovereign state, and request Your Excellency to ask the two Condominium Powers to recognize the

---

34   East Africa and Rhodesia, Nov. 10, 1955, pp. 330-1, quoted in Oduho and Deng, p. 32.
35   East Africa and Rhodesia, Dec. 29, 1955, p. 609.
36   The Arabic text reads 'has become', as is pointed out by M. Abd al-Rahim in Imperialism and Nationalism in the Sudan, Oxford, 1969, p. 226.

declaration forthwith"[37]. (There were two other paragraphs, dealing with the election of a Supreme Commission to exercise the power of Head of State, and the formation of a Constituent Assembly).

The presence of the paragraph on federal status for the South came about after intense negotiations between the Southern MPs and leaders of the Northern political parties who sought unanimity to pass the independence motion. This was the first time that any recognition at all has been given to their claims, they took the Northerners for their word and agreed to support the resolution. It passed unanimously on December 19th, and the Sudan became independent on January 1st, 1956.

---

37   East Africa and Rhodesia, Dec. 12, 1955, p. 648.

CHAPTER 4

The Election of 1958 and the Army Coup

It did not take the Southerners long to realize that they had been out-manoeuvred on the matter of the independence motion. In September 1956 a 46-man Constitutional Committee was appointed by the government to draft a new constitution. Of these 46 members, only three were Southerners: Bullen Alier and Stanislaus Paysama representing the Liberal Party, and Father Saturnino Lohure[38] representing the Christian churches. The committee resolved in one of its by-laws that "majority rule be adopted as the deciding factor"[39] in its deliberation,

---

38   Born about 1921 in Lornyo near Torit, educated at Okaro and Gulu seminaries, and on 21 December 1946 was ordained a priest at Gulu. Fr.Saturnino was perhaps the most energetic and able leader of the Southern independence movement. He was elected to Parliament in 1958, where he led the Southern Bloc. During the Abboud regime he escaped with other politicians into exile in December 1960, and with William Deng and Joseph Oduho founded SANU in Leopoldville. He continued to be the patron of the movement, supplying arms and equipment to the freedom fighters, until his death in January 1967. The circumstances of his death while resisting arrest by the Uganda army may be found in the The Reporter, (Nairobi) Mar. 10, 1967.

39   Oduho and Deng, p. 34

thus rendering automatic the defeat of the Southerner's proposal for federation. In December 1957 the three Southerners walked out of the Committee, leaving it to draft its own centralized form of constitution.

Meanwhile, elections for a new parliament, which would also serve as a constituent assembly, were being prepared. On the basis of the 1956 census the boundaries of the constituencies were revised, and in addition, the total number of seats was increased, with the result that the South received 46 out of a total of 173[40]. The old Liberal Party, however, was badly demoralized, and not in good condition to fight an election. This was largely due to its leaders having become discredited in the eyes of younger educated Southerners because of their willingness to cooperate with Northern politicians. For example, Buth Diu, Secretary-General of the Liberals, changed to N.U.P. late in 1955. Many other well-known Southerners, such as Bullen Alier, Dak Dei, Santino Deng, Gordon Ayom, Siricio Iro and Philemon Majok were at various times members of Northern parties – Six MPs in fact changed party after being elected as Southern Party members. Money was undoubtedly at the root of many of these defections in 1953[41]. Finally, the Liberals were split by a leadership and policy quarrel between Benjamin Lowki and Stanislaus Paysama which continued from 1955 to 1957.

Faced with this disarray, various groups of young Southern intellectuals undertook the task of political reform. One of these groups began to meet secretly at Wad-Madani in late 1955 at the house of Ezbon Mondiri[42], at that time an employee of Shell Oil. A cipher was invented for recording

---

40   As was noted above, however, the 1956 census was held while the South was still suffering from the after- effects of the mutiny, and therefore almost certainly under-represented the number of the Southerners.

41   Information from Akuot Atem.

42   Born 1926, Ezbon Mondiri Gwanza, was at elementary school in Lui and intermediate at Loka. He attended Nabumali High School in Uganda 1947-1950, and University College of Khartoum (in Arts) 1951-1955. Until 1953 he was correspondence secretary to Michael Watta, the first president of the Liberal Party. Mondiri founded the Federal Party in 1956, but after being elected MP. in 1958 was arrested and imprisoned until 1964. Became a Southern Front cabinet minister in the care-taker government 1964-1965, then resigned and entered the bush to work with the Anya-Nya. Was secretary for defence in ALF under Oduho 1966-1967 and travelled widely in the South, accomplishing a great deal in the way of unification. Following the Angudri Convention in August 1967, Mondiri was not included in Jaden's cabinet, partly because of suspected communist affiliations. Since 1967 he has been living in East Africa.He led the SSLM/Anya-nya delegation to the Addis Ababa peace talks with the Government in 1971.that culminated in the Addis Ababa Agreement in February 1972.

notes and minutes[43]. The first secretary of the group was Severino Fuli, who handed over to Maurice Agili when Mondiri moved to Khartoum in 1956. A draft constitution for the Sudan along federal lines was prepared[44], and copies were sent to certain members of the Liberal Party organization in the three Southern provinces for approval. These representatives were Marko Rume (Juba), Dominic Mourwel (Wau), and Louis Rweng (Malakal). Early in 1957, in preparation for the election, the "Southern Sudan Federal Party" was registered with Mondiri president and Fr. Saturino treasurer. The message of the Federalists and the new Liberals was a simple one – the old MPs had betrayed the movement and must be replaced by new ones.

Another group whose aim was to arouse the political consciousness of Southerners was the Dinka Youth Organization[45]. This group, whose president was Alfred Wol Akoc, had two constitutions – one public and one private. In cooperation with the Liberal and Federal Parties, they selected "progressive" candidates in all 15 Dinka constituencies in Bahr el Ghazal and managed to get 14 of them elected[46]. Throughout the South, it was the same. A total of 40 of the Liberal/ Federal Party candidates of February 1958 were elected[47] (almost all of whom in fact campaigned as Liberals, but supported Mondiri's federalist platform). The successful candidates included Mondiri, Fr. Saturnino, Joseph Oduho[48], Elia Lupe,

---

43   Information from Ezbon Mondiri

44   See K.D.D. Henderson, Sudan Republic, London 1965, p. 180 for a brief account of some of Mondiri's proposals.

45   Information from Alphonse Malek, one of the original organizers.

46   The fifteenth was Camillo Dhol, who was defeated by Santino Deng but was subsequently nominated to the Senate.

47   Henderson, p. 181; Holt, p. 179; Mohammed Omer Beshir, The Southern Sudan, Background to Conflict, London, 1968, p. 78.

48   Oduho was born on 15 December 1927 near Torit. He attended Nyapea Secondary School in Uganda in 1947, then sat (unsuccessfully) for his Cambridge School Certificate at Rumbek. After teaching at Bussere T.T.C. he joined the institute of education at Bakht-er-Ruda 1953-1954, and after graduation taught at Mundri and Maridi. He was elected MP for Torit East in 1958, and following the military coup became headmaster of Palotaka Intermediate School. When threatened with arrest he left the country in December 1960, met Fr. Saturnino and William Deng, and travelled to several African and European countries presenting the case of Southern Sudan. Was the first president of Sudan African National Union (SANU), and published (with Deng) The Problem of the Southern Sudan (London) 1963. After losing the presidency of SANU in 1964 to Aggrey Jaden, Oduho formed the Azania Liberation Front in 1965 and continued as President until 1967. Long known as one of the uncompromising proponets of Southern indepedence, he became associated with the Anya-Nya National Organization of Joseph Lagu.

Dominic Muorwel, Marko Rume and Pancrasio Ochieng. Buth Diu was elected as an independent, and Bullen Alier, Gordon Ayom and Benjamin Lwoki among ethers were defeated[49].

A strange incident, the arrest of Ezbon Mondiri, occurred immediately after the election. The story, as told by Mondiri, is as follows. When the original draft of the federalist proposal was written in 1956, it included a clause which never became part of the election platform but which was nevertheless in Mondiri's opinion vital. This clause stipulated that federation would be sought by legal means, but if these failed, then other methods would have to be used. By this Mondiri meant a U.D.I. for the South - the Southern MPs would all gather together in one place and declare themselves an independent state. Force if necessary would be used, even if it meant plunging the country into civil war[50]. This clause was naturally kept secret, but the original document of which it formed part was kept in Mondiri's files in his house near Amadi, together with a number of other things in cipher. While Mondiri was campaigning in his constituency, a supporter of rival candidate apparently noticed some papers on the desk of Mondiri's secretary Maurice Agili that looked incriminating. Agili's house was searched by the police, one or two things found, and then Mondiri's house searched and his files confiscated. Besides the U.D.I document other papers were found which led to his immediate arrest. The background of these other papers is as follows.

Following the mutiny, most of the active mutineers eventually surrendered. Others went into exile, but a few remained inside the Sudan and lived as outlaws, harassing the government with occasional raids and ambushes. These men included Lotada Hillir in the Imatong and Dongotono Mountains, Lasuba Tadayo near Yei, a man named Philip near Kapoeta, and some fighters directed by Paul Ali Gbatala in the Maridi area (Paul Ali himself was in Congo). Of these, Lotada was the most effective[51]. He was an army man who later transferred to the police:

Following the mutiny he took his rifle and moved into the bush.

---

49   A complete list of elected MPs is available in: Akol, Lam, South Sudan; From Colonial Neglect to National Misrule, London: Gilgamesh, 2009, pp. 246 – 247.

50   See the articles on Mondiri in the Times, May 21, 1958.

51   Information from Serahpino Swaka, Mondiri, Joseph oduho and Elia Lupe.

Others joined him, and by the time of his death he had 21 armed men (some say only 7) and many more unarmed in his camp in the Dongotono Mountains. In one of his operations in 1958, he killed a Lango chief (Chief Lapponya, who had attended the Juba conference in 1947) and wounded the A.D.C. Torit on their way back from meeting Ugandan authorities on the border. Lotada was killed in November 1960, according to one source[52]. Lasuba Tadayo, unlike Latada, was only one man with a gun[53]. He was a Kakwa trader who operated entirely on his own from early 1956 until betrayed to the army by his wife in 1958. Nothing is known of the early operations (if any) of Paul Awel, Philip from Kapoeta, or Paul Ali Gbatala's men. Mondiri's connection with these outlaws was an indirect one. What he did was to write threatening letters in their name to various Northern government officials, saying that they and their families would die if Southerners continued to be ill-treated. This was a rash act on Mondiri's part, but it was rasher still to leave in his files original copies of the letters in his own handwriting (from which Maurice Agili typed them). At his trial in March 1958 these letters, together with the U.D.I. document, obtained for Mondiri a sentence of 9 years[54].

The result of all this was that when parliament convened, the Federal Party was without its leader. Twenty-five of the more radical Southern MPs formed what they called the Southern Bloc[55], and elected Fr. Saturnino as their leader[56]. The important item of parliamentary business was the approval of a new constitution, and in May 1958 the unitary draft produced by the 36-man committee was tabled. Mohammed Ahmed Mahgoub, the Foreign Minister, announced that they have "given the Southern claim for federation very serious consideration, and found that it could not work in this country."[57] The Southern MPs responded by walking out. They returned briefly on June 16th to explain their point

---

52   Other sources say he lived until 1963-64

53   Information from Elia Lupe and Joseph Lokule.

54   According to Bona Malwal (Sudan and South Sudan....op.cit.pp. 91-92), he was sentenced to 20 years imprisonment and was released in 1964 by Prime Minister Sirr el-Khatim.

55   P.M. Holt, A Modern History of the Sudan, London, 1963, p. 179, puts the number of the Southern Bloc at 40.

56   Dominic Mourwel was the vice-chairman, Luigi Adwok the secretary-general, and Joseph Oduho assistant secretary-general

57   Oliver Albino Battali, The Sudan: a Southern Viewpoint, London 1970,

of view before withdrawing once more. Father Saturnino was their spokesman on this occasion:

> "Mr. Speaker Sir, the South has no ill-intentions whatsoever towards the North; the South simply claims to run its own local affairs in a united Sudan. The South has no intention of separating from the North for had that been the case nothing on earth would have prevented the demand for separation. The South claims to federate with the North, a right that the South undoubtedly possesses as a consequence of the principle of free self-determination which reason and democracy grants to a free people. The South will at any moment separate from the North if and when the North desires, directly or indirectly, through political, social and economic subjection of the South"[58] .

This speech, as will be seen, had a deep effect on some of the members from the non-urban areas of northern Sudan. The issues which it raised influenced the outcome of the political crisis which paralysed the country during the summer and autumn of 1958, which resulted in the military coup of November. The background of this crisis must be sketched briefly.[59]

Azhari's declaration of independence of December 19th, 1955 did not, it seems, have the full backing of Ali al- Mirghani and the Khatmiyya sect. As Sayed Ali was also the patron of the NUP, this was a serious matter, and Azhari was soon faced with the withdrawal of the Khatmiyya element from his government and the formation of the rival PDP (People's Democratic Party). In July 1956 he was defeated in a vote of censure and a new government was formed consisting of a coalition of the Umma Party and the PDP. The Prime Minister was Abdallah Khalil, the Umma Secretary General.

In the elections of February-March 1958 the coalition was returned to power, the distribution being Umma 63 and PDP 27 for a total of 90,

---

58   Oduho and Deng, p. 36.

59   See Yusuf Fadl Hassan, "The Sudanese Revolution of October 1964", The Journal of Modern African Studies (1967), pp. 491 – 509, for an excellent discussion of events prior to and during Abboud's regime.

as against NUP 45 and Southerners 38[60] (total 83). Despite his parliamentary majority, however, Khalil was unable to obtain an approval for a new constitution, partly because of lack of Southern support[61] and partly because of his determination to propose Abd al-Rahman al-Mahdi , the son of the Mahdi, as titular head of state. A further source of discussion was the question of accepting American economic and technical aid, which was barely approved by parliament in the face of opposition by members (including the PDP) who were socialists or pro-Egyptian[62]. Rather than face mounting criticism over the affair, Khalil adjourned parliament. According to Hassan[63], during the succeeding months Khalil became disillusioned about the prospects of any parliamentary government providing the country with a firm and stable administration, and instead invited the army to take over. This the army did, on November 17th, 1958, just one day before parliament was due to reconvene. There is however another factor which Dr. Hassan does not mention, but which might well have proved an even stronger reason for handing over to Abboud. This was the response which the Southern demand for a federal system of government met with from the Nuba, Beja and Fur people of Northern Sudan.

In the Nuba mountains, in the Beja hills near the Red Sea, and in the far west in Darfur, there are vast areas which are as underdeveloped and "backward" as the most inaccessible parts of the south. The MPs from these areas resented being dictated to by Khartoum, and were pressing for a larger say in the running of their own. They welcomed the Southern call for federal government. At a meeting of Dr. Balier and other Beja notables on August 13th in Port Sudan, to which the Prime Minister and cabinet were invited, a petition was presented requesting

---

60   These figures, which come from Hassan , op. cit., indicate that at least 8 of the 46 elected from Southern constituencies joined parties other than the Libera/federal party. Accurate figures on these matters seem hard to obtain.

61   Note that Khalil had appointed three Southern ministers to his cabinet, but not the men nominated by the Southern Bloc (Holt, p.179).

62   It is interesting that Father Saturnino supported the American aid proposal, rather than bring down the government, and in consequence lost his position as Leader of the Southern Bloc. He was replaced by Elijah Ajith. It was argued that in his fear of rejection American aid (and hence perhaps opening the door to the Russians) Fr Saturnino had put the matters of ideology above matters of national (i.e., Southern) interest. (Information from Alphonse Malek).

63   Hassan, op. cit., p. 493.

a high degree of local autonomy[64]." It is significant that there were visits to Port Sudan by Southern MPs both before and after this meeting. The Southerners also made contact with Nuba and Fur leaders (although they were not allowed to enter Darfur), and found ready acceptance for their ideas. The recognition was fast gaining ground that a federal system of government was the most suitable for a large country with a heterogeneous population like the Sudan. Things apparently even progressed so far that it was informally agreed among leaders of the "indigenous" or African people of the country, who numbered 58% of the population, that if they gained control in parliament they would choose as Prime Minister a member of Khalil's cabinet called Ali el-Tom-of Dongola.[65] But matters never got this far. On November 17th , the very day on which a Fur conference was due to be held, and at which it was expected that federation would be endorsed, power passed to General Abboud, and all political activity was banned.

The last few days of Khalil's government were a time of intense political activity and last-minute attempts to find a political alternative to military rule. Perhaps the truth about these events will never be fully known, but the following account by Elia Lupe of a session on the night of November 15th is of interest. Khalil apparently invited him, Elijah Ajith and Nicanora Choor Malek to his house, and there and then offered to form an Umma/Liberal coalition government. (Khalil was known to be mistrustful of the PDP at that time, because of the latter's Egyptian connections.[66]) The three Liberals present asked what the Umma would offer the Liberals, and were told two cabinet posts. They replied that this was not enough - their terms were that the Umma Party must support the idea of federation. But the answer was that the new constitution had already been drafted on a unitary basis and could not be changed. Khalil stressed that what was being discussed was a last chance for parliamentary rule: if the offer was rejected he would have no alternative but to hand over power to the army. The Southerners said so be it, and in two days'

---

64   Oduho and Deng, p. 36.
65   Information from Joseph Oduho.
66   Holt, p. 183; Henderson, p. 110.

time it was.[67] Thus ended the only period in which the South has had reasonably full and competent representation in a Sudanese parliament. Later, when parliamentary government was restored in 1965, the South was opposed to elections, and when these finally took place in 1968 many of the most able Southerners had given up the hope of achieving anything by legal means and were fighting in the bush. It is doubtful whether a group of legislators comparable to those of 1958 will ever be assembled.

---

67   One exception was Dominic Mourwel, who took seriously Mondiri's idea of armed resistance and left the country soon after the army coup. He went to France, where he was rumoured to have obtained promises of military assistance. He then returned to Sudan and travelled to Yambio. Government spies were following him, however, and he was arrested as he was trying to leave the country. He was taken to Wau, beaten very badly, and kept in prison until he was released in September 1962. He later played a part in the liberation movement in exile, being vice-president of SANU for a time, but disagreed with the other leaders over the best military methods to adopt in the South. Mourwel rejected the idea of guerrilla warfare, and insisted that the only way was to capture a major town, and then appeal for international military assistance and/or intervention. When his ideas were not accepted he retired to Central African Republic, where he now resides (1970). (Information from Mondiri and Alfonse Malek. See also the Kenya Weekly News, Jan. 8, 1965, p. 18.)

Chapter 5

The School Strikes
of 1960 and 1962

With the advent of the military regime, all political activity came to an end. The Southern members of parliament dispersed into the South and took up other employment[68].

There they were lectured by Governor Ali Baldo on the evils of politics:

"We thank God that by the virtue of the marvelous efforts of the Revolution Government, the country will remain forever united. You should turn a deaf ear to any evil talk which comes from politicians, as you well know what has come of them in the past few years and you certainly don't want 'bloodshed again in the South'. You are aware that anybody who interferes with public peace and tranquillity will be dealt with severely and at once.

---

68   Though not, according to Holt and Henderson, before another attempt was made to form an Umma/NUP coalition. (Holt, p. 183; Henderson, p. 110.)

During the days of Parliament, the Southern Parliamentary members advocated a federal government for the South. Such ideas are gone with politicians".[69]

On the side of education, the government pursued a policy of arabicisation and islamicisation whose general lines had been laid down as early as 1954 by an International Commission on Secondary Education[70]. This Commission, none of whose members were Sudanese, saw no virtue in providing elementary education in a combination of English and the vernacular as was then the practice. Instead, they considered that Arabic would be both easier to teach (being already, as they judged it, the lingua franca of the South) and more in keeping with the policy of national unity. The Commission recommended that all mission and private schools in the South should be taken over by the government, in order to facilitate the putting into effect of its educational policies.

The years 1957-1964 saw the progressive implementation and logical extension of the Commission's findings. In February 1957 the Minister of Education announced that all mission and private schools in the South would be taken over, although somewhat inconsistently private schools were allowed to continue unmolested in the North. This was discriminatory in that it had the effect of allowing Northern parents a choice of education for their children, while Southern parents had no alternative but to accept the type of schooling provided by the government. At the same time the Ministry of Education pressed ahead with its programme of making Arabic the sole medium of instruction and establishing Koranic schools in many parts of the South.[71] Six Intermediate Islamic Institutes were opened in various centres, while "the military governors and administrators devoted much of their time and energies to spreading Arabic and Islam and to suppressing the opposition."[72] Unfortunately, however, this programme suffered from a lack of qualified teachers who could teach in Arabic. The rapid two-year post-elementary course in

---

69   Oduho and Deng, p. 40

70   See M. O. Beshir, The Southern Sudan, London 1968, p. 74.

71   According to The Tablet of Feb. 16, 1963, a total of 350 mission schools were taken over by the government. 50 Koranic schools were opened in 1960-61, and another 50 in 1962, and 100 more were planned for 1963.

72   M.O. Beshir, p. 81.

Arabic for Southern teachers proved to be totally inadequate. As a result, when Southern schoolchildren came to sit their examinations at the end of intermediate school, the great majority of them failed in both Arabic and English.[73] The inadequacies of the government's policy are under-lined by the fact that even in 1970 most of the teaching in southern schools is conducted not in Arabic but in English.

A natural extension of the government's educational policy was to change the day of rest in the South from Sunday to Friday. This was done in early 1960.[74]The change, however, provoked a vigorous reaction of protest from students in southern schools. The centres of this protest were Rumbek and Juba Commercial Secondary Schools, which had been transferred to the North following the mutiny but returned in 1958. At each of these schools a revolutionary group of students formed, the leaders of which were Edward Nyiel, Matthew Obur and John Tongun at Rumbek, and Alphonse Malek at Juba Commercial. A strike involving all schools in the South was organized, the word being spread throughout the country by the students. Eventually the ringleaders were arrested, and Nyiel, Obur and Tongun each sentenced to 10 years in gaol (later reduced to 3 years, together with 5 years for Fr. Paulino Doggale, an ex-M.P. who had used the duplicating machine at Rumbek Catholic Mission for printing strike literature). The strike of 1960 was an expression of popular sentiment in the South, and lasted only a relatively short time before the students returned to school. The strike of 1962, on the other hand, was a much more serious affair. It emptied southern schools of 3/4 of their pupils, many of whom never returned but stayed in exile or joined the freedom fighters. The direct cause of the strike was a series of letters written from outside the country by Marko Rume, as will be explained.

With the banning of the Liberal Party in 1958, an underground movement arose with branches or cells distributed in many parts of the South. The nucleus of this organization seems to have been situated in Equatoria and Bahr el Ghazal - Upper Nile was not fully covered until 1964.[75]

---

73   Oduho and Deng, p. 48.

74   Friday had originally been observed in the South, but the day was changed in 1918 with the transfer of the Lado Enclave to the Sudan.

75   Information from Gordon Muortat.

The membership of the individual branches consisted mainly of Southern officials and educated men. There was no regular meeting time, but meetings were held whenever there was news or business to discuss. The meeting place was always *el nugta el mu'ayina* – "the agreed place of meeting" ~ and members arrived and departed separately.

About the middle of 1962 letters began to circulate among the branches from Marko Rume, the former secretary of the Juba committee who had moved into exile. These letters said that preparations were being made for military intervention and that Ugandan independence (October 9th 1962) would be the signal for an armed invasion of the South. For fear of reprisals, students should leave schools; people should withdraw money from banks, etc. These letters were, of course, complete fabrications, but the effect they had was enormous.[76] On October 9th people were to be seen departing from towns with their belongings, and many students left the country either for their own safety or to join the expected invading forces. Since that time, schools in the South have never operated normally.

The invasion, of course, never took place. The only event of any significance that occurred in 1962 was an attack on a small police post at Kajo Kaji. But before the activities of the freedom fighters are discussed, something must be said about the Southern Sudanese political movement in exile.

---

76   Marko Rume apparently later defended the letters by the argument that if he had not written them, the progress of the liberation movement would have been slower.

CHAPTER 6

The Creation of SANU

In December 1960, a plot was discovered to arrest certain former Liberal Party politicians on Christmas Eve. They were forewarned however, and escaped into Uganda on December 23rd[77]. In February 1961 they were joined by William Deng,"[78] an A.D.C. at Kapoeta who was a trusted civil servant and had even written a letter to the Governor of Equatoria, criticizing an article in *The Times* which had described

---

77 Oduho and Deng, p. 41. Joseph Oduho, Pancrasio Ochieng and Natheniel Oyet left from near Torit; Fr. Saturnino from near Yei.

78 Deng was born about 1926 near Tonj, and was educated in Catholic elementary school at Mbili, intermediate school at Bussere, and at Rumbek. He joined the Sudan Civil Service, and following independence studied public administration at the University of Khartoum. He was A.D.C. at Kapoeta at the time of his leaving Sudan in 1961 to join the liberation movement in exile. With Fr. Saturnino and Joseph Oduho, he founded SANU, and published jointly with Oduho The Problem of the Southern Sudan in 1963. In 1965 Deng split SANU by deciding to return and work in Khartoum for a peaceful settlement of the Southern problem. He formed alliances with parties such as the Nuba independents and the progressive wing of the Unma Party, and was elected to parliament in 1967 and 1968. Immediately after his election in 1968 he was assassinated on the road near Rumbek.

the plight of the South in a convincing fashion[79]. Nevertheless, Deng proved to be an effective advocate of the Southern cause, and following a meeting in Kampala in July 1961, he, Fr. Saturnino and Joseph Oduho visited different African countries to put their case[80]. In January 1962, Fr. Saturnino and Oduho attended the All African Peoples Congress in Lagos (the "Monrovia Group"), where they were not allowed to present a petition but met African heads of state and held a press conference. Returning to Leopoldville in February, they were joined by Deng and founded the "Sudan African Closed Districts National Union" (SACDNU) with Oduho president and Deng secretary-general. This was not a secret organization but an open political movement: by June all the well-known Southern politicians in exile had joined it.

After a lucky escape in Leopoldville in April when Oduho had avoided being deported back to the Sudan by jumping out the window of his hotel, he and Fr. Saturnino went on to more African countries including Congo Brazzaville and Central African Republic. They then met up with Deng again in Europe, where Deng wrote a letter to the Secretary- General of the United Nations and Oduho gave an interview which was reported in *The Observer*[81]. Deng's letter was followed by a 28- page petition to the United Nations, presented when Deng was in New York in April 1963.[82] This petition bears the name SACDNU: at some time not long after its presentation the simpler name SANU (Sudan African National Union) was adopted[83].

Other publicity ventures at this time included Oduho end Deng's The

---

79   The article appeared in The Times on Nov. 18, 1959, and Deng's letter is reproduced in Basic Facts about the Southern Provinces of the Sudan, Central Office of Information, Khartoum, 1964, pp. 97 - 98.

80   Information from Joseph Oduho and Lawrence Wol Wol.

81   Deng's letter is reproduced in the Sudan Daily of Dec. 24, 1962, and Oduho's interview appeared in The Observer of Dec. 16. On Dec. 30 The Observer reported on the reaction of the Sudan embassy to the interview.

82   A copy of this petition is in the Southern Sudan archive in the libraries of Makerere University and the University of Chicago. Besides those of the three founders, the petition bears the names of Marko Rume (vice-president), Ferdinand Adyang, James Wek, Pancrasio Ochieng, Valeriano Oregge, Aggrey Jaden, Akuot Atem, Alexis Mbali, Philip Pedak, Chief Basia Renzi, and Nathaniel Oyet.

83   According to Oduho the reason the name SACDNU was chosen originally was that it was hoped to include other closed districts of the Sudan in the movement, such as the Nuba mountains and Darfur.

Problem of the Southern Sudan, (London 1963), and the founding of The Voice of the Southern Sudan, a quarterly edited in London by Lawrence Wol Wol from February 1963 until December 1965.

The three leaders returned to East Africa at different times between November 1962 and July 1963. Oduho, who returned in January 1963, immediately began to organize not only the political but also the military side of SANU[84]. It was mentioned earlier that letters from Marko Rume, the vice-president, had given warning of an imminent military invasion of the South, although all that in fact occurred in 1962 was a small attack on a small police post at Kajo-Kaji. When Oduho heard of the attack he immediately wrote to Rume to call off any future operations of this kind, in which the participants were armed only with pangas. But at the same time Oduho and Fr. Saturnino began planning much more serious military activities. These will be described in the following chapter: they began with series of attacks in September 1963 in central and eastern Equatoria and in Upper Nile. Although the SANU executive was very much involved in planning them, official disclaimers were issued which 'denied any knowledge of or sympathy for these operations'[85]. Nevertheless, enough information leaked out to cause the Uganda Government to arrest Oduho on October 15th, charging him with managing an unlawful society and raising an army. He was sentenced to 9 months and released in August 1964.

Meanwhile branches of SANU were being opened in many different countries. In at least some cases these branches took the form of "plebiscite support" unions - i.e., unions whose object it was to agitate for a plebiscite to be held in the South as a first step toward self-determination. In Ethiopia, for example, the branch was known as "PSE" (Plebiscite Support Union in Ethiopia). The first meeting of PSE was held in February 1963 following receipt of letters from Deng.[86] Other branches were reported to be named PSK (Kenya), PSC (Congo), PSU (Britain), etc. In Ethiopia, however, as will be seen, the real activities of the group lay not in agitating for a plebiscite but in planning military operations.

---

84   Information from Oduho.

85   See for example The Observer of Oct. 6, 1963, in which Oduho describes the Any-Nya as a terrorist movement, likely to harm than help the cause of self-determination.

86   Information from Alphonse Malek.

At the time of the founding of the movement in exile, agreement and harmony seem to have characterized relationships among the three leaders. But this state of affairs did not last. A split developed between William Deng and Fr. Saturnino, which came out into the open at a SANU executive meeting in Aru, Congo, on the 19th and 20th of February 1964. The causes of the disagreement seem to centre around the way money being received by the leaders on behalf of the movement was being spent. Each leader seems to have had his own account, and seems not to have regarded himself as answerable to the others for the spending of the money.

These differences and troubles made for a difficult SANU executive meeting in February 1964[87]. The President, being in jail, did not attend, and the main part of the meeting seems to have been devoted to accounts by the Secretary-General and the Patron of their activities over the previous eight months, and to answering allegations brought against them. From what they are reported in the minutes to have said, it would seem that they were either unwilling or unable to lay at rest doubts concerning their candidness if not their honesty[88]. The meeting ended with a proposal that the executive committee be reorganized, but it is not known whether any such reorganization was ever carried out. In any case, the rank and file of the party seem to have lost patience with the founders, for at the first national convention of SANU held in Kampala in November 1964 they were replaced by an entirely new executive.

The SANU convention from the 6th to the 16th of November occurred at approximately the same time as the OAU Commission on Refugees met to take evidence in Kampala[89]. There was thus a double reason for Southern refugees leaders to travel to Kampala. It was decided at the SANU convention, that there should be proportional representation by provinces, with seven official voting delegates from each. Unfortunately

---

87 Information from Elia Duang, who was present. The agenda and minutes of the meeting are in the Southern Sudan archive mentioned above.

88 For example, Deng apparently never explained why he published the French translation of The Problem of the Southern Sudan under his own name rather than jointly with Oduho. And Fr. Saturnino claims that the exact amount given to him for the movement by Catholic charities in Italy was "what he did not bother to know".

89 The author has unfortunately not yet seen a copy of SANU's memorandum to this commission.

not all the delegates showed up, so that in the end Equatoria had seven delegates, Upper Nile 5, and Bahr el Ghazal 2[90]. The most notable absentees from the Bahr el Ghazal delegation was William Deng, as will be explained below. The results of the voting were as follows:

NAME	POSITION
Aggrey Jaden	President
Philip Pedak	Vice-president
William Deng	Secretary for Foreign Affairs
Dominic Muorwel	Secretary for Special Affairs (mainly defense)
Elia Lupe	Secretary for Interior
George Kwanai	Secretary for Information
Michael Wal	Secretary for Finance
Lawrence Wol Wol	Secretary for Education
Joseph Oduho	Secretary for Constitutional Affairs (Justice)
Oliver Albino	Secretary for Refugee Affairs
Fr. Saturnino	Patron (Spiritual head, would swear in officers, etc.)

On paper, this seemed to be a fine collection of officers. But unfortunately SANU was immediately split by the most severe dissension it had yet experienced, and hence Jaden's[91] executive never had a chance to function normally. The cause of this schism was William Deng, who despite appeals for him to return was at the time of the convention absent in Europe. There the news reached him of the fall of General Abboud's military government at the end of October, and without consulting

---

90   Information from Lawrence Wol Wol.

91   Aggrey Jaden was born about 1922 in Loka.. He was educated at Yei elementary school, Loka intermediate school, and Nabumali High School in Uganda. In 1948 he went to Gordon College, where he studied Arts followed by Public Administration. He was posted to Torit as a sub-mamur in 1954, then transferred to El Fasher and Malakal, where he left the civil service after one or two incidents which made him suspect in the eyes of Northerners. For a while he lived in Juba, then left for Uganda in January 1961. There he participated with Ibrahim Nyigilo in the organization of the Sudan Christian Association (a group for helping refugees). Following his election as president of SANU he organized SANU and SALF, and was vice-president of ALF from December 1965 to April 1966. At the Angudri convention of August 1967 he was elected president of the Southern Sudan Provisional Government, with headquarters at Bungu. Jaden retired from the S.S.P.G. in September 1968, and since then has not been active in any of the succeeding groups.

anyone Deng immediately wrote to Khartoum suggesting (i) that SANU be recognized as a political party to fight the coming general elections on the policy of a Federal Sudan, and (ii) that a roundtable conference on the South, with observers from neighbouring African countries, be convened. What exactly prompted Deng to write this letter without consulting his colleagues is not clear. It has been said that his main quarrel was with the military regime and the restrictions on personal liberty and free speech that it imposed, so that when Abboud fell, Deng was willing to re-establish communications with Khartoum. This may well be true, but in any case, the impact of Deng's diplomatic initiative on SANU was severe. The movement became divided between the militants, who could see no useful purpose in negotiating with Khartoum, and those who hoped for a peaceful solution, perhaps along the lines proposed by Deng. These developments will be traced in the next chapter but one.

Chapter 7

The Rise of the Anya-Nya

As was said earlier, armed men such as Lotada and Lasuba were active in the countryside from 1955 onwards. As early as 1957 their activities had brought reprisals upon the civilian population, when authorization was given to the army to burn 700 houses near Yei[92]. And on November 16th 1962 a small police post at Kajo-Kaji was captured by a group of Southerners armed with pangas[93]. But it was not until September 1963 that serious guerrilla fighting broke out in the South: this was the time of the formation of the Anya-Nya.

According to Joseph Oduho, the name Anya-Nya was adopted at a meeting he convened in September 1963. Fr. Saturnino had earlier suggested "Pan-African Freedom Fighters", but endorsed the new name when it was conveyed to him in the bush (he had gone on ahead with the soldiers). The name originated as follows.

In the 1930's, there occurred in Madi country a very serious outbreak of poisoning by Madi witches. The poison was made from snakes and rotten beans, and was given the Madi name Inya-Nya, which was corrupted to

---

92   Henderson, p. 185; Oduho and Deng, p. 41

93   One policeman was killed and two rifles seized.

Anya-Nya in the Lotuko language. Such was the fear engendered by this poison that the very mention of the name Anya-Nya in Madi, Acholi or Lotuko areas cause people to flee. One of the first manifestos issued by the Anya-Nya in 1963 read as follows:

> Our patience has now come to an end and we are convinced that only the use of force will bring a decision …From today onwards we shall take action …for better for worse …we do not want mercy and we are not prepared to give it[94].

From the beginning there was an air of mystery surrounding the operation and command of the Anya-Nya. The rumour was circulated, for example, that the Anya-Nya leader was Lotada Hillir, although other evidence indicates that Lotada died well before 1963. Much more remains to be learned about the early operations of the Anya-Nya. The following is a rough outline of them.

The attacks had originally been planned to start on August 18th the anniversary of the outbreak of the mutiny in 1955 which many Southerners observe as their National Day. But delays occurred and the date was changed to September 19th .On that day several parties of men, each with a few arms, entered the Sudan and launched attacks on police and army outposts near the border. These expeditions met with varying success. The most westerly of them under Paul Ali Gbatala, which was aiming for the area between Maridi and Yambio, was intercepted by Congolese authorities before it could enter Sudan. Except for Paul Ali and one or two others who managed to escape, all 35 members of this group were captured and imprisoned in Congo for two months. In central Equatoria, in the region around Yei, attacks were made at Kajo-Kaji again, and at Lasu and Kaya. Not many details of these attacks are available, except that at Kajo-Kaji 5 Northern policemen were killed and 3 rifles captured. The freedom fighters in central Equatoria started with 25 rifles at the

---

94 From the SANU memorandum to the OAU commission for refugees, November 1964, quoted in M.O. Bashir, p. 84. Three manisfestos were issued: one to the Sudan government, one to the Southerners and one to the Northern and Greek merchants living in the South.

most. In eastern Equatoria they started with only 6- 8. In that region there were attacks at Nimule, Pajok, Katire,Ikotos and Chukudum. The first major attack in Bahr el Ghazal came later, when a force of 99 men attacked Wau in January 1964. But by far the biggest engagement, involving forces which numbered in the thousands, took place in Upper Nile at Pochalla on the Ethiopian frontier. This battle will be described in the review of the build-up of Anya-Nya forces by regions which follows.

CHAPTER 8

Upper Nile

An important fact which should not be lost sight of in discussing the part of Upper Nile which borders Ethiopia is the identity of peoples and of terrain on both sides of the boundary. The Baro-Pibor salient of Ethiopia, in fact, was administered by the Sudan government from 1928 to 1954. Hence many people on the Ethiopian side still feel themselves to be Sudanese. The Nuer and the Anuak tribes are each dissected by narrow international river-boundary extending across country that is uniformly flat on both sides. Another significant fact is that the border people have for a long time possessed firearms. The British administration permitted this, to enable them to repel Ethiopian raiders. The rise of the Anya-Nya in the area must be seen against this background.

In 1962 and 1963 many soldiers, police and prison warders in Upper Nile responded to the formation of SANU and its "plebiscite support" branch in Ethiopia by deserting and forming themselves into the "Southern Sudanese Land Freedom Army".[95] The principal recruits to

---

95   The name seems to have originated with William Deng. The name Anya-Nya was not used in Upper Nile until 1964, people preferring to call themselves simply "freedom fighters" or "Dej Dor" (A Nuer expression meaning: "bush army").

this army were four men named Paul. Paul Adung, a Chollo (Shilluk), was formerly a sergeant in the police at Kodok. He organized a camp near Kodok and recruited numerous other Chollos[96]. Paul Ruot was a Nuer from the region of Thul near Waat who graduated from Juba Commercial Secondary School in 1962, the only one of the four with secondary education. He had been a military cadet at school, and joined the freedom fighters in late 1962 or early 1963[97]. Paul Awel, a Dinka police corporal, left Akobo to join the freedom fighters in Ethiopia on July 30th 1963 with 75 other people[98]. The last Paul was Paul Nyingori Ojulo, an Anyuak from Akobo who completed intermediate school at Atar about 1958 and then did a farm management course and became a farmer at Akobo before leaving for Ethiopia about the end of 1962[99]. These four men, with many others, assembled at a large Anya-Nya camp seven miles from Pochalla in August 1963.

Fighting in Pochalla

The choice of Pacholla was not by accident, nor was it straightforward. It so happened that the news had spread of the attack of Pochalla in

---

96   Adung's real name is Paul Ogol Deng Nyikwec, but commonly known as Paul Adung. Born in Pachodo village of Kodok District. He was given command of the Northern battalion of Upper Nile province. He was wounded at Akoka in August 1964 and died of tetanus.

97   Ruot was put in charge of the Anya-Nya forces at Pochalla, and continued as commander of Upper Nile till his death. He was according to one of his friends a poor administrator but a magnificent fighter {"when there was peace the soldiers were unhappy with him, but when there was war they flocked around"). Ruot was killed in a fierce battle near Pibor in March (or May) 1965.

98   Awel, born in 1936 near Bor, attended Atar Intermediate School and joined the police in 1956. Following the death of Adung, he took over the command of both the Northern and the Western battalions of Upper Nile. He attended the Angudri convention in 1967, where he was appointed assistant commander-in-chief to Taffeng, and in 1969-70 was of the Nile Provisional Government forces.

99   Nyingori was second in command to Ruot at Pochalla, and after Ruot's death became commander of all Anya-Nya forces in Upper Nile. He established his headquarters in Anyuak-land, between Akobo and Pochalla (for a description of this part of the country see: Tom Stacey, "The Army that Fights on a Diet of Crocodiles", Daily Telegraph Magazine, April 26, 1968.) In August 1969, Nyingori was replaced as military leader of Upper Nile by Joseph Akuon. After that he stayed in his village till the Addis Ababa Agreement when he was integrated into Prisons service as a Lieutenant Colonel.

July 1954 by an Anyuak Kingdom claimant to the throne, Abala Agwa Didumo, and his supporters[100]. Thereafter he had retreated to safety in the countryside. This encouraged the freedom fighters to look for this safe place. The group tasked Paul Nyingori to lead them to where the rest of the people who were with Abala Agwa were. In July 1963 the four Pauls went to Pochalla area to be directed to the place. They arrived Dhaldim, in Ethiopia, where Prince Agole Akway Medho lived and found him surrounded by his people. Paul Nyingori introduced his group to the prince and told him the reason for visiting him. The Prince was suspicious that the group may be government agents wanting to get him arrested. He asked them to go back and not to disclose his whereabouts. They went back to Akobo, and after three months the four Pauls returned with a good number of people. They camped far from where the prince was, only the four leaders went to meet him. This time the prince was cooperative and gave them a place in the nearby forest.

The reconnaissance of the freedom fighters around Pochalla noticed that three policemen in Pochalla used to cultivate near the riverbank every morning leaving their guns nearby unattended. One day, the freedom fighters went to the place very early in the morning and laid an ambush. They succeeded to take the three guns and went back to their camp. When Prince Agole saw the three 303 rifles, he was excited and immediately took two strings of Dimui (a valuable Anyuak cultural bead for marriage price) and sent two of his people to Pinyudo to sell and buy bullets for the Menlechier rifle to be used in attacking Pochalla. He told the commanders that when the bullets arrive he will lead the attack and they together with his people follow him. Indeed, when the bullets arrived, he led the attack. The attack of Pochalla started on 17 September 1963 and was captured on the 19th. Sgt Abbas and two others were killed. One of Abbas' daughters was wounded and captured[101].

---

100 Abala Agwa Didumo was claiming to be the Anyuak king instead of King Agada Akway Medho. King Agada reported the matter to the government authorities in Malakal. Abala attacked Pochalla to show his hostility to the government that sided with his rival. Prominent among the attackers were Agole Akway Medho, Gilo Araw and Ojulo Wer Akoc. The government threatened to destroy Anuak Kingdom around Pochalla if the rival of King Agada who attacked Pochalla does not give himself up to the government. To save his people, Abala Agwa gave himself up in 1955 and was subsequently hanged to death.[Information from Stephen Ogut Obongo].

101 Information from Stephen Ogut Obongo who took part in the fighting

On hearing the news of the fighting in Pochalla, the armed forces in Akobo sent a force to repulse the freedom fighters. Sudanese forces arrived Otalo village, spent the night there and the following morning they came to Ajuara village while the ambush was laid between Ajuara and Pochalla; they were hit at and one G-3 rifle was captured and two soldiers killed, but they continued to advance towards Pochalla.

On the 20th, bombardment by air started around Pochalla, but didn't stop the fighting which continued then. At the end of seven days a strange event occurred which swung the battle in favor of the government forces. An airplane normally used for spraying crops appeared, dropped two bombs which failed to explode, and then was damaged by small-arms fire and forced to land. To the horror of the local Anyuak tribesmen a single Englishman emerged from the plane, fired his pistol in the air and was escorted into the post. The Anyuak irregulars quickly departed, saying that the freedom fighters had told them they were fighting the Arabs but now it seemed they were fighting the English as well. Without their support the siege of Pochalla came to an end.

The situation before the attack of Pochalla was that by August, about 300 men had assembled in the freedom fighters' camp near Pochalla[102]. The order of command was as follows: (1) Paul Ruot, (2) Paul Nyingori, (3) Paul Adung, (4) Paul Awel, (5) Daniel Chuol Chagor. Fighting began, as mentioned, on September 17th , when Pochalla was surrounded for three days by the freedom fighters. Pochalla was a police post at that time, not an army camp, but army reinforcement soon started to arrive from Akobo[103]. Despite ambushes by the freedom fighters (in one of which Nyingori was slightly wounded in the leg) the army succeeded in reinforcing the 35 police at Pochalla with 250 soldiers. But the numbers of freedom fighters also increased greatly, and when the main attack on the post was launched on 19 September 1963, a total of 1,000- 2,000 men armed with 181 guns took part. Of these guns, only 21 belonged to the freedom fighters, the remaining 160 belonging to Anyuak tribesmen who joined in for the fight[104]. Pochalla was

---

102 Information from Paul Awel. According to him, the 300 men included only 3 Dinkas, 4 Shilluks (Chollo) and about 30 Anyuaks, the remainder being Nuer.

103 During the rainy season, steamers used to travel from Nasir to Jekou to Gambella and along Akobo river. For instance, in September 1963, a steamer was ambushed and set on fire at Ulang, a police post near Nasir.

104 Information from Paul Awel and Alphonse Malek.

besieged for seven days, during which time The attackers had captured the camp but driven out when the reinforcement of the army arrived from Akobo. Pochalla was then besieged for seven days, during which time the attackers entered the camp more than once. All four Pauls fought in the front line together with their most experienced man, an ex-army sergeant named Peter Wal who operated one of the attackers' three bren guns until he was hit and killed.

Who won the battle of Pochalla? Inasmuch as the post eventually remained in their hands, the Sudan army did. But casualties there were considerably higher than in any previous engagement (one estimate places those on the Northern side at 80; no figure is available for Southern casualties). Pochalla was the signal for the start of a long guerrilla war in Upper Nile, and remains to this day one of the largest engagements ever fought in the 1955-72 civil war[105].

Earlier Attacks

Although Pochalla is generally reported to have been the first engagement fought in Upper Nile, there had actually been earlier attacks made by the freedom fighters for the purpose of obtaining arms. One of these attacks is described as follows[106]:

In July 1963 a number of freedom fighters gathered at a camp near Yom, 30-40 miles northeast of Nasir. This camp was commanded by Daniel Chuol Chagor, a Nuer from Nasir. An attack was made on the police post at Yom at 2:00 a.m. in the morning by 80 men armed with 17 old rifles and 21 bullets. Although the freedom fighters suffered heavy casualties from the police weapons, which included three bren guns, the post was overrun. Of the 15 Southern policemen manning the post, 4 were killed and 6 taken prisoner, 4 of whom later joined the Anya-Nya. Eight rifles and two bren

---

105   Pochalla remained impregnable for over seven years, until it was attacked and ovr-run by the Anya-Nya on January 5th 1971

106   Information from Alphonse Malek, who was present. Malek graduated from Juba Commercial Secondary School in 1960, where he helped organize the Suday Strike. He then made his way to Ethiopia, and was elected presidentof PSE in February 1963. He went to East Africa in 1964 where he stayed until the Addis Ababa Agreement was signed

guns (one damaged) were taken. Following the engagement, the party moved down toward Pochalla. A detachment of the Sudanese army was in Jakou at the time, but could not come to assist the police at Yom because the rains were falling and the country was knee-deep in water.

The Camps of Upper Nile Province

The first camps in Upper Nile Province were organized by the four Pauls: Col. Paul Ruot, Col. Paul Adung, Col. Paul Ngingori and Col. Paul Awel. The four were together at the fighting in Pochalla.

After Pochalla the four Pauls split up. Paul Awel and Paul Adung went to a camp near Nasir, where with 800 men and 221 guns they fought a pitched battle against six companies of Northern soldiers who attacked them on March 27th 1964[107]. Soon afterwards Ruot and Nyingori rejoined Awel and Adung, and the four remained together for a month and constructed the general headquarters for Upper Nile Province. This was the last meeting of the four Pauls. Paul Nyingori left in April to open a camp near Pibor, and Paul Adung left in June to begin operations in the region of Renk. Neither ever returned: Nyingori quarrelled with Ruot and refused to come back, while Paul Adung was killed on his way back to headquarters in September. The circumstances were these. The split between Ruot and Nyingori had led to Ruot's resignation, but when the resignation was sent to the political wing of the movement in Ethiopia for ratification it was rejected, and Ruot was reinstated. Ruot then sent a letter to Adung that he was resuming command, and asked him to return to headquarters. It was on his return that he met a force of Northern soldiers at Akoka, 50 miles north of Malakal. In the engagement, 15 Anya-Nya were killed; Adung wounded and died of tetanus[108].

Following Adung's death, Paul Awel was given command of Adung's forces as well as his own. At the time there were three battalions

---

107 The fighting extended from 7:30 a.m. until 10:00 a.m. the Freedom Fighters lost 49 killed and 11 wounded, and the Northerners (unconfirmed) 111 killed or wounded. (information from Paul Awel).

108 Adung may have been returning from an incident in Kodok in August 1964 where a large number of civilians and government officials were killed by Northern troops. Victor Anon gives a slightly different version (see below).

of three companies each in Upper Nile, distributed as follows. The Northern battalion (formerly Adung's) operated in the region of Renk and Kodok. After Adung's death its operational commander was Daniel Chwogo[109]. The Western battalion (Awel's) had as its area Malakal itself, Fangak, Bor and Bentiu Districts. Second in command to Awel was Daniel Chuol Chagor. Finally, the Eastern battalion operated in Nasir and Akobo districts, under the command of Paul Nyingori assisted by George Ngut. Note that the Pibor area is not included in this list. The reason is that at the time the DC at Pibor was a Murle named Hassan Nyachingol, who persuaded the Murle people to be loyal to the Khartoum government and not to cooperate with the Anya-Nya. Nyachingol was killed in 1967, but the sympathies of the Murle remained the same[110].

In March 1965 the Anya-Nya suffered severe loss with the death of Paul Ruot. He was proceeding to a meeting with Nyingori on the Ethiopian border, and on the way took some cattle from a small village between Akobo and Pibor. He then retreated, knowing that the Northern troops would follow him. The pursuing force was however larger than anticipated, coming up from Malakal in lorries passing through Waat along dry-season roads, and the ensuing battle was a grim one. Forty-two Anya-Nya died, some of thirst and the defending force was cut off from water, and the number of Northern casualties was estimated to have been

---

109 Chwogo, a Shilluk, had a remarkable history. He joined the police about 1959 and was pressured into becoming an informer for the C.I.D., which he did reluctantly. He was imprisoned for drunken driving and escaped in 1963, making his way to Pochalla. Adung was about to shoot him as a spy but the other Pauls interceded on his behalf and he was kept on probation, being tied up each time the freedom fighters went for an ambush. On one occasion he was given a gun, though watched closely by Adung, and performed so bravely that he was thereafter trusted. A daring fighter, he was responsible for the Abu Anga incident (see below) and continued to operate in the vicinity of Malakal until he was betrayed by one of his men in 1967. This man, Kalkon, conspired with a certain Shilluk and Northern officials and killed Chwogo at night while he was sleeping. After his death, the Shilluk Anya-Nya command fell apart. (information from Matthew Obur)

110 According to one report, Nyachingol was killed by the Northerners for reasons unknown. Relations between the Murle and the Anya-Nya were strained by an incident in September 1969, when the Bor Anya-Nya force took part in a Dinka tribal raid upon the Murle, killing large numbers of the latter (see the London Times, 15 Sept. 1969, where the victims are described by Khartoum as "rebels").

85[111]. Ruot himself wounded in the shoulder and the right leg, each time returning to lead his men once more before being finally hit in the head: he was buried where he fell by his men. In the same battle, Samuel Gai Tut sustained seven gun shot wounds, Matthew Pagan Nyilek a gun shot wound in the arm and Pamet Ajobong (Othol) was killed. After the death of Col. Paul Ruot, Lau camp that was under his direct command got split into two camps: the larger group was under the command of Major Samuel Gai Tut and the other group was commanded by Lt. Pajok (Dhoal)[112].

Following the death of Ruot, Awel and Nyingori planned to meet, but Awel who was in the region of Malakal had 30 wounded men with him and could not make the journey to Nyingori's camp[113]. During the whole of 1965 there were constant fighting around Malakal, and to anyone who took note of the frequent ambushes and Anya-Nya raids it must have been a mystery where they got their ammunition. The answer in simple: they purchased it in Malakal. It seems there was an Arab dealer there who had an officer friend who took the bullets from the armoury and sold them. The price was 10 piasters per round and many thousands of rounds were purchased in this way. One authority estimates that every thousand rounds sold by the army officer cost the army 60-70 dead. No doubt there exist parallels to this story in the history of warfare.

The deaths resulting from the fighting in Upper Nile, and indeed throughout the Southern Sudan as a whole, were not confined to the belligerent forces. The principal sufferers were the civilian population, This is illustrated by the *Kal-Liri* incident. Kal-Liri is the southernmost suburb of Malakal town inhabited by the Liri Arabs and their cattle. Early August 1965, it was attacked by a small force of the Anya-nya inflicting casualties on some residents and the force withdrew driving away some cattle with them. In retaliation, the Sudan army descended on Warajwok, the nearest village, on 4 August 1965, and killed 89 people,

---

111 Anya-Nya estimates of casualties among the opposition are usually unverified and must be treated with caution. The figure given of their own losses is probably fairly accurate, since the normal propaganda value of minimizing losses is counter-balanced by the propaganda value of demonstrating the sufferings of the Soutern people.

112 Dhoal in Nuer language refers to a person who has no marks on his forehead that signify having grown from a boy to fully grown man. Pajok didn't carry those marks, hence the name given him.

113 Information from Paul Awel.

all males. This is by no means an isolated incident. It frequently happens that when the Northern forces are defeated by the Anya-Nya they vent their anger and frustration on the civilians. For example, in October 1970 the Anya-Nya over-ran the police post at Bur Math near Akobo and killed 18 men. In retaliation, the army killed 80 civilians in Akobo. The details of the Bur Math fight were as follows[114]. In October 1970, the police post was overrun by an Anya-Nya Company commanded by Captain Daniel Deng Opyienyi deputized by Captain David Oman Didumo and 1st Lt Victor Anon Laa as platoon No. 3 leader. In that attack the post was temporarily occupied by Anya-Nya force from 10:15 a.m. to 3:30 p.m., the same day. The post was evacuated on arrival of the army reinforcement from Akobo garrison. Enemy casualties were: 15 policemen and 3 Haras Watani (local militias) killed, 10 Abu Ashra (303 semi-automatic rifless) and one (1) Light machinegun captured and one (1) Commer lorry destoyed by a landmine near Akobo. Anya-Nya casualties were: Captain Daniel Deng Opyienyi and 6 other ranks killed in action and 18 others wounded.

Returning to the Anya-Nya leadership in Upper Nile following the death of Paul Ruot, Awel was unable to meet Nyingori and remained in the vicinity of Malakal for the whole of 1965 and most of 1966. During that time groups of soldiers were sent to Congo to buy arms: they walked the thousand odd miles there and back and returned with a few modern automatic weapons[115]. In late 1966 Awel and Nyingori received letters from Ezbon Mondiri, then Secretary for Defence in Oduho's Azania Liberation Front (See Chapter 15) inviting them to attend a meeting at Mondiri's HQ near Amadi. This invitation was declined by Nyingori but accepted by Awel, who went to Equatoria in late 1966 and did not return until 1971. A large Upper Nile meeting was held however in 1968 without Awel, and this meeting established the pattern of Anya-Nya military and civil organization in the province wich still largely prevailed during the war.

In March 1968, a large Upper Nile meeting was held at Tedo between Akobo and Pochalla with delegates from every district. In that meeting,

---

114 Information from Victor Anon Laa.

115 The story of these arms in Congo will be discussed more fully below. They were sent originally to the Simba rebels by Algeria and the UAR, but eventually found their way into the hands of the Anya-Nya.

Paul Nyingori was confirmed as the overall commander of the provincial forces. Samuel Gai Tut was given the command of Akobo, Nasir and Fangak forces deputized by Daniel Nyang Rundial. The command of Ngok, Dingjol, Nyiel and Abilang was given to Paul Awel who was not present in the meeting, to be deputized by Peter Mabil Riak. The command of Northern and Southern Shilluk, i.e., Kodok and Tonga, was given to Anthony Kur Nyidhok who was by then under arrest.

Peter Ayul Ajak was made to act till Anthony Kur is cleared of the charges against him. On the civil side, the province was divided for administrative purposes into 5 areas, with a district commissioner in charge of each:

1.   Malakal, Renk and Kodok districts – Antipas Ayiei.
2.   Nasir and Waat districts - Gabriel Gany Juc
3.   Bor district - Job Adier.

No DCs were named for the other two areas, namely, Fangak and Bentin districts and Akobo district (including Pibor sub-district).[116]

The nature of the terrain in Upper Nile meant that certain areas had double administrations. In some regions the administrative officials of the Khartoum government were never seen – these areas were under the effective control of the Anya-Nya. In other regions the Khartoum officials toured during the dry season, collecting taxes and establishing their presence with the help of mechanized transport. The Anya-Nya officials toured the same areas in the wet season, when roads were impassable and the only method of transport was on foot. It would be interesting to know whether the people in these doubly-administered areas paid their taxes to Khartoum, to the Anya-Nya, to both, or to neither.

Joseph Oteo Akuon takes command

Col Paul Nyingori who was confirmed in 1968 as the overall commander of the Upper Nile forces continued to operate from the Anyuaks camp

---

116 Information from Victor Anon Laa and Stephen Ogut Obongo both of whom were
      present in the meeting

near Pochalla. Early 1969, his force clashed with the Ethiopian forces[117] and captured three (3) guns from the latter: one machine gun and two AK-47.

The Ethiopian government asked for the captured guns to be returned. Paul Nyingori Ojulo didn't accept to return the Ethiopian captured arms, in his authority pointing out that the capture of these arms cost lives.

In 1969, an Ethiopian Anyuak official in Gambela approached Joseph Oteo Akuon[118] asking about the captured guns from Ethiopian armed forces in the gold mine. Joseph Akuon replied that he heard something about that whereupon the official told him that the Ethiopians are planning to chase the Anya-Nya out of their territory and work to persuade other countries that help the Anya-Nya to severe their relations with them if the arms are not returned.

From there Joseph Akuon got into contact with some of the Anya-nya rebels from Anyuak and talked about these guns. He met some of them including Stephen Ogut Obongo and discussed the matter at length. So they concluded to go down to Tedo where Nyingori was to talk to him personally. Akuon and the Anya-Nya with him left Pingbago and went to Tedo arriving there in August 1969. They immediately started talks with Nyingori who was adamant that under no circumstance will the guns be returned to the Ethiopians.

At last they declared removal of Col Paul Nyingori from the position of Commander of the forces and detained him. They addressed the soldiers in a parade that Nyingori was refusing the work to go forward, elaborating that they would have got thousands of guns long time ago if Nyingori had agreed to return the three Ethiopian guns. But he refused

---

117 The reason for the clash was that the Anyuak Anya-Nya were selling cattle to Ethiopian traders to buy bullets. The Ethiopian Police complained to their army accusing the rebels of encouraging the Anyuaks to raise prices of goods. It seems the Ethiopian forces didn't bother to talk to the rebels and used force instead. Information from Stephen Ogut Obongo.

118 Joseph Oteo Akuon is from Ajwara village of Pochalla Anyuak. He studied at Obel Intermediate School and left for Khartoum before completing. He had a relative there, Buobo, who was a policeman. There he joined the American Commercial High School in Omdurman. All this time Joseph Oteo Akuon was not present in the camp, he was working in Pinybago village on Baro River in Gambela region farming. However, he was in contact with the Israelis since 1967/8. While in Pinybago, Joseph Akuon used to help in the medical treatment of the Anya-nya wounded. He joined Joseph Lagu in March 1968 and visited his HQ at Owiny-ki-bul. Information from Stephen Ogut Obongo.

making things difficult for the prosecution of the war. They concluded that with the return of these guns, arms would flow like water.

Joseph Oteo Akuon was chosen to replace Paul Nyingori. A committee of seven was selected to assist him, namely, Ochala Gilo, James Oman Didumo, Opoli Abala, Stephen Ogut, Simon Makwac Adhom, Opat Opiew and David Owok Aruangi. Akuon and his committee prepared to meet the other groups in the province.

They left Tedo in August 1969 and met other Anya-nya groups in Owilo village. Their leaders were: Peter Mabil Riak, Paul Awel Ruac, James Adiang, Simon Agwenyang Odan and Daniel Deng Opyienyi. Joseph Akuon and members of the committee met these groups and told them what happened regarding deposing Paul Nyingori and being replaced by Joseph Akuon, The reaction of the group was rather surprising. They said the discussion of the matter should be deferred for a later time, thus endorsing Joseph Akuon as the overall Commander of Upper Nile. It didn't seem to bother them that a commander chosen by a meeting of the whole province could be removed in such a manner.

Not long after these developments, Joseph Oteo Akuon was promoted to the rank of Brigadier General by Major General Joseph Lagu and made him his second in command (2-i-C).

In 1970, now under Joseph Lagu, Brigadier Joseph Akuon decided to unite the camps in Upper Nile province into one Brigade under his command. He appointed Major Matthew Pagan Nyilek as his Adjutant to remain at his HQ at Tedo near the Ethiopian border.

In December 1971, Brig Gen Joseph Akuon accompanied by Major Matthew Pagan left his HQ to visit Chollo camp which was under the command of Major Peter Ayul Ajak. At the end of his tour of Chollo land, Brig Gen Joseph Akuon decided to take the whole Chollo camp with him back to his HQ. On his way, the whole force was attacked at Bag-jwok area by an enemy force while on move following river Sobat's northern bank. In that attack, Brig Gen Joseph Akuon was killed in action together with six other soldiers.

On arrival to the main HQ at Tedo, Major Matthew Pagan was sent in February 1972 to Addis Ababa to join the Anya-Nya negotiation team in the peace talks taking place then with the government.

The Chollo Camp of the Freedom Fighters

Colonel Paul Adung Deng, Lt. Colonel Daniel Chwogo Nyikango, Major Anthony Kur Nyidhok[119], Captain David Bol Apiek[120] and Captain Isaac Mapilo Jwodho appeared in northern Upper Nile in June 1964. They were accompanied by some few Chollo soldiers. They came from Tedo, the main Anya-Nya camp near Pochalla police post close to the Ethiopian border, through Maban area to Akoka area.

Col. Paul Adung decided to organize his group into two camps. The decision was not political but to ease their mission of recruiting Chollo and Dinka youth and also to cover the whole areas of Kodok and Renk districts before the dry season sets in. The two groups were organized as follows: the first was commanded by Col. Paul Adung himself, deputized by Major Anthony Kur and Captain Amos Kwanyireth to be in charge of administration of the new recruits. The second group was commanded by Lt. Col Daniel Chwogo Nyikango deputized by Captain David Bol Apiek with Captain Isaac Mapilo Jwodho in charge of administration and training of the new recruits.

Col Paul Adung's group was able to recruit some few men from Melut and Akoka areas on the eastern bank of the White Nile, but his biggest success was in the western bank where he recruited a large number of Chollo youth from Manyo to Pachodo. He put these recruits into a three-month training programme. After graduation, Col. Paul Adung started military operations by attacking Akoka police post. The Anya-nya forces nearly overran it, but due to shortage of ammos they withdrew to a nearby Dinka village for reorganization after the battle. The following morning, an enemy reinforcement mounted on horses arrived from Melut and went straight to attack the Any-nya force in their camp near Akoka police station. In that fight, Col. Paul Adung sustained a gunshot wound. The wound got cured, but later on, in September 1964 Col Paul Adung Deng died of tetanus. He was buried there. Lt Col Daniel Chwogo visited his

---

119 Anthony Kur Nyidhok, escaped to Ethiopia where he joined the Ethiopian Police. He escaped from there to Pochalla with his rifle.

120 David Bol Apiek, after completing the Intermediate School, joined the Teachers Training Collge in Khartoum for Elementary School teachers. He was in his final year when he decided to join the armed struggle. Information from Victor Anon Laa.

grave in November the same year[121].

Lt. Col Chwogo's group crossed the Nile north of Akoka post to the western side passing through Detwok Elementary School[122] and went straight to Pabo village west of Kodok town. From there, they started recruitment. The group passing through Wic-rek rested at Biew village for some time. They left Biew passing by Obwa village at night. There, and precisely at Owangliny, they fell into an enemy ambush[123]. There were no casualties and the group continued its march southwards establishing a military camp at Wunlam, and the training of the new recruits started in earnest.

In August 1964, Lt. Col. Daniel Chwogo led a small number of his men to attack Atar El Ardeiba police station. With the help of L/Cpl Womo Anyong and Pvt Ajang Landit who were in the police post, they were able to capture the police post without own casualties. In Atar El Ardeiba, the rebels captured one Bren gun (a light machine gun) and two 303 rifles (Abu Ashra). The news of the rebel success in overrunning a police station spread all over the area and within a week Wunlam camp was full of new recruits from all tribes and walks of life; teachers, school boys, policemen, government officials and youth.

Main battles fought in Chollo land

The first two engagements between the rebels and the enemy in Akoka and Atar El Ardeiba have already been mentioned. Other battles fought include:

1 An attack on Khorflus prison warders post executed by Lt. Col. Daniel Chwogo in October 1964. In that attack the rebels managed to overrun the whole post capturing four prison warders with their weapons and some ammos. Among those captured were Samuel

---

121 Information from Victor Anon Laa

122 At Detwok Daniel Chwogo killed a Northern tailor who they found there. It is believed that the subsequent reaction of the government by arresting and killing teachers in Kodok was triggered by this incident.

123 The story behind the ambush was as follows. At Biew village, Daniel Chwogo wrote a note to Amum Okyiec, who was his colleague in the Police, informing him that he will pass by his village, Obwa. Amum passed the information to the army and was given a platoon. It was that platoon that carried out the ambush.

Ajang (from Thworo) and Jago Nyibong (from Obai).

2   While they were taking rest after a very long journey, the Anya-Nya soldiers were surprised by an enemy dawn attack in Odwar village. The rebels defended the village fiercely and managed to push back the attackers, but with heavy losses on both sides. Their only light machine gun was destroyed by the enemy mortar fire. The battle took place on Christmas day, 25 December 1964.

3   On 29 September 1965, the Nile steamer Abu Anga, empty of passengers, was about to tie up to the bank at Tawfigia, a few miles south of Malakal, in order to take on firewood. It was ambushed by a platoon of Anya-Nya led by Daniel Chwogo. As soon as the captain perceived the attack he cut the connection between the second- and the third-class barges, and the engine and the second-class departed, leaving the third- class behind. There had been 15 army troops guarding the second- class, but none on the third, which was promptly captured and sunk by Chwogo.

4   In March 1966, the enemy mounted a surprise early morning attack on the rebels camp near Ologaji village west of Kodok town[124]. The rebels withdrew putting up a stiff resistance. The enemy entered the camp and burned it down. The Anya-Nya casualties were two soldiers killed in action and one soldier wounded.

5   When their force withdrew from Ologaji, Lt. Col Daniel Chwogo moved with 18 soldiers to Detang village, opposite Malakal town on the western bank of the White Nile. The rest of the force remained at Pamath village. The following morning, on 18 March 1966, an enemy force moved to Detang and found the rebels ready. The ensuing fight started at about 10:00 am and lasted for twenty minutes. The rebels

---

124   The attack wasn't going to be a surprise were it not for the negligence of the officer on duty, Thubo Hakim. The Inspector of Local Government in Kodok, Ben Lado, took the courageous step to send his driver, a certain Malual from Bor, on his Commer car to the village where Anthony Kur was to inform him that an enemy force was moving from Kodok to attack them. Anthony instructed Thubo to run and inform Col Daniel Chwogo. He didn't do so.

force lost two men, and the enemy lost a Major and six soldiers.

6   An attack on the enemy police station at Kaka claimed the life of four soldiers including Captain Akwey wa Nyalyiech, the commander of the force. Enemy casualties were not known.

7   An enemy force supported by Nuer natives attacked an Anya-nya camp near Wathkech in 1967. The fight started at 6:00 am and continued until sunset the same day. The rebels suffered heavy casualties both in men and materials. On hearing this news, Col Daniel Chwogo who was preparing to cross to the western side of the Nile cut his mission short and returned to the camp from where he mounted a punitive attack on the Nuers that took part in the fighting.

8   The enemy force that was trying to cross Duolpi stream between Obaang and Dor villages of Nyilwak was ambushed by the Anya-Nya. The enemy suffered heavy casualties.

9   In January 1972, a large enemy force left Malakal by land and river looking for the Any-Nya fighters. They met the Anya-Nya at Bag-jwok that extends a distance of some fifteen miles from Bom village in the south to Nyanachan village in the north. Contact was established at about 7:00 am till 6:00 pm the same day. The rebels lost six soldiers killed in action, including the overall Upper Nile forces commander Brigadier General Joseph Akuon. Enemy casualties were not known.

Various trips to Congo

The first trip to Congo was undertaken by Matthew Obur Ayang who was sent by the Southern Front members to survey whether arms could be purchased from Congo. He found out that arms and ammos are bought illegally there in Aba, Congo. He then wrote a letter to James Ogilo Agor asking him to send ten strong men with some cash to him in Juba town.

Mr James Ogilo Agor led the second trip accompanied by Major Anthony Kur Nyidhok, 1st Lt George Kulang Diing and four other soldiers. The group left Malakal on a steamer. When the steamer arrived Bor town, James Ogilo and 1ˢᵗ Lt George Kulang Diing disembarked to go buy some food items for the journey to Juba. On coming back to board the steamer, James Ogilo was shot by a government soldier who was waiting to arrest them at the river bank. 1ˢᵗ Lt George Kulang Diing managed to get on board the steamer and continued the journey to Juba with the rest of the group. James Ogilo was arrested in Bor, and after investigating him, he was released and returned to Malakal. After two months in Congo, Major Anthony Kur came back to Malakal area bringing with him the following weapons:

- One RPD-44 machine gun (Doctor Yub)
- One Rocket Propelled Grenade (RPG-2) launcher
- One FN rifle (Fal)
- One Pistol sub-machine gun
- Three (3) AK-47 rifles
- Large quantity of ammos.

The third trip was led by Captain Isaac Awow Aban. This group was composed of mainly students who wanted to go to East Africa to continue with their education and some few of them who wanted to join the movement. The number of soldiers in this group was about two platoons. They returned with some few arms and ammos.

The fourth group was led by Captain Peter Awol Alijok. This group left Upper Nile Province on the 4th of February 1966 and arrived in Garamba area near the national park bearing that name in the Congo. There the group linked up with the Chollo soldiers that had remained behind when Captain Isaac Awow left Congo. In Aba, the group found out that Matthew Obur Ayang and Nyirath Kwong Dak Padiet had just left the town for Kampala, Uganda, leaving Albino Awang Akot Ajawin doing the work of purchasing arms and ammos all alone.

The fifth trip was led by Captain Simon Acwil. The group left Upper Nile Province in March 1968. On arriving at the Congo border, the whole group was arrested by Akuot Atem who was Minister of Defence in the Nile Provisional Government led by Aggrey Jaden. Akuot Atem's reason for arresting them was that the Chollo soldiers led by 1ˢᵗ Lt. Daniel Deng Opeyienyi left the depot at Garamba on 10 December 1967 without orders from the C-in-C who was by then Paul Ali Gbatala. Albino Awang Akot and Lt. Victor Anon were with that earlier group claimed to have left Garamba without permission. The group leader, Captain Peter Awol Alijok, left Aba for Kampala around September 1967.

Friction with the Nuer of Fangak District

By 1967, the trips to Congo were facing resistance in the Gawar area of Fangak district. A sizeable number of the population there was won over by the government. This situation prompted Col Daniel Chwogo to think of an alternative route to Congo that does not pass through that area. His decision was to use the western side of Bahr el Jebel through Bentiu District. He took the best weapons in his camp and moved to Kilo 50 so as to cross to the western side of the river to survey a route that would be used by his soldiers to go to Congo. Before crossing, news reached him that the government troops accompanied by armed natives of the area attacked the rebels on move from their camp near Fangak town, which Col Daniel had left four days earlier. It was a devastating attack in which many officers and other ranks were killed in action and others were wounded. The soldiers were dispersed. The preponderance of the enemy, coupled with the inadequate armament of the rebels led to the significant losses sustained by the rebels.

Col Daniel Chwogo moved with speed in the Jwach Bor area in Fangak District. He reached a location about half-way between Kilo 50 and Wathkech at about 2:00 pm and decided to spend the night there. He sent some soldiers to the Nuer village to look for food. The soldiers were met with hostility by the natives, returned back empty-handed and reported the matter to their commander. Col Daniel Chwogo deployed his force in round defence and prepared for the night. At dawn, the natives attacked, and a fierce battle ensued ending in the dispersal of the attackers. Col Daniel Chwogo mounted a punitive campaign against the villages he found on his way from that location to the location in which his soldiers were dispersed some days earlier. By the end of that campaign, it was estimated that around 3,000 Nuers lost their lives.

Col Daniel Chwogo did not waste time embarking immediately on regrouping his soldiers. After that, he moved with them to the Toic of Papwojo village in Tonga area. When the camp was in good shape again Col Daniel Chwogo was confronted with two immediate problems to deal with: the consequences of the attack and a mutiny that had taken place while he was in Kilo 50, just before the force was ambushed on move by a force of armed natives.

The mutiny and the attack by the Nuer

When Col Daniel Chwogo left for Kilo 50, he left Captain Michael Oywach (from Athidhwoy) in charge. He was not the most senior officer. This action angered the senior officers. After Daniel Chwogo left, Captain George Kulang Diing (from Pakwar) made a coup and put Captain David Bol Apiek (from Panyidwai) in place of Michael Oywac.

Captan David Bol advised him against such a move telling him that his relationship with Col Daniel Chwogo was not good already and anything of the sort will immediately be interpreted that he mutinied against him. George Kulang insisted and went ahead with his plan. He persuaded the other officers and they disarmed the Captains except Captain David Bol Apiek who he asked to assume the command. The Captains arrested were: Samuel Ajang, Isaac Awow and Michael Oywac. Capt Ayul Ajak was too sick to be arrested. Not long after that David Bol moved with the force from Toic to go to Thiang in Fangak area. On their way the force fell into an ambush laid by the Nuer. Own casualties were 28 killed 11 of them were officers including Captain George Kulang Diing. The RPD-44 (Doctor Yub) was captured by the enemy. Among the survivors was Captain James Adiang.

It was Captain Michael Oywac and William Nyuon Bany who went running to where Col Daniel Chwogo was and informed him that they were attacked by the Nuer early morning that day. Captain Michael Oywac reported that Captain David Bol Apiek had staged a coup against Daniel Chwogo by disarming officers suspected of loyalty to him and that he was supported by 1st Lt Ezekiel Kujo Deng[125].

---

125 Information from William Kak who was with Col. Daniel Chwogo

Signs that the Nuer population in the area were won over by the government were already clear to the rebels, as evidenced by their obstruction of groups travelling to Congo through their territory in Gawar area. However, things were not that clear around Fangak town. The news that the enemy accompanied by armed Nuer natives were planning to attack the camp came in the evening of the day before the attack.

The Execution of David Bol Apiek

As soon as Col Daniel Chwogo regrouped his soldiers he turned his attention to deal with the mutiny that took place in his absence. Captain David Bol Apiek was detained accused to be the plotter together with others including Kalkon from Dedigo, Panyidwai, and Nyiyom Lwal from Obai Dhego. Captain David Bol Apiek was sentenced to death by a firing squad and executed. Each of the two mentioned above was lashed 70 strokes and released. The killing of David and their lashing made Kalkon and Nyiyom angry with Daniel Chwogo.

Many in the camp were unhappy about the execution of David Bol Apiek, and there is no doubt that the subsequent assassination of Col Daniel Chwogo has something to do with the disaffection that was caused by this episode.

The death of Col. Daniel Chwogo

The Chollo Anya-Nya suffered a devastating loss with the murder of their commander, Col Daniel Chwogo Nyikango, in August 1967[126]. The incident took place at Dedigo village some 15 kilometres south of Malakal on the western bank of the White Nile. A conspiracy was hatched by Kalkon and Nyiyom in collaboration with some of his men. The details of the incident were as follows.

---

126   Information from Victor Anon Laa and Awer Akol Bienyo. Awer was with Daniel Chwogo and remained at Canal Mouth to follow him together with the rest of the force the next day..

Col. Daniel Chwogo left Papwojo with the forces to Konam (Anakdiar) to look for Nyodho wa Okyiec who was suspected of collaboration with the Arab forces. He was not found, his brothers were detained and the force returned. Upon their arrival to Canal Mouth from Konam, Daniel decided to go to Dedigo to see his friend, Anthony Kur, whose wife was from Dedigo. He went with only two of his bodyguards: Pio Yukwan Deng and his nephew (son of his sister). He ordered his forces that were with him in Canal Mouth to follow him the following day.

When Daniel arrived Dedigo, Kalkon and Nyiyom who were stationed at Owaci got information about his arrival, and they planned to get rid of him. On the fateful day, they went to Dedigo at night with other people who planned with them. Daniel was sleeping in his separate hut while his two bodyguards were away in the village. Kalkon and Nyiyom attacked him at midnight hitting him to death with metal rod and sticks. They dragged his body, threw it into a small stream nearby, and the two of them escaped to Malakal to join the government.

The bulk of the force moving from Canal Mouth heard about the killing of Daniel when they arrived Obai Dhego. They immediately proceeded to Dedigo and were told upon arrival that their commander was missing. Awer Akol Bienyo led the group that went to inspect the hut where Daniel Chwogo was sleeping in. He found the destruction of things in the hut and followed the traces of the blood stains from the hut up to the stream and found the body dumped under the grass in the water. After that Awer returned to Dedigo and informed the forces.

Awer and the forces went to collect his body and took it in a canoe. Awer and a trusted few were selected to bury him in a secret location so that the grave is not to be found by the government forces[127]. The commander of the bodyguards, Lt Pio Yukwan Deng, was detained but was later released.

After the death of Col. Daniel Chwogo, the command passed to Captain Peter Ayul from Obwa, and the force moved to northern Chollo.

---

127 Information from Awer Akol and Yolong Kur Chol who took part in the burial. They add that the Any-Nya were keen that his burial place shoud not be known by the enemy lest they may exhume the body. The body was buried in the small wood between Obai Dhego and Obai Agugo and the grave levelled with the ground and covered with natural vegetation to hide it from view.

Chapter 9

Eastern Equatoria

As was mentioned above, the first guerilla fighter in Eastern Equatria was an ex-policeman named Lotada Hillir, who operated out of a camp in the Dongotono Mountains between 1955 and 1960 with perhaps a dozen armed supporters, including his son. Lotada's most notable attack occurred in 1957, when he ambushed a car containing three Lango chiefs and the A.D.C. Torit on the Torit/Madi Opei road[128]. The chiefs were returning from a meeting at the border with Ugandan authorities, and Lotada apparently considered them to be cooperating too closely with the Sudan government. Chief Lapponya, who had been at the 1947 Juba conference, and Chief Ingingo of Logir were killed, and Chief Marcello of Dangotono died later of his wounds. Mustafa, the A.D.C., escaped into the bush and eventually made his way back to Torit.

The date and manner of Lotada's death are unknown, but he seems to have died sometime in 1960. The rumour which circulated at the time of the first Anya-Nya attacks in September 1963 that Lotada was

---

128 Information from Ali Ayume.

the Anya-Nya "field marshal" is false[129]. The commander in fact was Emidio Taffeng[130], who upon his release from prison in Northern Sudan in 1961, began immediately to organize armed resistance. Unlike the political leaders who left Sudan in 1960, Taffeng never went into exile, but proceeded directly to his village in the Horiok section of Lotuko country south of Torit and began to gather people around him. Lotada's men, who had scattered after Lotada's death, came together in November 1962, and the following February they were joined by Taffeng's group in a training camp named Agu[131]. During the next month Dr. Obote, the Prime Minister of Uganda, visited General Abboud in Khartoum, and to mark the occasion all those who remained of the 10,000 Southerners imprisoned following the 1955 mutiny were released. Some of them found their way to Agu camp, notably such ex-S.D.F. servicemen as Marko Lohuyoro, Solomon Lobiala, and Lazarro Mutek[132].

Agu camp engaged in training only up until September 19th, 1963, when the first Anya-Nya attacks were made. In Eastern Equatoria these occurred as was stated earlier at Nimule, at Pajok near Palabok, at Magwi, at Katire saw mills, at Ikotos and at Chukudum south of Kapoeta. Of these the most successful was at Chukudum. The Anya-Nya force under command of Mutek, an ex-sergeant major in No. 2 Coy in 1955, left Agu camp on September 19th and walked northeastwards for a week

---

129 John Osman writing in the Sunday Telegraph, Nov. 10 1963, states Lotada to be the Anya-Nya leader. He also gives a picture of a captured guerrilla named Cipriano Lokori, and a broken bridge on the Torit Katire road.

130 Taffeng, like Ali Gbatala, was a former sergeant in the SDF who was promoted to second Lieuenant. Having been arrested in Juba following the Saturlino affair, he took no part in the mutiny. After his release from prison, Taffeng was commander of Eastern Equatoria from 1963 until early 1967, and following the Angudri convention, he was made commander-in-chief of all Anya-Nya forces for SSPG. He attended the Balgo-Bindi convention, but in June 1969 broke away and became chairman of the revolutionary council of the Anyidi government based in Morta. Taffeng has no active responsibilities or command in the Any-Nya organization of Joseph Lagu, which absorbed Anyidi in April 1970.

131 Information from Mario Coho and Joseph Oduho. Agu camp was in the vicinity of Mt. Kinyeti, the highest mountain in Sudan, being in fact situated not far from the house of Saturlino Oboyo. In December 1962, 200 men armed with spears, knives, bows and arrows were found by the Ugandan Rifles near the Sudan border, preparing to take part in a Sudanese insurrection, and 20 of them were gaoled for a year (see the Reporter, Nairobi, Jan. 5 1963, p.19).

132 See the Weekly News, Nairobi, Nov. 8 1963, p.17. The paper wrongly gives the date of Obote's visit as May rather than March.

before arriving at their destination. The actual attack at night failed, but the next day a car was intercepted trying to leave the post and 5 rifles and a bren gun captured. Mutek and his men then went on to capture Nagishot (Nangichot), the former British administrative centre high in the mountains overlooking Chukudum. Nagishot has remained continuously in the hands of the Anya-Nya ever since. Government forces based at Chukudum have made periodic attempts to recapture Nagishot for years, culminating in a sustained assault in December 1970, but have been unsuccessful. Conversely, the Anya-Nya troops at Nagishot have never succeeded in overrunning Chukudum.

Soon after the initial attacks in 1963, the Anya-Nya forces in Eastern Equatoria were reorganized into three companies under the overall command of Taffeng. The first of these, A Company, was based at Idale in tho Lopid mountains about 50 miles north of Torit. Its commanding officer was Marko Luhuyoro[133], like Mutek an ex-sergeant major in the Equatoria Corps, and was said to have been particularly favoured by Father Saturnino whose home village of Loronyo was only fifteen miles from Idale. Father Saturnino was able to send Lohuyoro arms and supplies from Congo, although in so doing he undercut the authority of Taffeng who came from a different section of the Lotuko tribe. The rivalries and jealousies thus engendered have left their mark all through the struggle. B Company, commanded by Lazarro Mutek, was based at the former mission station of Isoke in the Dongotono Mountains. Mutek also constructed a more secure company headquarters at Dito, directly above Isoke at an altitude of 7,000 feet[134]. The third company, C, was Taffeng's headquarters company, based at Lorifa near Katire. These three companies were all there until the end

---

133 Lohuyoro, a brave and illiterate soldier, stole a gun just before the 1955 mutiny with the intention of shooting an Arab officer and spent seven years in prison. Father Saturnino transferred him briefly to "C" group in central Equatoria in 1963, but he soon returned to the east and remained in charge of A Company until replaced in 1966 or 1967 by Joseph Lagu.

134 It was at ISOKE that Mutek was visited in 1965 by the journalist Anthony Carthew, who published an account of his visit in the London Daily Mail, 31 Jan. and 2 Feb. 1966. There is a description of Dito, and of its temporary capture by Northern forces on April 18th 1967, in an interview with Joseph Oduo published in Sudan Informazioni, Milan, No. 13, 10 March 1968, pp. 12-16. Dito was also attacked in May 1966, the Northern forces being repelled with the loss of 2 rifles, 4,000 rounds of ammunition and 92 two-inch mortar shells (Southern Sudan Archive, Document 2C- 30, p. 3).

of 1964, when D Company was formed by an Acholi officer named Obale. D Company was recruited mainly from the Acholi and Madi peoples, and established a number of camps in the Nimule/Magwi area. Later still, an E Company was established in the vicinity of Kapoeta under a Toposa named Raymond Lokinei. As will be seen, however, circumstances have not favoured the Toposa people taking much active part in the liberation movement until fairly late.

Side by side with the military activities of the Anya-Nya, political work was carried on amongst the people living in the countryside. This political work was quite distinct from, though in theory controlled by, the activities of the SANU politicians in exile. It consisted of visiting the people in the villages, explaining to them the nature and the purpose of the guerrilla war being fought by the Anya-Nya, and enlisting their cooperation and support. Unfortunately, although this aspect of the work of the Southern Sudanese movement would seem to be fully as important as the military aspect, it does not seem (at least to the outside observer) to have been as well organized or as enthusiastically pursued as the fighting.

One political officer was appointed for the whole of eastern Equatoria, and he took up his duties in January 1964. He was based in the Imarok mountains north of Magwi, but spent most of his time on trek, visiting chiefs and village headmen in all the areas he could reach. Since the people of whom he was theoretically in charge were spread out over an area of more than 10,000 square miles, and since he could go no other way but on foot, he obviously could not be very thorough. He did however succeed in organizing a system of poll-tax collection, as well as an annual collection of what was known as "association money". Poll-tax rates were S£1 per household per year, while gifts of association money depended on what people could afford and were used exclusively for purchasing weapons. The political officer's estimate of 75% of the rural population paying both poll-tax and association money is probably over generous. In later years, owing to the progressive impoverishment of the countryside and the policy of attrition of the Khartoum government, tax collections have declined considerably.

Relations between the political officer and the guerilla forces were not always good. In one region where they broke down completely, the effect on the civilian population was disastrous. This was in east Lotuko, where

Lazarro Mutek dispensed with the services of the political officer and began to deal directly with the civilians himself[135]. The results were deplorable. East Lotuko had been extremely rich in cattle, but they were eaten at such a rate by the guerillas that in a few years the country was completely denuded. This shows the damage that can be done where a military commander is a warlord having absolute power over his region. The situation in east Lotuko forms a contrast with that in Horiok region, where Taffeng took great care to protect people's property. Because of the tsetse fly, there are few cattle there, but Taffeng prevented his soldiers from molesting the herds of sheep and goats on which the prosperity of the region depended.

The bad relations established between the civil population and the Anya-Nya in east Lotuko were in large part due to the lack of a political force which could mediate and act as buffer between the two. Ideally, this political force should take the shape of a full-scale civil administration to provide framework within which civilized life is possible. This framework appears to have been totally lacking in east Lotuko during the years 1955-67, and the repercussions of Mutek's policies travelled outside his area. Further east the Toposa, who are even more attached to their cattle than the Lotuko, saw what was happening and resolved to have nothing to do with the Anya-Nya. For this reason, and also because they had few educated leaders to explain to them the *raison d'etre* of the movement, the Toposa have in large part remained aloof from the struggle until the last years.

During 1966 the split mentioned above between Taffeng and Fr. Saturnino deepened, and when A and D Companies came together under command of Joseph Lagu[136] and under the patronage of Fr. Saturnino, B

---

135 Information from the political officer and from Joseph Oduho

136 Lagu was born on November 21 1931 of madi parents. His father was employed by Archdeacon Shaw in Malek, near Bor. He went to intermediate school in Tonj and speaks among other languages Dinka. At Rumbek Secondary School he was known for his forceful and outspoken views, and when on graduation he joined the Sudan Military College many of his schoolmates were implicitly aware of his intentions. He was commissioned second Lieutenant in 1960, and in 1963, then a 1st Lt, left the Sudan for Congo, where he was one of original group who planned guerrilla operations. He remained as commsnder of all Anya-Nya forces in Central Equatoria until the end of 1965, when he went to the east and engaged n a power struggle with Taffeng. In 1968, he and Oduho laid the foundatons of a new Anya-Nya military organization based in eastern Equatoria. This organization absorbed Anyidi and the Nile Provisional Government in 1970 and was headed by Lagu.

and C Companies united in opposition under Taffeng. The split persisted even after the moving of the political HQ of the Azania Liberation Front to Lorifa and then to Tul in 1966, showing that where divisions exist in the Anya-Nya the politicians are by no means always able to overcome them. The divisions continued after the death of Fr. Saturnino in January 1967, in fact becoming so bad that a big meeting of all notables in Eastern Equatoria was held at Lorifa in March 1967 to resolve them. This meeting was the first large-scale meeting held in Eastern Equatoria. Over 300 people attended, including almost all the important chiefs, political figures and Anya-Nya officers. A regional government for Eastern Equatoria was set up, following the pattern laid down by ALF in its division of the Southern Sudan into 8 administrative regions[137]. On the military side, it was resolved that Taffeng should have the rank of major general and be commander of all Anya-Nya forces in Eastern Region, while Lagu should be in charge of the mobile force. Unfortunately, the Lorifa agreement was short-lived, and Eastern Equatoria drifted without much guidance or leadership until a new basis of organization was established by Lagu and Oduho in mid-1968.

To conclude this chapter on the early development of the Anya-Nya in Eastern Equatoria, one or two passages will be quoted from the report of a Southern politician in exile who visited parts of the area in January 1966. The report is an excellent illustration of the difficulties and frictions that can arise between the military and political wings of any independent movement.

> The Anya-Nya. This is a difficult body to handle. If any politician claims that he had the loyalty of the Anya-Nya in his area, such a politician is deceiving himself. During my short stay, I have noticed that the bosses have developed the tendency of independent attitude from the politicians such that they have openly claimed too that the present arms so acquired are their own property and nobody else. Even the poor citizens who contributed the money are looked at as people of low-ebb...

---

137 The territory of Eastern Region (as it was called) included Torit district, Kapoeta district, and the non-Bari-speaking areas of Juba district east of the Nile. Eastern Region was to be administered by a Regional Commissioner and a Regional Assembly, with responsibility for finance, education, health, agriculture, police and prisons. See document 2C-30 in the Southern Sudan Archive for details of this.

I must point out that the few educated fellows now in the field are being hated by the present bosses and have even gone so far as forbidding using the English language. I must point out too that to have immediate remedy on the situation some prominent members of each locality should forthwith come to the field or pay periodical visits to the Anya-Nya so as to avert the ill practices over the poor citizens. The presence of such personalities would do a lot of good because, till now, the Anya-Nya bosses believe and openly say that they are fighting and being killed alone and when the war ended it would be the politicians who did nothing would enjoy the harvest of their labour. But if we now step in and stay together, go to the ambush together, be chased about by Arab air-raids and endure all odds together, they will then know that we are serious about the war. They will then and only then forget some of their grudges they have piled against the politicians and learn to be one and to know that the war against the Arabs is being fought by all citizens of the South. Not all the Anya-Nya bosses can be discredited. There are some brilliant junior officers together with their men who give no trouble to the citizens but fight the Arabs. They have excellent characters and are brave too. These groups together with conscripted educated class, could form the nucleus for future Azania Armed Forces. Nevertheless, the preceding paragraph does not apply to the Headquarters of the Old Man because he is a good soldier and is an excellent administrator in his work too. All the work at the Headquarters is run on the Governmental line. He has set up an all-officers council whose duty is to deal with war planning, discipline, etc. He is the final authority in this council and its sub-committees. Given the authority of the unified Eastern Command, he would have the situation well in hand and would facilitate the smooth running of the Anya-Nya in that region which would be exemplary in the entire South wherever such functions exit. I have high hope on him, and I was relieved of my anxiety during my short stay with him.[138]

---

138 Document 1C-287, p. 4, Southern Sudan Archive.

CHAPTER 10

Central Equatoria

Serious planning for military operations in Central Equatoria began about February 1963, when Father Satunino and Elia Lupe[139] met in Aru. It is true that an earlier attack had been made on the police post at Kajo-Kaji in November 1962, but this was a hit-and-run affair conducted without arms and without plans for any continuation. At the meeting in Aru, Fr. Saturnino put forward the idea of capturing Eastern Equatoria by conventional warfare and then advancing westward, but this idea was dropped when it became apparent that the supply of weapons would be wholly inadequate. Instead, it was decided to adopt guerilla tactics and capture weapons from the enemy[140]. At a second meeting in Aru in June,

---

139   Elia Lupe Baraba, the son of a former Kakwa paramount chief, was born in 1924
near Yei, and graduated from Nabumali High School in Uganda in 1947. He entered
the police, and returned from a training course at Scotland Yard to become Deputy
Commander at Juba in July 1955. In 1956 he transferred to the civil administration, and
became A.D.C. at Maridi, but then resigned in 1958 to enter politics. He was a member
of the Southern Bloc in parliament, took up coffee farming near Yei during Abboud's
regime, and left the country in October 1962. Since then he has been active in the
liberation movement, and became Chief Commissioner in the civil administration set up
by Joseph Lagu's organization.

140   . Information from Elia Lupe.

when the other two were joined by Joseph Lagu, plans were made to attack simultaneously at three points with three groups of 25 men each. Group A was to enter Sudan from Congo near Maridi under command of Paul Ali Gbatala. Group B, under the command of Lagu, was to enter slightly to the west of the Yei-Aba road, and under Marko Lohuyoro, Group C was to enter at Kaya post near the point where Sudan, Congo and Uganda meet. The date of entry was originally fixed for August 18th, but at a third meeting at Aru, it was postponed for a month. Fr. Saurnino himself gave the order to the three groups to start, travelling throughout the night of September 18th in his car.

The three groups met with varying fortunes. Group A had no weapons at all, and were arrested by Congolese authorities as they were about to cross the border. Only five men including Gbatala escaped, Gbatala eventually making his way through Sudan to near Aba by the end of 1963. There he was given a gun and some supplies and returned to the Maridi area, entablishing his camp about 30 miles south of the town. His soldiers meawhile were imprisoned in Congo, and (except for the three who were killed) came and joined the camp when released a couple of months later. In March 1964 Gbatala's men killed Chief Sali and anothor sub- chief who were informing on the group'a activities. In August, at Gangara Osman, seven miles west of Maridi on the Yambio road, a van belonging to a Northern trader was burned and the driver and another man killed. No weapons were captured until December of the same year when eight Northern soldiers were killed two miles from Maridi prison and two guns taken.

Group B meanwhile met with fewer difficulties. The party entering Sudan, which included Lagu, Bernardino Mou[141] and Philip Angutua, proceeded northwest along tho Congo border to a heavily forested area 35 miles from the Yei-Aba road. There they established their camp at a place called Tungu. Their armoury consisted of 7 ancient munzle-loaders collected from the chiefs in Yei district (powerful but almost as

---

141 Mou, a Dinka corporal in the SDF, crossed into Central African Republic in 1961 or 1962. He led the attack on Kajo-Kaji in November 1962, and after only a short time in B group was withdrawn by William Deng to open operations in Bahr el Ghazal. Mou was wounded and captured during the attack on Wau of January 11th, 1964, and was executed in late February (See the Daily Telegraph, 22 February 1964). Many consider him the best soldier ever to fight in the Anya-Nya.

dangerous to the user as to the enemy), 3 rifles and 2 shotguns. Their first action on September 19th consisted in burning the shop of an Arab trader at Yei district at Avukaya on the Yei-Maridi road. This brought the army in armoured cars and trucks, and during the following days and weeks, there were constant ambushes, including one at Larumbe 35 miles from Yei where 4 Northern soldiers were killed. Group B captured its first weapons in July 1964, when 5 rifles and 2 sten guns were taken from an army car destroyed on the Yei-Maridi road[142]. The party was not without its troubles, however. The people living in the vicinity of the camp - mostly Avukayas and Bakas - were not very friendly. (Following an often-to-be-repeated pattern which shows the lack of unified political, social and military thinking in the movement, no political officer was appointed to the group.) Food could not be purchased locally but had to be supplied from Congo. In January 1964 the camp moved eastwards across the Yei-Aba road to Akepa, near the tea and coffee plantations of Kabengere. There the Kakwa chiefs were generally firm supporters of the movement, and so welcomed the group which by that time had grown to about 200 men.

Upon entering Sudan (and in the process carefully avoiding Uganda which was considered hostile to the movement), Group C established it camp at Onyako on the Kindi river. The party possessed 1 automatic weapon, 2 rifles and 2 shotguns. As in the case of Group A and B it began by attacking Arab traders, burning 3 or 4 shops near Morobo. The army were not long in arriving, and the usual pattern of ambushes ensued in which several soldiers were killed but no weapons captured. In December 1963, Group C attempted an ambitious operation which nearly resulted in their being wiped out[143]. They attacked Tombili police post at Jebel Gumbira, about 50- 60 miles from their camp. The attack failed, owing to the preparedness of the police who had dug trenches around the post, and the Anya-Nya lost one man killed[144]. Worse still, the police summoned the army by radio, and the attackers soon found themselves being followed back to their camp. The army captured one man and forced him to lead them, he tired and was shot; they captured another; the next morning,

---

142 Information from Elia Lupe
143 Information from Oliver Albino
144 Joseph Lagu's brother.

when the Anya-Nya awoke in their base camp, they found themselves surrounded.

It was a hopeless situation, but miraculously only two Anya-Nya were killed, one of them being the B group commander Yosia Yenki[145]. The rest escaped by creeping under the river bank to a secret camp nearby. Following this incident, Joseph Lagu, who had overall responsibility for all operations in Central Equatoria, diagnosed the trouble as too many men with too few arms and sent most of them back to the Congo border for training. The camp itself was moved to Alutu near Akepa, and placed first under command of Samauel Lolika, a Lotuko, and then in July 1964 under David Dada and Ali Ayume. C group continued to grow, and by early 1964 numbered over 300 men.

In 1964 there occurred an event which, for better or for worse, was to have a profound influence on the scale of Anya-Nya operations and ultimately on the whole of the Southern Sudanese movement. Then was the "Simba" rebellion in Congo, which began in September 1963 under the leadership of Pierre Mulele, Antoine Gizenga and Christopher Gbenye, and which reached the Sudan border at Aba in August 1964. At first, it was hoped that the Simbas would be friendly to the Anya-Nya, and Fr. Saturnino even suggested that a mission be sent to Stanleyville to meet their leaders. But it soon became apparent that, far from being friendly, the Simbas were working closely with the Khartoum government, and in fact received a large part of their military supplies from Algeria and U.A.R. via Juba. The Southern Sudanese leaders in Aba and Aru, upon receiving word that the Simbas intended to arreet them and turn them over to the Sudan army, were forced to cross hurriedly into Uganda, where they remained from August 1964 until the defeat of the Simbas by the Congolese National army in the later part of 1965.

The Simba period, during which the Anya-Nya forces in Central and Eastern Equatoria were partially or wholly out of touch with their representatives and sources of supply in Congo was not as much of a hardship as might be thought. In the first place, a formal cease-fire between the Anya-Nya and the army extended throughout the South from November

---

145   Yenki had replaced Lohuyoro after entering Sudnn.

1964 until June 1965[146]. This cease-fire was frequently broken, particularly in Upper Nile, but by comparison with what went before and after it was a time of peace and relaxation. In the second place, the Simba period resulted in a fantastic windfall of weapons and equipment for the Anya-Nya. This came about as follows.

When the Simbas were defeated by the Congolese National army, they abandoned the weapons they had so recently received from the Sudan in large numbers. These arms the Congolese, who resented their being supplied by Khartoum in the first place, felt no reluçtance to sell or give to the Anya-Nya. Detachments of freedom fighters came from all over the South to the Congo borders to acquire weapons, and it is estimated that at least 6,000 guns changed hands in this way. This would have been enough to equip (for purposes of illustration), the entire Uganda army, and the arms so acquired have formed the basis for all Anya-Nya resistance since 1965.

Although the cease-fire ended in June 1965, it was not until after the Juba massacre on July 8th, that military operations in Central Equatoria began again in earnest. With large numbers of weapons now in the hands of the Anya-Nya the fighting became much more severe. To take an example of the battles fought, in about August 1965 Group B ambushed a convoy of 8 military trucks on the Kabengere road 8 miles from Yei and destroyed them, the tank escorting them being forced to return to Yei. All except one of the 40 - 50 soldiers in the convoy were killed. In the words of one Southern leader the latter part of 1965 was "the bitterest time, the most active time", and it would be true to say that the Anya-Nya's military control of the South reached a peak at the end of 1965 which it has not regained since[147].

The period from May 1965 onwards saw a considerable increase in the number of Anya-Nya camps established throughout Central Equatoria. In 1963 and 1964 these camps were for the most part located close to the Congo border, but in 1965 many were opened deep inside the country.

---

146 This was the period in which Clement Mboro was Minister of the Interior in Sirr el Khatim's caretaker government.
147 With the possible exception of Upper Nile in the last part of 1970.

Camp C1, for example, was established by Michael Lorwe[148] at Bereka northwest of Lanya corner in Pajulu country. At about the same time C2 was opened by Simoni Jada at Su'bi among the Baris south of Juba. Jada was a prolific founder of camps, opening also in 1965 Moli south of Su'bi and the camp known as Saigon[149] far to the north of Juba in Mondari country. In the area of Group B, B1 was established north of Yei by Richard Wari.

The founding of Anya-Nya camps in Central Equatoria and elsewhere was by no means as straightforward as the labels C1, C2, B1, etc. imply. The subject would make a fascinating study for a sociologist. Perhaps the most interesting camps are those which are not opened by other camps or by Anya-Nya leaders, but which spring up spontaneously in the countryside for no other reason than that the people living in the area want them. An example of such a camp was one established in Pajulu country in August 1965 by a man called Henry, who the month before had run away from the Juba massacre[150]. Henry was a clerk, with no military experience. He gathered together the people of his own clan, talked to them about the history of their sufferings and the necessity of liberation, and got them to agree that he should be given money to buy arms for them in Congo. The members of his clan were far from wealthy, but they succeeded in collecting £500 (part money, part in goats), with which Henry purchased 23 arms, together with ammunition, cartridge belts and mines. On his return, he became the leader of 240 men, all in his own clan, who became Anya-Nya. This was a completely self-contained group, a "little army", held together by clan loyalties and owing allegiance to its leader largely in virtue of the fact that he could arrange for the purchase of weapons. Later on, members of other Pajulu clans were admitted to the group, but only in sporadic cases non-Pajulu, because "you don't entrust keeping a gun to a member of another tribe". In its early days, Henry's camp belonged

---

148 Lorwe was formerly a businessman in Torit vho did his Anya-Nya training under Josoph Lagu and Ali Ayume. He rose to become Commander of No. 3 Company in Central Equatoria in 1965. He was killed on 28 June 1969 at Bungu.

149 The origin of this name in unclear, but its choice no doubt reflects a desire to identify with the Vietnamese people in their struggle for independence which was in the news those days.

150 The author is indebted to the notes of Nelson Kasfir's interviews with Henry and with Eliaba Surur for the information which follows.

neither to Group B nor Group C, but in March 1966 an (abortive) attempt was made to bring all the Anya-Nya of Central Equatoria under a unified command, and a meeting was called in Henry's area to decide which group to affiliate with. At first, the men were against any merger, but Henry reasoned with them and eventually, they agreed to join Angutua's Group B. People initially opposed the affiliation because Angutwa was of a different tribe (Avukaya). Still, in the end, they were mollified because his mother was a Kakwa (Bari-speaking, like the Pajulu) and because he came from not very far away. The reader will judge, from this example, how difficult it is for individual Anya-Nya units to weld themselves into a unified fighting force.

Henry's group is not an isolated case, but exemplifies a strain of parochialism and self-sufficiency which characterizes the founding of many Anya-Nya camps. Even C1 and C2 exhibited it. Lorwe and Jada were both members of Group C, it is true, which at the time was under the command of David Dada, but when they went to their respective home areas and collected money for arms-buying they did not give what they had collected to Dada. Instead they went directly to Congo and brought the arms themselves. Dada would certainly have preferred them not to do this, for the result was that the men of C1 and C2 looked to Lorwe and Jada rather than to Dada for leadership. But he kept quiet about it, and in any case, C1 and C2 still remained within the orbit of C group in the sense that they always obeyed order from HQ concerning military operations. For example, when C group besieged Kaya post in November 1965, both C1 and C2 sent platoons to take part in the battle. If one were to look for a single unifying thread on which to hang a history of the devolopment of the Anya-Nya, it would probably be the gradual replacement of the initial single-minded loyalty of the guerrilla fighter to his clan, his tribe, and his local camp commander (coupled with mistrut of other clans, other tribes and other camp commanders) by a willingness to participate in an integrated Southern Sudanene force. This process was on-going throughout the struggle.

The problem of Anya-Nya leaderehip in Central Equatoria has always been a difficult one, and has been made worse by frictions and jealousies between those who live east and those who live west of the Nile. From as early as May 1964 there were attempts to replace Joseph Lagu by a west bank man, and at one point Lagu is even said to have been tied up by a group of disgruntled west-bankers. Lagu, however, had the firm support of Aggrey Jaden in SANU, and continued as Jaden's chief of staff until the end of 1965 when he and Father Saturnino returned to the east. 1965 was Lagu's most active year, in which he trained many Anya-Nya and supervised the distribution of thousands of Simba arms. A significant step in the process of unification of the region occurred in late 1966 or early 1967 when B and C groups finally came together under a single HQ at Morta[151]. The Central Equatoria forces have constituted a battalion with companies, Gbatala'a men becoming part of a separate battalion based at Maridi.

It was mentioned above that in the early days the Anya-Nya in Central Equatoria - particularly B group - suffered from having no political officers who could act as a liaison between the guerilla fighters and the civilians. (Note incidentally that political officers would be unnecessary in an Anya-Nya camp such as Henry's.) In 1964 two people began doing this liaison work in C Group, although they were not formally appointed as political officers until mid-1965. B Group followed later, with its first political officer in 1966. In June 1967 a full-scale system of civil administration for Central Equatoria region was started, following like the system in Eastern Equatoria the pattern laid down by ALF. Daniel Jumi was appointed regional commissioner, being succeeded in February 1968 by Eliaba Surur[152]. The civil administration in Central Equatoria has the reputation of being the best organized of all the regions in the South, as is evidenced by the large number of schools operating in the area.

---

151 Morta was located west of Gulumbi near Jebel Kojiko, and replaced an earlier camp named Nyambiri. It continued as the civil and militnry HQ for Central Equntoria until captured by the Sudan army on October 1st 1970.

152 Surur was the headmaster of Lanya Technical Intermediate School until he escaped into the bush at the time of the Juba massacre. He remained regional commissioner of Central Equatoria until mid-1970, including the period of the Anyidi government, and was in charge of education in Elia Lupe's civil administration.

CHAPTER 11

Western Equatoria

In this chapter, which deals with developments in roughly the areas of Maridi and Yambio districts, we shall include Moru-land, although since 1963 the Morus have associated themselves at least as closely with the Central as with the Western region of Equatoria. The Zande area has always been somewhat separate, from the rest, and has followed its own patterns of growth.

The Moru-land

The Anya-Nya owes its establishment in Moru-land to two men, Stephen Ali Baba and Jackson Garanga, who in April 1964 set up a small camp at Bangule. Ali Baba was one of the four men who had escaped capture from the Congolese with Paul Ali Gbatala in September 1963, and after helping Gbatala found the camp at Maridi he decided to move into his home area. Jackson, who like Ali Gbatala belongs to the Kediru section of the Moru tribe, had worked in the forestry department at Katire before returning to Moru area in early 1964. He had also been in contact with

Ezbon Jodi[153], a Moru political and liaison officer based at Aba. Ali Baba and Jackson met by chance at Bangule, about 60 miles south of Mundri, and set up their camp there.

The camp at Bangule remained very small until July 1964, when Jodi despatched a party of eight, with four guns, from Angudri[154]. The group was under the command of El Hag Beshir, a Baka (or Mundu) ex-sergeant of the S.D.F., and included Repent Sunday Gideon[155], Aggrey Peter and Mondiri's former secretary, Morris Agili. The party picked up others along the way, and by the time they reached Bangule numbered over a hundred. The Anya-Nya force so constituted named itself Group F (later in June 1965 changed to Group D), and although the name indicated that it was independent of Groups A, D and C, there was until 1967 a close but not always clearly defined relationship between Group D and Gbatala in Group A. Shortly after July 1964 Jackson broke away from the others and went to found a separate camp in Kediru area: this camp he declared to be part of Group A and as such not under the command of El Hag. This was the beginning of a long-drawn-out quarrel between the Kediru and the other Moru Any-Nya, a matter which, as will be seen below, implicated eventually Ezbon Mondiri and many others.

In June 1965, there began a period of heavy fighting in Moru area, marked by the destruction of Lui hospital[156]. The sequence of events was as follows. On June 19th an Anya-Nya attack was made on a military and police post at Chief Jambo's village at Mide, 29 miles southeast of Lui. A bridge on the Juba side of the post had been destroyed the previous night, in the hope that no reinforcements would be able to come from Juba. But

---

153 In December 1963 the Anya-Nya took £500 in payroll money from Jodi, who was manager at a large tea and coffee plantation at Iwatoka. Jodi was suspected of complicity by the police, was arrested, and when released escaped with 700 plantation workers to Congo. Some of these labourers returned after the fall of Abboud and resumed work, but there was another exodus in July 1965, and the whole plantation including the tea factory was burned in 1966.

154 Informntion from Ezbon Jodi. Angudri, on the Congo border between Yei and Maridi, was for a long time the depot camp for arms buyers from all over the South. Every major tribe had its own camp there, under the overall control of a camp commandant.

155 Repent Sunday went to a TTC in Yei, then to Khartoum Technical Institute, and was a schoolbook illustrator in Juba until he left for Congo in 1964. He became the commanding officer of Moru area in March 1967, the position he held till ca 1970.

156 Lui was built in 1920 by Dr Fraser of the CMS and was housing a medical centre, a school and a church which was erected in 1922.

as luck would have it, unknown to the Anya-Nya an army detachment already happened to be staying in Mide *en route* to Maridi, and the attack was therefore repulsed. The detachment in question left for Maridi the next day, was ambushed again between Lui and Mundri, and informed the commander at Mundri. The Anya- Nya at Mundri were certain that the army would return the next day and attack Lui hospital, so at 6:00 a.m. they began moving medicine and equipment and loading it into a car[157]. But at 8.00 a.m., before the car could be driven away, the army arrived, and a fight took place in which two patients and a hospital cleaner were killed. (Fortunately, the majority of the patients had been sent home the day before.) Over the next two months, the entire hospital was burned by the Northern troops, and most of the hospital staff went to work with the Anya-Nya. By this time the Moru HQ had been moved to Mayaya about 40 miles south of Lui, and two small hospitals were set up there, one military and one civil. In addition, there was established a chain of 16 dressing stations throughout the country, all manned by Lui hospital staff. This medical service in Moru country has continued to function ever since, although in later years it was very much handicapped for lack of supplies.

Ezbon Mondiri Gwanza arrived in Moru-land from Khartoum in April 1965, and for two years was a dominant but controversial force in the area. Although no soldier, Mondiri had a genius for organization, and took an early hand in military operations. After an unsuccessful attempt to capture Mundri in October 1965, which was frustrated by an aerial bombardment from planes based at Juba, Mondiri turned his attention to the Kediru, who since 1964 had operated quite successfully on their own without being integrated into the main Moru forces[158]. He visited the Kediru chiefs, who agreed that integration should take place and complained to Mondiri that out of £20,000 collected and given to Gbatala and others they had so far received only 4 arms and 500 bullets. Mondiri replied that the money should be given to El Hag, not to Gbatala, but promised to ask the latter what had become of it. Following this meeting the chiefs gave an additional £90 to a soldier, who instead of giving it to El Hag took it to Jackson the Kediru military leader in Congo. Jackson bought a bren gun and returned via Maridi, complaining to Gbatala on

---

157 Information from the medical assistant in charge of the hospital.
158 Information from Francis Wajo and Elisapana Kabi.

the way about Mondiri's interference. On arriving home Jackson arrested the Kediru chiefs who had met with Mondiri. Mondiri was incensed, and on December 31st despatched a military force under Sunday to subdue the Kediru Anya-Nya. This was duly accomplished a number of Kediru soldiers being killed and 2 or 3 more fleeings to Rumbek for safety.

But when the Moru forces returned from this rather shameful operation, they came to the conclusion that it was with Mondiri rather than with the Kediru that the fault lay. What exactly were their accusations against him is not clear, but in any case, they arrested Mondiri with three other Moru officers and beat them. Then they released him and because Mondiri was Secretary of Defence in SANU[159], they sent him to Congo with a letter to Aggrey Jaden, Elia Lupe and Joseph Lagu to try him. Needless to say, Mondiri did not deliver this letter, but instead gave instructions to William Hassan, Peter Cyrillo and some other Anya-Nya officers he found at Angudri to proceed to the eastern boundary of Moru-land at Lomilingwa and build a new national Anya-Nya headquarters. Mondiri then left for East Africa, where Joseph Oduho appointed him Secretary of Defence in the newly-formed ALF.

Lomilingwa was built in the early months of 1966, and was intended to be a national HQ with soldiers from all parts of the South. Many soldiers in fact did come, including a lot of Dinkas from Rumbek, and given time Mondiri might have been able to weld them into a truly national force. But, unfortunately, the Morus refused to recognise Lomilingwa. They had their own HQ at Ngiri (the successor to Mayaya) and the Moru people in the area of Lomilingwa were only with difficulty persuaded to supply the new HQ with food. Given the hostility between Ngiri and Lomilingwa it wan apparent that sooner or later there would be an explosion, and what eventually triggered it off was an abortive military

coup d' etat staged against ALF in February 1967. The nature of this coup will be described below. Suffice it to say that after a bewildering series of arrests and counter-arrests the Moru forces of Ngiri attacked and defeated the forces of Lomilingwa during March and April 1967[160]. Estimates of casualties range around 30, including Solomon Manyang,

---

159   And because the news of the replacemet of SANU by ALF had not yet reached them —
see below.

160   There is a Moru song about the battle which has beon recorded on tape.

an officer from Rumbek. Lomilingwa was destroyed, Mondiri escaped into the bush, and what was probably the most negative and destructive chapter in Moru Anya-Nya history was ended.

Mundri area was under the independent command of Major Sunday Gideon. This area extended up to Jambo area[161]. Under his command were Captain John Maluk, Captain Arnold de Mamur, Weseley, Christopher Dabile and others. His forces conducted successful operations against the enemy forces in Mundri, Lui, Amadi, Yere, Manyolo and Jambo establishing full control of the countryside. When he joined the SSLM under Joseph Lagu, the whole of the Western Equatoria Region had thus become part of the new set-up. An incident of great military and political significance occurred in December 1971 in the area under the command of Major Sunday Gideon[162]. A Sudan Airways Fokker plane missed its destination to Juba and crashed in the area. The surviving passengers, which included some officers, were rescued, treated for injuries, and well looked after. The dead were properly buried. On the orders of Lagu, the surviving passengers were released and escorted by the Any-Nya to a point near the Mundri garrison to be received by the Sudan army. The humane treatment of the victims of the plane crash shown by the Anya-Nya in this incident had a tremendous impact in changing the image of the Anya-Nya in the North from the hitherto "terrorists" and "highwaymen" to mature and responsible people. This positive gesture had a significant impact on the May regime of Nimeiri and contributed in no small way to the acceleration of the search for peace by then.

The Zande Region of Western Equatoria

In the Zande region of Western Equatoria, the Anya- Nya owes its establishment to the work of Dominic Dabi[163]. Dabi was an agricultur-alist working for the Sudan government who in September 1962 went

---

161 Magaya, M.A.,T he Anyanya Movement in South Sudan, 1962-1972, Kisubi: Marianum Press, 2014, p. 70.

162 Alier, op. cit. p103-5 gives a detailed account of this incident.

163 Most of the information in thie chapter comes from Dominic Dabi, Michael Ngamunde, Samuel Abujohn, Joseph Lokule and Philip Nvue.

to Congo and made contact with SANU. He was assigned the job of organising the refugees in the Yambio area with the purpose of starting up military operations, and placed a man, Allison Magaya, in Gbatala's ill-fated party. In early 1964, Dabi opened Naangere camp about 20 miles northeast of Yambio, leaving Ismail Kpatakpari in charge. Naangere was followed in rapid succession by Biki camp near Ezo, established by Matayo Mwangi and Richard Babiro, Birisi camp east of Yambio opened by Dominic Cassiano and William Sebit (called "youth" camp because it contained mainly schoolboys), and Ringasi camp southeast of Nzara founded by Habbakuk Kefu Soro[164]. None of these camps started with any weapon besides spears, bows and arrows, and muzzle-loader, but modern arms were gradually obtained through "black marketing"[165]. Dabi remained in Congo for this purpose. Each camp operated independently until about May 1965, when they came together under the leadership of Habbakuk. Two later camps were opened at Tambura (1965) under Dominic Cassiano, and at Ibba (January 1966) under Dominic Dabi.

As was generally the case throughout Equatoria Province, the largest battles with the Sudan army took place during the latter part of 1965. One of the biggest in Azande-land was the battle of Uze river on June 26th 1965, when an Any-Nya force of 56 men ambushed 300 Northerners who were coming to attack Birisi youth camp. The Northern force split into 3 columns, and when the centre column was ambushed the two outer columns fired inwards on their own men. In the dense bush, it was impossible to tell friend from foe, and Northern casualties were reported to have reached 150[166].

Not all the camps located in Zande-land were started by Azande. In July 1964, a camp was opened at Zangambaro between Tambura and

---

164 Habbakuk, the son of Chief Soro, gradunted from Rumbek in 1958 and joined the game department. In September 1963 he crossed into Congo, narrowly escaped being killed by the Simbas in the forest when he managed to run away with the rope tied along his waist, and re-entered Sudan early in 1964. He was commander of the Anya-Nya forcea in Zande area from early 1965 until May 1968, when he became second-in- command to Samuel Abujohn. With regard to Habbakuk's narrow escape in Congo, it is worth noting that many Azande were killed by the Simbas, though apparently only after the Simbas started to lose ground.

165 For Southerners, the term "blackmarket" applies exclusively to the purchase of weapons and ammunition, not in general to the buying of scarce commodities at high prices.

166 Information from Samuel Abujohn.

the border of Central African Republic by Ferdinand Goi[167], who later moved his sphere of operations to Western Bahr el Ghazal. Goi's camp, which had earlier, in 1963, been located inside C.A.R. and which had no name but was known simply as the Bellanda camp, was supplied by a civilian committee in Tambura town[168]. These committees sprang up throughout Western Equatoria early in 1963 following the receipt of letters signed by Dominic Dabi and William Deng: they had as their purpose the collection of funds to be used for the purchase of clothing, camp materials and weapons. The Tambura committee sent an average of £50 per month outside to Dabi, in addition to supplying Goi'a camp. Even the Greek merchants of Tambura helped by providing supplies. In early 1965, when there was an active branch of the Southern Front in Tambura, the scale of donations increased, and £700 was collected in two months, much of which went to Biki camp. At that time the SF branch, although collecting a lot of money, was harassed by C.I.D. informers in Tambura town, and eventually went to Goi with a list of 15 Southerners believed to be government spies. Goi's camp arrested and executed them. Also at the same time, Goi's first ambush took place two miles from Tambura on the Wau road, when two army trucks were burned. Life became very difficult for the SF committee, and when on February 12th the Northern troops opened fire in the native lodging area of Tambura, they left *en masse* for one of the Anya-Nya camps near Tambura.

---

167 Goi, a Ballanda from Baggari near Wau was a legendary figure. He left his studies in a seminary in Milan in 1962, made contact with SANU in Congo, returned to Wau to inform people of his plans, and then entered the forest about May 1963. In November, he succeeded in taking a gun from a policeman at Bussere, and from his camp at Tambura he made many successful raids on army and police posts. During a double attack at Tambura and Source Yubu in 1965, Goi is said to have killed 18 police singlehanded with a machine gun. Toward the end of tha year, Goi took over command of all the Anya-Nya camps in western Bahr el Ghazal from Filbert Ucini, and extended the chain of camps as far as Raga. In early 1967 he was in Central Equatoria and was the main leader of the coup against ALF. When he returned to his HQ near Wau had a coup of his own (i.e., against him) and was arrested. He was released after 3 months, but never fully regained his power and left Bahr el Ghazal in late 1968. He was appointed Deputy Minister of Defence in Jaden's SSPG but declined the post. Toward the end of his life he was much troubled by illness: his right hand was paralysed in a battle at Kpaile near Wau in early 1966, and Goi was forced subsequently to fight only with his left. He went to Italy in 1969 to be treated for a heart condition, and died in hospital in Gulu, Uganda, on November 8th 1970. He was about 35.

168 Information from Michael Tawil Ngamunde

The departure of their supporting committee from Tambura did not result in any diminution in tho activities of Goi's camp. Following receipt of a fairly large amount of money from Wau, Goi purchased a good number of modern weapons in Congo, and in August 1965 made a big attack on Tambura and Source Yubu. Tambura was surrounded and nearly fell (an announcement to this effect was broadcast on Radio Omdurman), and the pressure on the government troops was so intense that supplies had to be parachuted to them[169]. A relief column from Wau took nearly a month to reach Tambura because of constant ambushes and broken bridges.

The other non-Zande camp in Zande-land was a camp founded at Li-Rangu near Yambio in January 1965, by a group of Dinka Anya-Nya from Bahr el Ghazal and Upper Nile. This camp, which was founded by Camillo Dhol[170] but was theoretically under the over-all command of Habbakuk, was intended merely as a transit camp for soldiers taking supplies from Congo into the interior. But owing to certain difficulties at home, the Bahr el Ghazal group under the command of Edward Nyiel remained for some months and took part in significant military operations in June and July 1965. On June 24th the Dinkas blocked the three roads linking Yambio, Nzara and Li-Rangu, destroyed 3 army lorries, and captured the airport and Li-Rangu hospital[171]. Seven days later the army counter-attacked, and lost 48 men in a 4-hour battle. The Dinkas occupied the airfield until July 10th, and when they departed left trenches

---

169   Information from A. Wanji. See alao the Uganda Argus, 7 August 1965 and The New York Times, 14 Aug. 1965. The Uganda Argus throughout the month of August reports heavy military activity in the South.

170   Dhol was born in 1924 in Aweil, went to Bussere Intermediate School, worked as an agricultural officer, and was elected to the Senate as a Liberal in 1958. When he left Sudan for C.A.R. in February 1963 his father, who was a paramount chief, was put in prison for 3 years because of his son's flight. Dhol organized various refugee camps in Congo as well as Li-Rangu, was chairman of the coordinating committee for Bahr el Ghazal, and was later chairman of the preparatory committee for the Angudri convention. He became vice-president of the S.S.P.G., and was subsequently a member of the Nile Provisional Government. Dhol is regarded as one of the founding fathers of tho resistance movement in Bahr el Ghazal.

171   Information from Camillo Dhol and Akuot Atem

dug in the runway so that planes were unable to land[172]. The hospital was destroyed and has not been used since. With the death of Edward Nyiel in mid-1966, the camp lost its most effective leader, and reverted to being a transit rather than an attacking unit.

In July 1966 Zande area set up a full-scale system of civil administration - the first region in Southern Sudan to do so. The events which led to the establishment of this system are of interest, and help to explain Zande-land's relative independence from the rest of Equatoria.

In February 1966 Michael Tawil Ngamunde, having previously met in East Africa, was sent on a mission by Habbakuk and the other Zande leaders to contact Joseph Oduho's ALF[173]. The purpose of this mission was to acquaint ALF with the situation in Zande-land, to say that the people were finding it increasingly difficult to pay their taxes to the movement, to point out that so far no help of any kind has been given the Azande in their struggle, and to ask for assistance. Ngamunde was cordially received by the leaders of ALF, but no firm commitment to help was forthcoming. When Ngamunde returned to Ringasi it was generally recognized that Zande region would have to stand on its own feet, without outside support or even contact with the national leaders. It, therefore, proceeded to establish a civil government based on the ALF pattern[174], but including such portfolios as Secretary for Foreign Affairs which indicated that it regarded itself as in some degree independent. At a large meeting in Ringasi in July 1966, to which delegates came from all parts except North area[175], Michael Tawil Ngamunde was elected Chairman of the Western Region, and Father Angelo He-Totuo Vice Chairman. Lt Col Habbakuk was confirmed as military commander.

The system of regional government worked in most parts very well. District Commissioners were appointed in Yambio, Tambura and

---

172   The Observer of 21 Nov. 1965 reports that Li-Rangu airfield was out of action. It also says that the role of R.A.F. pilots in dropping arms and supplies to Sudan army units cut off by the Anya-Nya proved "vital" in helping to combat the rebels. Later, in 1966, the army built 2 more airfields at Yambio and Nzara near the army barracks: the field at Li-Rangu was abandoned.

173   Information from Michael Tawil Ngamunde

174   Ngamunde diocussed the ALF pattern of govornment with Elia Lupe, the ALF Secretary for Internal Affairs on his way home through Aba.

175   It was decided to organize first in Zande-land, and then if successful to extend the system to Moru area. The extension, however, was never made.

Maridi, with an A.D.C. in Ibba, all reporting to a Secretary for Home Affairs and Local Government at headquarters. There was initially some jealousy in Yambio, where the commanding officer saw the new civil government as eroding some of his powers, but this was settled at a new conference in March 1968. Only in Maridi did the system break down completely, where Paul Ali Gbatala dismissed Simon Mohandes, the newly-appointed D.C., following a meeting in August 1966 with a delegation from ALF. This delegation, which included Elisapana Kabi Mulla, Peter Cyrillo and Severino Fuli (Mondiri came later in October), took a dim view of the new government in Zande-land, which seemed to them to be proceeding entirely independently of ALF and hence to be working againat the rest of the South. Hence, they persuaded Gbatala to have nothing to do with it, and Mohandes was appointed political officer for ALF instead of D.C. for the Western Region. In the long run this has probably been a bad thing for the civilians of Maridi area, for in the absence of a strong civil administration they have suffered as much from the Anya-Nya as from the Northern troops. Most keenly felt was the lack of an agricultural officer to encourage food production for the Anya-Nya: when food grew short there were quarrels and fights, and some people living in the countryside had to return to Maridi town (and the protection of the Khartoum government) for safety. These troubles in Maridi area continued up until March 1970, when the commanding officer was killed in circumstances that are not entirely clear following his arrest, and replaced by a new man who recognized the authority of the Western Equatoria military commander.

Since its formation in 1966, the government of Western Equatoria has continued on its own way, only beginning in 1970 to have very much contact with the civil administration in other parts of the South. Its decision to remain aloof from Jaden's Southern Sudan Provisional Government will be discussed below: suffice it to say that Azande were divided on this issue, and that at meetings called to discuss it in March and May 1968 the military leadership passed from Col. Habbakuk to Col.

Samuel Abujohn[176], Habbakuk remaining as second-in-command. Later, however, close links were once more forged between Zande area and the rest of the South.

The separate existence of Western Region of Equatoria came to an end in 1969 when they joined Joseph Lagu who had assumed the leadership of the Anya-Nya that year. Lagu invited the leaders of Western Equatoria to meet him for discussion on the future of the Anya-Nya. Col. Samuel Abujohn and Major Allison Magaya were delegated to take up the mission. The two travelled to Uganda through the Congo where they met Joseph Lagu. He explained to them why he decided to take over the leadership of the Anya-Nya Movement from the politicians and the then military commander, Gen. Emido Tafeng. He also informed them that the Israelis had agreed to support the Movement under his leadership. After a 4-week joint mission with the Israelis to Eastern Equatoria, Joseph Lagu promoted Col Samuel Abujohn to the rank of Brigadier to be the third in command and Brigadier Joseph Akuon of Upper Nile was the second in command in the army and Southern Sudan Liberation Movement (SSLM) was adopted as the political wing of the Movement with Joseph Lagu as Chairman[177]. Brigadier Samuel Abujohn moved to Owiny-ki-bul, the new HQ of the Anya-Nya, and Habbakuk Soro took over again the command of Western Equatoria.

---

176   Abujohn, who is the first non-Avungara in history to become a Zande military leader, was educated at Rumbek. He attended the Sudan Military College, and in 1954 was the first projected Southern officer to be commissioned since the uprising of Ali Abdel Latif in 1924. Abujohn took no part in 1955 mutiny, and his name was on none of the mutineers' lists of future Governors, D.C.'s, etc.: this fact doubtless saved him from imprisonment. Dismissed from the army in 1961, partly because he was a Southerner and partly because of his friendship with Brigadier Shenan, he worked in radio and was a translator for the Round Table Conference. In April 1965 he joined the Anya-Nya, taking charge of training, and became the commander of Western Region in May 1968. He was a Brigadier in Joseph Lagu's Anya-Nya organization.

177   Magaya, M.A., op. cit., pp. 66-9.

CHAPTER 12

Bahr el Ghazal

The story of the rise of the resistance movement in Bahr el Ghazal begins in the refugee camps of Congo and Central African Republic. Following the school strike in 1962, the first group of students from Rumbek arrived at the Congo border in December of the same year, and were joined by others including a few ex-police and army men. Refugee camps were opened at Isiro, at Naangere (over 400 men, mostly Dinkas), and at Rindimbia (150, mostly Zandes). Large sections of these camps were militarily oriented, and training was carried out in secret using sticks instead of riles[178]. A coordinating committee of 5 members was set up, under the chairmanship first of Dominic Muorwel and then of Camillo Dhol, which directed operations both outside and inside Sudan.

The firat expedition to enter Sudan was led by Captain Bernardino Mou. This was the famous attack on Wau the night of January 11th 1964. Mou entered from Central African Republic with a force of 50-100 men, including Captain Thomas Dhol, Lt Henry Deng Monywiir and Lt Peter Utu Goi. NCOs included RSM Daniel Deng Kawac and RSM Philip

---

178 Information from Elia Duang, Camillo Dhol, Gordon Muortat, Akuot Atem and Victor
     Kwol, who supplied most of the Dinka material for thia section.

Nanga Mariik[179]. The force attacked on the strength of information that he would be supported by an uprising of police and prison warders within the town. Unfortunately, the promised support failed to materialize - some say that the man supposed to signal the start of the attack by cutting off the town's electricity was late; others that an informer betrayed the plan of attack and the sympathetic prison warders were replaced[180].

Although very poorly armed (Bernardino seems to have had the only rifle, and there were one or two muzzle-loaders besides) the guerillas pursued their attack until Bernardino was wounded[181]. Bernardino ordered his soldiers to abandon him and run for their lives: he was captured and hanged a month later[182]. The remainder of his force retreated to their base camp in C.A.R. under Ajing Daw.

In June they were back again, a force under Ajing entering from C.A.R. and another under Joseph Kuol Amoum proceeding through the forest from Yambio to Tonj. The two were to meet near Tonj, but Ajing's party delayed in order to send back to Congo for 3 sub-machine guns, following the seizure of £1,000 from an Arab hashish buyer. The other force went ahead and attacked Tonj in July or August. They had about 7 automatic weapons and almost succeeded in capturing the town, but were held off by one wounded man operating a bren gun until reinforcements arrived the following morning.

After Tonj, Kuol Amoum's group made several smaller attacks in the area against Arab traders and civilians, and then proceeded to near Gogrial to await the party from C.A.R. This group had its difficulties, being attacked at Raffili Mission while crossing the Namatina River and

---

179　Poggo, p. 68. Poggo does not mention Ajing Daw who was the second in command of Mou.

180　According to Arkangelo Wanji, who was in Wau two days before, every Southerner, including small children, knew that the attack was coming.

181　Bernardino, at the army HQ, had 5 succesaive mis-fires with his rifle before passing it to his second-in-command Ajing Daw, who shot and killed a major and a sergeant. Running a little later toward the Governor's house Bernardino was shot and wounded in both legs by a Northern soldier when silhouetted against the light. There seems no truth to the rumour that he was shot in error by one of his own men. Information from Paul Duang.

182　The Daily Telegeroph of 22 Feb. 1964 says that 2 other Southerners were hanged with Bernardino, 5 sentenced to life imprisonment, and 15 to various other prison terms. Following the Wau attack, many people were tortured and put in prison all over Bahr el Ghazal.

losing three men, but finally joined up with the others in late August. Philip Nanga[183], who had replaced Ajing and had been slightly wounded at Namatina crossing, took command of the united force. It called itself "Gur Mou" (the force to avenge Mou) and conducted ambushes and other operations around Gogrial until fighting stopped in October 1964.

Lakes, Jur River and Aweil Districts

The cease-fire following the overthrow of Abboud was relatively effective in Bahr el Ghazal. Anya-Nya officers and men mingled freely with people in towns during the day, retiring to their camps at night, and the very distinction between guerillas and civilians became blurred. In the absence of military activities, the guerilla force split in three according to districts: Lakes District (Rumbek) under Nanga, Jur River (Tonj) under the SANU political officer Albino Mathiang, and Aweil under Ajing Daw. These were all Dinka groups. In Western District, whose population comprises a large number of small tribes, the Anyn-Nya under Filbert Ucini operated independently of the Dinka camps, and will be discussed later.

The cease-fire, which lasted until about June 1965, was broken in a rather spectacular way on 22 January 1966 at Ler. This village, which until the expulsion of the missionaries had been the site of an American Presbyterian Mission station lies in Bentiu District, and so forms part of Upper Nile, but the attacking force was led by Paulino Arop, an ex-sergeant of the S.D.F. who was sent by Philip Nanga from Bahr el Ghazal[184]. Hence the event will be mentioned in this section. The attacking force arrived with 4 guns and were assisted by the local Nuers, as well as by 2 policemen who joined in the assault on their own post with their rifles. The post was overrun, 15 Northern policemen killed, and 4 more Southern police taken into the Anyn-Nya where they have apparently

---

183 Nang, like Ajing, a former sergeant in the Sudan army, became the Anyn-Nya commander in Lakes District. He was executed in 1968 by the SSPG, allegedly for indiscipline.

184 Information from Victor Kwol and from Kuaclieth Banak, a Nuer law student at the University of Khartoum who had come south following the riot of December 1964 and who joined in the attack.

remained. Twenty rifles, 1 Bren and 3,000 rounds of ammunition were captured, the largest amount hitherto obtained in the South.

An attempt was made to re-opon the police post in June 1966. But this was resisted by the local population, who demonstrated the Nuer quality of tenacity by fighting a Northern force 19 miles from their village back to the river.

Returning to Bahr el Ghazal proper, splits and dissensions among the Anya-Nya leadership continued to develop throughout 1965. The end of that year represented the nadir of disunity: in 1966 the work of rebuilding and regrouping began and has since proceeded fairly steadily, though not without setbacks. The process has been an extremely involved one, and its complexities are not easy to grasp.

During the Simba rebellion, the Dinka Anya-Nya field commanders in Bahr el Ghazal were cut off from their leaders' coordinating committee in Congo, and as mentioned above split into three districts. Each collected its own taxes and brought its own arms[185]. But then Albino Mathiang, who was in theory political officer for the whole province, dismissed Ajing Daw in Aweil, and a long struggle between Mathiang and his opponents ensued. The opposition was led by Elia Duang[186], also from Jur River, who resigned from William Deng's branch of SANU in June 1965 and was one of the main architects of reconciliation. Duang arranged for Mathiang to be arrested by Kuol Amoum, but Mathiang bided his time and awaited the arrival of Camillo Dhol from Li-Rangu. It should be said at this point that in the Dinka areas of Bahr el Ghazal, Anya-Nya officers appear to have sought guidance from their civilian and political leaders far more than was the case in Upper Nile and Equatoria. The

---

185 For example, Lakes District sent £1,000 to Congo in June 1965 with Nanga, who returned in August with 11 Chinene bren guns and a numbor of automatics. (Information from Victor Kwol.) In order to avoid problems in exchanging Sudanese money, transistor radios were sometimes purchaned in the towns and re-sold in Congo.

186 Duang graduated from Rumbek in 1961 and went to Congo in December 1962, where he became secretary of the coordinating committee. He went to Khartoum with Deng's wing of SANU in February 1965, attended the Round Table Conference, and in July began his work of organizing the Anya-Nya. He succeeded in uniting Aweil and Jur River Districts, then in July 1966 left to take up the position of Minister of Animal Resources in the SSPG. Later he became associated with the Nile Provisional Government and has continued his work of organization and coordination. The author owes much of the informntion in what follow to the notes of a series of interviews with Duang by Nelson Kasfir.

coordinating committee in Congo was the highest authority recognized - in practice operating independently even of SANU - and its powers seem to have been considerable. Hence the arrival of its chairman Dhol was awaited with expectancy.

Dhol left Li-Rangu with 80 men, all armed, on August 15th 1965 and halfway to Tonj met another force of 355 sent by Mathiang to fetch weapons[187]. This group reversed direction, and the whole force proceeded to Tonj under the military command of Tito Athuai Mahmud. Arriving in September, Dhol re-instated Mathiang. Kuol's forces were disarmed[188], Duang was put in "prison" (meaning that he was isolated from other people with a guard), and the whole body moved slowly toward Aweil. But once there, Dhol could not succeed in reconciling the two districts. Kuol and Mathiang said that Ajing and co. were rebels because they broke away from Mathiang's authority. Ajing said they broke away because of Mathinng's mistakes and were not rebels. This was a dilemma, and because he could not resolve it Dhol lost authority. One day Kuol got up at 4:00 a.m., released Duang and went off with his men saying that Duang was free to leave. Tito Mahmud also took his force back to Jur River (and was betrayed and killed by the Northerners in January)[189]. Dhol became leader of Aweil, his own district. This was November, the lowest point of unity.

On December 26th 1965, Mathiang called a meeting of all educated people in Jur River, and about 300 attended. At this meeting, a district committee of 5 was elected to carry on all the political work in Jur River. Duang and Mathiang both became members, but when Duang was elected Committee chairman Mathiang refused to accept his leadership and went off to Li-Rangu to seek a fresh mandate. But this time he was unsuccessful: the coordinating committee had disintegrated, and Edward Nyiel refused to give Mathiang military support. Instead, he put him in

---

187 Information from John Macham.

188 In the whole of Jur River before the arrival of Dhol there were 600 soldiers but only 30 guns. Aweil had 1,000 soldiers and 20 guns.

189 Mahmud and another officer called Deng had ordered a soldier named Dut to be lashed. Dut looking for revenge, led some Northern soldiers to a village named Mayen where Mahmud and Deng were spending the night with their wives. Mahmud took up a spear in his hut and was shot through the window. Deng was captured, taken to Khartoum and later executed. (Information from Benjamin Bol.)

detention and said his case would be heard when the group returned to Bahr el Ghazal. Nyiel was killed by Northern troops in the middle of 1966, however, and it was not under him but under Emmanuel Abur Nhial[190] that the force eventually returned in January 1967.

Meanwhile, in Jur River, the work of integration proceeded. In November 1965 the Anya-Nya in the district had split into three groups – one in Thiet and two in Gogrial - and these came together on February 20th 1966. Kuol Amoum became military commander and Elia Duang, the top civil administrator. Chiefs were confirmed in their posts as long as they were (a) loyal to the movoment and anti-Arab, and (b) acceptable to the people. (Note that certain chiefs who did not satisfy condition (a) had run away to the towns; new ones had to be appointed in their places. In making new appointments (a) and (b) were all that mattered. Such things as whether a candidate came from a clan that traditionally produced chiefs or whether he had any administrative ability were not considered of much importance: "Anyone can become a chief. There is no training school.".) As of February 1966 Jur River was run by an organization which controlled all weapons in the district and provided a civil administration, but which was affiliated to no larger or national body in the movement.

Once Jur River had settled its internal affairs, it began looking to neighbouring areas. Overtures were sent to Rumbek, but Philip Nanga had been in contact with Ezbon Mondiri and had agreed to affiliate Lakes District with ALF, in return for which Mondiri had appointed Nanga commander of all Bahr el Ghazal. Hence Rumbek was out of the picture for the time being (showing the danger of integrating regions from the top rather than the bottom), and the next step was the uniting of Jur River and Aweil. This was accomplished by means of an elegant administrative structure. In September 1966 a four-man civilian coordinating committee was set up with two members from each district, and a HQ established near Kwango River on the districts' common border. A headquarters force was created to

---

190 Abur, who is from Gogrial attended Rumbek where he was one of the ringleaders of the 1962 strike. He arrived in Congo in December 1962, became a member of the coordinating committee, and was assistant to Josoph Lagu in 1965. He also attended University in Kisangani for a year. In January 1967 Abur was put in charge of the united Aweil/Jur River force, and later in 1969 became military commander for the Nile Provisional Government. He then became commander of the Bahr el Ghazal Anya-Nya under Joseph Lagu.

which each district contributed 1/3 of its guns: the resulting unit had more weapons than Aweil, though fewer than Jur River. This situation, which in fact amounted to the establishment of three separate armies, was not wholly satisfactory, and a better arrangement was achieved when Abur arrived with the remainder of Mahmud's force (40 men and 23 guns) from Li-Rangu. A unified command with three battalions was set up under Abur: in choosing him, the committee abandoned seniority and adopted education as its standard. A new constitution was drawn up in which Jur River, Aweil, and a section of Western District inhabited by the Bahr el Ghazal Luo[191], were divided into three "theatres", one for each battalion. D.C.'s and A.D.C.'s were assigned to these theatres, the principle being that no man should serve in his home theatre. The army was integrated by transferring a certain proportion of officers and men in the same way. By January 1968 the organization was working smoothly, and when Duang received a message from the SSPG that he should come with a detachment to their HQ near Yei he made plans to hand over to his deputy, Arkangelo Kwac. In July 1968 he departed, taking with him £5,000 in money and arms as his region's contribution to the national government.

The Western District

In the Western District of Bahr el Ghazal, the growth of the Anya-Nya proceeded more or less independently of the other districts until early 1969[192]. The founder of armed resistance in that area was Filbert Ucini Vomongo[193], a Belanda from Diem Zubeir. Sometime in 1963 Ucini established a guerilla camp near Mboro in the vicinity of Wau. This camp had no fixed abode but shifted about. It acquired a few muzzle-loaders from chiefs, and toward the end of 1963 is reported to have carried out

---

191 The Luo were under the command of Col. Mayen, an ex-policeman who captured a rifle shortly after Bernardino's attack. Col. Mayen brought 100 men and 20 guns into the organization.

192 Most of the information in this section comes from Arkangelo Wanji

193 Ucini, who like Goi is from the Bviri section of the Belanda tribe, was born about 1918 and became a policeman. He was elected to the Senate in 1958, and in 1962 went into exile and became SANU representative in C.A.R. After being deposed by Goi as the leader of the Western District in 1965, Ucini returned to private life.

some ambushes on the roads around Wau. Ucini and his men did not participate in the attack on Wau of January 1964.

Although he had few arms, Ucini had plenty of money. He succeeded in organising an efficient system of donations whereby each villager contributed £1 per year and officials in Wau considerably more. These donations were not stopped by the arrests and persecutions which followed Bernardino'n attack - if anything they increased. And in April or May 1965 Ucini's financial assets were swelled by an unexpected windfall, when a man named Godi arrived in the camp with £32,000. It came about like this. Godi was the driver of a car taking payroll money from a bank to a government office, and the Northern officer accompanying him stopped off to do some shopping. Godi started up the car and drove it 2 or 3 miles out of town, and then abandoned it and carried the money to the camp. Ucini gave him £1,000 and kept the remainder. The question was, what to do with it? Here Ucini committed errors of judgement which eventually led to his downfall. Instead of buying arms and prosecuting the war against the government in a vigorous way, which might have won him the support of the younger, more educated and more idealistic men of the area, Ucini provided his camp with luxuries[194]. The amount allocated for weapons is not known exactly, but seems to have been less than £10,000. This money was given to Uvoyo, Ucini's second-in-command, a senior and extremely tough soldier, who set off with it to Congo.

Meanwhile, as was mentioned earlier in the section on Western Equatoria, Ferdinand Goi had established a camp at Bakiri near Tambura. Bakiri lies in a pocket of Zande-ized Belanda, who speak both Belanda and Zande, and Goi had attracted to his camp a group of educated young men. He integrated them into his forces. Goi travelled to the Central African Republic leaving Alfonso in command, and while he was away, Alfonso did manage to capture 13 arms in an ambush near Mboro. During this period the chain of Anya-Nya posts, which had previously stopped at Diem Zubeir, was extended westward as far as Raga.

From C.A.R. Goi went to East Africa, then led the attempted coup against ALF at Angudri, then returned to Western Bahr el Ghazal in March 1967 and resumed command from Alfonse. He tried to persuade

---

194 For exnmple, instead of kerosene lamps Ucini is reported to have bought Tilley lamps, which for a guerilla camp would seem to violate rules not only of economy but of safety.

his soldiers to accompany him back to Angudri to make another attempt at overthrowing ALF, but they rebelled at this and arrested him. Goi was an extremely autocratic leader, and there is no doubt that many of the younger officers would have been happy to see him deposed. But after three months Frederick Fodul, who had been with Ucini since the early days and who was married to Goi's sister, staged a counter-coup and released him. There followed a purge of the young officers' ranks (presumably under orders from Goi, although this is not entirely clear) and four at least were shot. Others ran away to the HQ of the Northern command at Kwango. This was in early 1968. The last act in the drama was Goi's departure in late 1968, and the arrival in February or March 1969 of the force sent by the S.S.P.G. under Simoni Jada to unite the whole of Bahr el Ghazal. This force, which had previously succeeded in uniting Lakes District with the rest of the province, was remarkably successful in accomplishing its mission, and Fodul was persuaded without much difficulty to accept integration. This ended the isolation of Western District, which has since been an integral part of the overall administrative and military structure of Bahr el Ghazal.

The End of Abboud's Government and the Round Table Conference

In the previous five chapters, we have tried to give a detailed account of the early activities of the Anya-Nya in the various regions of Southern Sudan. We have also shown how systems of local administration were created in the areas under Anya-Nya control. In subsequent chapters, we shall describe how the various Anya-Nya groups and administrative systems were drawn into larger and more centralized organisations. In the present chapter and the next, however, we shall be talking more about events at the national level, affecting the Sudan as a whole, and the way in which these influenced and were influenced by events in the South.

At the end of February 1964, not long after Bernardino's attack on Wau, the Sudan government took the step of expelling all foreign missionaries from the South. Approximately 250 missionaries were deported, 214 of whom were Roman Catholics[195]. The reason given by the government was that the missionaries had encournged anti-government and separatist feeling among their parishioners, even going so for as to assist the Anya-Nya[196]. Another possible reason is that the government planned severe reprisals against the civilian population following the Wau attack in January 1964, and did not wish to have any independent witnesses who might report the matter to the outside world[197]. If the latter, then the government delayed a month or two too long in expelling the missionaries, for when they left they brought with them stories of suffering some of which only readers of books like Koestler's *Darkness at Noon* will recognize. These stories have been collected together under the title "Genocide in the Southern Sudan"[198]. Whether they are true or not depends on the veracity and powers of impartial witness of some 33 missionaries, most of them now living in Italy.

> On February 22nd, 1964, while returning from Wau, I noticed hundreds of people of the Belanda tribe along the Kuru-Diem Zubeir road who were living in temporary habitations made out of branches and straw while they were building their huts. They were victims of the retaliatory measures taken by the Arab soldiers and policemen against those of their tribe who had fled to the forest for becoming guerillas. Not only the huts of the Belandas had been destroyed but also their granaries containing their last harvest had been burnt…The populace, deprived of their food stores and forbidden to enter the forest for game or honey, had already begun to starve. As no crop could be harvested for many more months, no one

---

195   The latter figure comes from The Black Book of the Sudan: An Answer, (Milan 1964) in which the Catholic missionaries reply to the charges brought against them by the Sudan government. A large majority of the 214 Catholics were Verona Fathers, the rest being Mill Hill Fathers. The Protestants, who have in general been much less politically-minded than the Verona Fathers, do not seem to have responded to their expulsion with any similar reply.

196   The Black Book (opt. cit.) gives the government's memorandum on the reasons for the expulsion, including quotations from documents purportedly demonstrating that such assistance occurred (see p. 190 ff.). The documents are all from the vicinity of Diem Zubeir, and concern the activities of Alfonse Dinia. Assuming they are genuine, they would at most involve only the Father Superior of Diem Zubeir Mission in giving help to Alfonse.

197   See for example, Dame Margery Perham

198   Reproduced in successive issues of Sudan Informazioni, Milan, beginning with No. 24/25, 25 August 1968.

doubted that many, especially the weak ones and the children, would soon die of disease and hunger. (S.I. 24/25, p. 38)

Around February the fifteenth, 1964, Dr. Salah, an Arab, went to Malakal prison, and brought three dying prisoners to the hospital. The following day he admitted four more. These seven were from a group of eighteen men, all of the Nuer tribe, whom I heard had been caught in the forest near the city of Nasir by the Arabs. The soldiers had probably taken them to be freedom fighters and so had carried them to Malakal to extort confessions from them. They seemed to be simple villagers to me as they spoke neither Arabic nor English. Only one of the seven could say "moya", the Arabic word for water.

Their beds were kept under guard by a soldier so I was not able to speak to them. They had been cruelly tortured. They bore the signs of having been flogged, and from head to foot, they were one great burn. I guessed that they had been tortured by fire. One in particular had a back that looked like an iron slate. Their hands and feet stank for gangrene. Surely they had been in that condition for a very long time. I have never seen anybody so suffering of tetanus as they were. They were about 29 or 30 years old. Two died the night after their admittance, the others not much later. The last, the strongest, died two days before my departure from the Sudan, at the beginning of March. (S.I. 34/35, p. 51.)

On the 15th of January, I gave the Last Sacrament to a Christian, in pitiful conditions, at the end of his life already. In tears, he told me that he had been seen in the woods near to the Ngangala road some ten days before as he was gathering wood with his son. A lorry of soldiers stopped and shouted something in Arabic. Then they began to beat him with sticks found on the ground and with the butts of their guns. They wounded him in the right arm and leg with his own spear which he had brought along to protect himself from wild animals. They also beat his fifteen year old son. He told me that he did not know why he had been beaten or what the soldiers wanted of him" (S.I. 39, p. 62.)

The end of October 1964, saw the fall of General Abboud'a government in Khartoum. The immediate cause of its downfall seems to have been an attempt by the police to break up a University discussion group on the South. In September the Supreme Council had appointed a 25-man commission to study the Southern problem, and when the Students' Union met and decided that no solution was possible under a military dictatorship, further discussion was forbidden. Rioting ensued, both at the university and in the city, and on November lst a respected civil servant, Sirr el-Khatim al Khalifa, was sworn in as Prime Minister of a new caretaker government[199].

In Sirr el-Khatim's government, there were at first two and then later three Southern ministers. These ministers were appointed by the Southern Front, a body of civil servants, that formed themselves into a political body to represent the interest of the Southerners in the negotiations for the interim government following the ousting of the Military junta. The newly appointed Minister of Interior, Clement Mboro, paid an extensive visit to the South to acquaint himself with the situation there.

The Southern Front had negotiated with the political parties led by al Sediq Abdel el Rahman al- Mahdi and the Professionals Front that represented the professional and trade unions. The Southern Front has declared its agenda to be[200]:

1. The interim government is to declare a ceasefire all over Southern Sudan,
2. The new government is to release all the South Sudanese political detainees,
3. The interim government is to prepare for the Round-Table Conference to be held abroad to discuss the resolution of the problem of the South,
4. Immediate contact would be made with the politicians in exile in order to plan for negotiations.

The implementation of this programme was swift, and many Southern civil servants moved back to their home areas. Clement Mboro's tour was an enormous success and resulted in a cease-fire that significantly reduced the level of military activity. A Southern Front delegation composed of Abel Alier, Darius Beshir and Lubari Ramba was despatched to meet SANU representatives in Kampala and elsewhere. It was a time of optimism and

---

199 See Beshir, The Southern Sudan, p. 88; Henderson, Sudan Republic, p. 207. Abboud's fall is the only instance at that time of an African military ruler being overthrown by a popular revolt.
200 Malwal, Bona, "Sudan and South Sudan: From One to Two", Basingstoke: Palgrave Macmillan, 2015, 92.

hope, marred only by tragic riot in Khartoum which showed that certain basic attitudes remained constant beneath the changes.

The day that Clement Mboro was due back from his tour of the South was a Sunday, December 6th, and a large crowd of Southerners gathered at the airport to greet him[201]. Unfortunately, his plane was delayed, and the rumour spread that he had been the victim of foul play. Led by a group who had been drinking heavily at the airport bar, the crowd swarmed into town, overturning cars and breaking windows. Once in Khartoum, they ran into an even larger crowd of Northerners emerging from a football stadium, and when some of them took refuge in the Christian Literature Centre the crowd set fire to the building and for over 4 hours prevented the fire brigade from extinguishing it[202]. During the night and the next day, a general man-hunt ensued, and it will never be known exactly how many Southerners perished. The official report says 44 (plus 8 Northerners and 1 Greek), but eye-witnesses estimates range from 300 to over a thousand. It is fairly obvious that political emotions and racial tension played a predominant part in the rioting. Demonstrators at the airport carried placards reading "South must determine her own future", "Down with the merchants' imperialism in the South", etc., and Luigi Adwok's comment to reporters immediately following the incident was that "there is racial hatred here, and any other explanation would be a lie"[203]. The riot serves as an uneasy reminder of what can happen once relations between North and South deteriorate past a certain point.

The Road to the Round Table Conference

We now turn to the events and political manoeuvrings, which led to the Round Table Conference. It was stated above that immediately after the fall of Abboud William Deng wrote to Sir el-Khatim suggesting that a conference be held. The idea was taken up by the government, who

---

201 Information: Henderson, op. cit., p. 211; from excerpts from the report of the official Commission of Enquiry reprinted in Sudan Informazioni 45, pp. 23-29; from news reports also reprinted in Sudan Informazioni 45; and from eye-witnesses Kuaclieth Banak, Serafino Swaka and Arkangelo Wanji.

202 See the excerpts from Report, loc. Cit., pp. 24 and 27.

203 New York Herald Tribune, 9 Dec. 1964.

sent various teams of envoys to Kampala to discuss the matter with SANU. However, SANU was badly divided on the issue. Deng, who had returned to Kinshasa from Europe in December and had then proceeded to Kampala with some Dinka colleagues, was in favour of negotiations with the government. Aggrey Jaden, elected president of SANU in November, did not oppose talks provided they were held either in Juba or in a neutral country. Joseph Oduho, who had just been replaced as president and who refused appointment as SANU Secretary for Constitutional Affairs, opposed talks in the belief that nothing would come of them. These three schools of thought prevailed throughout January and February, with agreement almost being reached at one point to hold the conference in Juba, until the deadlock was broken by Deng's departure on February 27th[204]. Deng arrived in Khartoum with 8 other SANU members including Elia Duang and announced that he was ready to negotiate.

Deng's entry into Sudan broke the deadlock in one sense, but at the same time, it created a whole new set of problems. By his action, he forced the hand of his colleagues not only in SANU but in the Southern Front as well. This is explained as follows. At its first full-scale convention in early February in Malakal, attended by delegates from branches that had been set up throughout the Sudan, the Southern Front declared its basic support of the aims and purposes of SANU in exile. As was mentioned, during the latter years of the Abboud regime there had existed an underground organization of Southerners in the Sudan that had supported SANU, and the Malakal convention to some extent brought this organization into the open[205]. Although a motion that the whole Southern movement in Sudan should declare themselves as SANU, was not carried the convention revealed that the ideological gap between the Southern Front and SANU in exile was minimal. At the convention, a resolution was passed that the Round Table Conference should be held either outside Sudan or in Juba, but not in Khartoum. Hence when the attempt to get talks started in Juba had failed, and when Deng nevertheless appeared in Khartoum and said he was ready to negotiate, the Southern Front felt as aggrieved as SANU in Kampala. Furthermore, Deng had said from the start that he

---

204 Henderson, p. 218; Beshir, p. 91; Albino, p. 51

205 In addition, the Southern Front seems to have formed more underground cells of its own. See Ray Moseley in the Kenya Weekly News, 8 Jan. 1965, p. 18.

was prepared to discuss federation as a solution to the Southern question. SANU and the Southern Front were probably prepared to accept federation, but wished to appear to reach this position as a compromise instead of offering it right away. In this way, they were being undercut by Deng.

In fairness to Deng, it must be said that the SANU leaders in Kampala were under considerable pressure from the Uganda government to talk to the Sudan government without preconditions. If they refused, it would seem to be they rather than the government who were being unreasonable and obstinate[206]. Furthermore, the SANU leaders' position that if talks in Juba or outside the Sudan could not be held, they would have no alternative but to allow the Anya-Nya to continue fighting, appeared to Deng ridiculous. Minister of the Interior was Clement Mboro, a Southerner. Would the Anyn-Nya fight against Mboro's own police force? It was, doubtless, considerations such as these which finally led Deng to make up his mind to return to Khartoum.

Nevertheless, Deng's arrival split the Southerners and destroyed their solidarity. Faced with the possibility that the Sudan government might negotiate with Deng and his group alone, the Southern Front urgently requested SANU in exile to send a delegation to Khartoum. This they finally agreed to do, and on March 15th they arrived. An immediate problem was created by Deng's claim that he rather than the new arrivals represented SANU. After an all-night debate, the issue was resolved by dividing the SANU delegation into two parts: 5 members from SANU in exile and 4 from Deng's group. The Southern Front sent 9 delegates[207]. One final problem was the insistence of the Northern political parties that Southerners holding opinions other than those of SANU and the Southern Front should also be invited. This would have had the effect of causing the Southern side to speak with many voices instead of one.

---

206 See the speech of the Minister of Defence, Mr Felix Onama, to the Uganda Parliament on 3 March 1965.

207 SANU in exile were represented by Elia Lupe, Lawrence Wol Wol, George Kwanai, Oliver Albino and George Lomoro; Deng's group by himself, Hilary Uchalla, Niknora M. Aguer and Elia Duang; the Southern Front by Gordon Mourtat, Abel Alier, Othwonh Dak, Gordon Abyei, Othwonh Bwogo, Natale Olwak, Lubari Ramba, Bona Malwal Ring and Romano Hassan. For the names of the 18 Northern delegates and the observers from other countries see Akol, pp. 252-255. Abel Alier, the only Southern judge in Sudan, was refused permission by the Chief Justice to take part in the conference and had to resign in order to become a delegate.

Chief among those to whom SANU and the Southern Front objected was Santino Deng, who had been the sole Southern minister in Abboud's government and who had founded the Sudan Unity Party early in 1965. Also unpopular were Stanislaus Paysama and Buth Diu, who had revived the old Liberal Party. After considerable discussion, both these small parties were excluded, and the government nominated 9 Southerners to represent "shades of opinion" different from those of SANU and the Southern Front. The desired diversity of opinion was not forthcoming, however, for once inside the conference, the specially-selected delegates announced that they entirely supported the views of the major parties[208].

The Round Table Conference

The Round Table Conference, attended by observers from Uganda, Kenya, Tanzania, Ghana, Nigeria, Algeria and U.A.R., opened on March 16th 1965 and lasted until March 29th. For the first (and, as of 1971, the only) time since the 1958 parliament, Southerners and Northerners were able to sit down together and discuss their common problems. Much can be learned by studying the results of the conference; why it failed and why it was not reconvened. Some small measure of progress is discernible during the meetings. The South dropped its initial demand for a plebiscite, and the North agreed to such things as the headmasters of Southern schools should be Southerners. Given good will and further meetings, perhaps agreement would have been reached. But, as will be seen, this is not what happened.

We now turn to the conference proceedings, the papers of which have been published in different places[209]. Their main interest lies in the proposals put forward by the two sides - the speeches of the leaders of the various delegations are with one or two exceptions tendentious and make the reader wonder how the different parties came as close together as they did. Following the conference rules, according to which each of the two

---

208 See Beshir, p. 92, and Albino, pp. 53 and 57. Henderson, p. 219, wrongly states Santino Deng to have been a delegate.

209 See Round-Tabla Conference on the Southern Sudan, (Sudan Information News Agency booklet, 1970) which also reprints various news reports on the conference. The main documents of the coference occur as appendices to Beshir, op. cit.

sides had to present a unified set of proposals, SANU and the Southern Front proposed plebiscite in Southern Sudan with the following choices:

1. Federation
2. Unity with the North
3. Separation (to become an independent state)[210].

The Northern parties, on their side, made a detailed and interesting proposal in which they rejected both federation and a centralized form of government, and suggested instead a system of regional government[211]. The Northern proposal is worth discussing at this point, since different versions of it have been put forward since 1965 under the description of local or regional autonomy.

The main reason given by the Northern delegates for rejecting a centralized government was that in a country as large and inhomogeneous as the Sudan, only the local authorities of any given region would be sufficiently knowledgeable and sensitive to its needs to be capable of meeting them. In making this point the Northerners might seem to be implicitly recommending federalism, but this was not so. Federation was rejected for three reasons. First, the South lacked the human and economic resources to administer a federal system. The latter was too expensive a form of government for the Sudan. Second, federation was felt to be a step towards separation, or at least would generate centrifugal forces which might lead to civil war. Third, federalism "encourages regions to reserve their resources for local as opposed to national development." This might act to the detriment of the more impoverished regions of the country. Put in this way, it appeared to be in

---

210 Beshir, p. 179; Albino, p 54
211 Beshir, p. 174.

the South's own interest to reject federation[212]. The Northern proposal then went on to outline a regional system of government. In this system, the South would have its own elected regional council, together with a (Southern) Governor appointed by the central government. The powers of the regional council were fairly narrow, comprising such things as the regulation of elementary schools, markets and cooperative societies, village planning and the building of roads. Local police were to be recruited, subject to the right of the central government to take over command when necessary. This may not seem to be much. On the other hand, the Northern proposal did meet some important Southern demands that had been made by William Deng and by the federalists in 1958. These included a Southern vice-president of the Republic, a Southern Council for economic development, an entirely Southern sub-commission of the public service commission, and a university in the South. It was a start, and the Southerners responded by producing their own proposals[213]. In these suggestions, which might be described as confederal rather than federal, North and South were each given control of their own economic planning, foreign affairs, armed forces and internal security. Linking the two territories were common services analogous to those found until recently in East Africa: currency, customs, posts and telegraphs, railways, university education. The demand for a plebiscite was dropped, and in its place was put a "Programme for immediate implementation" which included the Southernization of all police and top administrative posts in the South, the re-transfer of schools that had been moved to the North

---

212 In the conclusion to his book, Beshir brings forward a number of general objections to federalism which would apply to any developing country. He quotes F.G. Carnell: "With its rigidities, technicalities, inefficiency, excessive legalism and conservatism, federalism is only for peoples of mature political experience, capable of playing the complicated game of circumventing such restrictions. There are quite enough forces enlarging the decline, if not extinction of parliamentary government in the new states without their saddling themselves with the additional burden of federal systems. Such systems will restrict the scope of national economic planning and thus greatly delay any possibility of the econoic 'takeoff'." ('Political implications of federalism in new states', in Federalism and Economic Growth, London 1963). To this it might be replied that man does not live by bread alone, and that individual freedom is also important. If federalism is the only way of allowing an important segment of a country's population to develop a sense of political identity, then economic take-off may have to be delayed.

213 Beshir, p. 180

and the withdrawal of the army from small towns and villages to headquarters that had existed prior to 17 November, 1958.

With these two proposals, it might seem that a dialogue had at last begun between North and South that might eventually have resolved their differences. At this point, the Round Table Conference adjourned, and further negotiations were left in the hands of a 12-man committee with instructions to report back within three months. Although no political agreement had been reached the conference adopted a group of final resolutions which included some of the South's immediate demands[214]. The implementation of these would have gone a long way toward creating the kind of trust that leads to settlement. If what Mohammed Omer Beshir says is true, settlement was not too far away:

> In a closed meeting, the Southern representatives agreed that the 12 – man committee would exclude any scheme which would imply the continuation of the status quo or which on the other hand might lead to separation. They also agreed to seek a solution within a united Sudan. But they asked, and the Northern parties agreed, not to make this part of the agreement public or part of the formal resolutions[215]

However, despite the guardedly optimistic note on which the Round Table Conference ended, all its good work was destroyed by the events which followed it. The conference was never reconvened, and none of its resolutions was kept. Even the agreement on the composition of the 12-man committee was violated. According to this agreement, SANU and the Southern Front were each to send 3 representatives, but when SANU in exile sent Peter Akol as their representative from Kampala, he was met by Deng's group who had remained in Khartoum and who also called themselves SANU. This time, instead of dividing the delegation between the two SANU's as was done for the Round Table Conference,

---

214 Beshir, p. 183. These resolutions are reproduced in Appendix 1 below.

215 Beshir, p. 95. This passage written in 1967, should be contrasted with a letter of Beshir's in The Times, 31 July 1965, in which the writer complains that the failure of the Round Table Conference was due to the unyielding demands of a small group of Southern politicians for separation. It would be interesting to know whether it was all the Southern representatives, or only Deng's group, which at the end of the conference agreed privately to seek a solution within a united Sudan. It is also significant to note that Beshir, in his letter, states that the Northern delegates 'did not close the doors to a federal solution".

the Kampala delegate was officially rejected by the Northern political parties.[216] From that time onward the dialogue was broken, and contact between Khartoum and the Southern leaders in exile ceased. The reasons for this breakdown will be considered in the next chapter.

---

216 See Albino, p. 58; the Reporter, Nairobi, 2 July 1965, p. 15, and the Voice of the Southern Sudan, London, Vol. 3 No. 2, (October 1965), p. 14. The rejection occurred on June 14.

CHAPTER 14

Government Oppression, June and July 1965

What was the reason for the sudden change of atmosphere following the Round Table Conference? Its resolutions were never implemented, and the conference was never reconvened. The answer lies in the fact that on April 6th, right after the conference, the Supreme Council announced that elections in the Northern Sudan would be held at the end of the month. From that moment Sirr el-Khatim al- Khalifa, who as a civil servant rather than a politician had decided not to contest the elections, knew that his term had only a short period to run, and his government became what the Americans call "lame duck" administration.

The background to the Supreme Council decision is an interesting one, and it seems probably that if the Southern Front could have its life over again, it would prefer to alter the choice it then made. It had all along been opposed to the holding of elections in the South, on the grounds that fair elections could not be held until the state of emergency was lifted, and in November it had refused to nominate a member to the newly-formed electoral commission.[217] But in April, when the four Northern members of the Supreme Council were evenly divided on whether or not to go ahead with elections in the North, Luigi Adwok gave his casting vote in favor.[218] The Southern Front must have foreseen that, first of all, that as soon as elections were announced the government would become even more indecisive, to the extent that it would be quite incapable of imple-

217   The New York Times, 21 Nov. 1964

218   See B. S. Sharma, "The 1965 elections in the Sudan", Political Quarterly 37(1966), p. 442; Keith Kyle in the Sunday Nation, Nairobi, 27 March 1966, p. 9. The Southern Front had explained that it instructed its member to vote against the motion for elections to be conducted and he was rebuked for voting otherwise [see Akol, L., Souh Sudan; From Colonial Neglect…., p. 189].

menting the Round Table Conference resolution[219]. Secondly, they should have foreseen the possibility of a weak government, which failed to do much positively for the South, being replaced by a strong government, which would act negatively against it. This is in fact what happened.

The April elections in the North resulted in an Umma/N.U.P coalition being formed with Mohammed Ahmed Mahgoub as Prime Minister. This coalition had three quarters of the seats and could govern without support from the smaller parties. With regard to the South, it was evident from the start that Mahgoub's policy was going to be one of extreme firmness. Such policy had in fact been advocated in a series of nine articles which appeared in the influential Arabic newspaper El Ayam in Khartoum during the month of April. These articles, which took a very critical line against what their author considered to be the weakness both of Sirr el-Khatim's government and of the Northern delegates at the Round Table Conference, probably did a fair amount to harden public opinion against the South. The articles were translated into English in The Vigilant[220], a paper published by the Southern Front, and give an interesting picture of how the Southern problem appeared to at least one Northerner.[221]

To return to the Southern Front, it seems fairly clear that their decision to allow the North to go ahead with elections in April 1965 was from their point of view an unwise one, and one which they lived to regret. The danger, of course, was that a government would be elected which would not only fail to implement the Round Table Conference resolutions, but would engage in repressive measures against the South. Of course, it is easy to be wise after the event, but to any observer of the

---

219 Gordon Mourtat, who as Minister of Works sat on a Ministerial Committee charged with implementing the resolutions, relates that every proposal made by himself or Clement Mboro met wit delaying tactics. For example, to the suggestion of appointing Southern Governors in the Southern provinces, the committee (which included the Prime Minister) replied, "No, this takes time and must be planned." "Then what about admitting some of the 60 Southern applicants to the Police College?" Again nothing was done and the new government took over.

220 The Vigilant appeared first on 23 March 1965, and was banned for six months for its reporting of the Juba and Wau incidents in July. It then resumed publication, and served as the only outlet for the expression of Southern opinion in Sudan until banned by General Nimeiry's government in May 1969.

221 A selection of these articles appear below in Appendix 2.

political scene in April there were signs that many groups in the North were becoming impatient with the caretaker government's Southern policies, and would prefer to see harsher methods adopted. Nor is it even clear that the government was above using harsher methods itself. For example, on March 17th, just as the Round Table Conference was beginning Joel Akec, a Dinka Senior Inspector of Police, was assassinated by his own Northern police subordinates in Bentiu[222]. It is reported that one month earlier, the Northern policemen had rebelled against him and forced him to delegate his powers to a police sergeant. On March 30th, the day after the conference ended, the village of Luigi Adwok near Kodok was burned to the ground. Adwok heard the news on April 8th and left immediately for Malakal to investigate[223]. When he returned he reported to Sirr el-Khatim and the cabinet in the following words:

"I found that Agodo, my village, which comprises 250 homes with property and life collections of about 700 persons, had been utterly and systematically destroyed on March 30, 1965, by the armed forces stationed at Kodok...

"The destruction of my village was ordered and effected on March 30, exactly on the day when Your Excellency and the Council of Ministers with the Southern member of the Supreme Council were trying to solve the itching problem of what was to happen after the expiration of the transitional period. Therefore the destruction was carefully planned...

"You and your government have found new formulas, new terms, to cover up your murders. You call a "security" measure the complete exter-mination of Southern Sudan; you call 'outlaws' all the non-Arab Southern Sudanese - me included, who still am by right a member of the Supreme Council of State."[224]

The Southern Front's reaction to these events was to prepare itself for a bitter struggle. In the last week of May, seven of their members flew to

---

222 Henderson, p. 220; Albino, p. 60; Voice of Southern Sudan, Vol. 3, No. 1, May 1965, p. 9; verbal information from Cleto Rial and Kuaclieth Banak.

223 Alexis Mbali, The Nile Turns Red, New York, 1967, p. 119. If Adwok had heard the news two days earlier, he might have cast his vote the other way in the matter of elections.

224 Mbali, pp. 119-122

East Africa to meet with SANU in exile and discuss common policies to be adopted during the expected reconvening of the Round Table Conference. To protest against continued government oppression, and to demonstrate the strength of their support, they called a two-day general strike throughout the South in June. But when it came to force, their strength was not equal to that of Mahgoub's government. In a policy speech on June 19th, Mahgoub undertook to annihilate "the terrorist gangs which abuse security". In the events which followed, he succeeded in annihilating much more than he had promised.

The overall picture of the events of June and July 1965 is still far from complete. The Juba and Wau massacres are fairly well documented. Less well-known are the killings, in Yambio , Torit, Maridi, Yei, Kapoeta, Mundri and Rumbek, all of which took place between June 25th and July 20th. These different incidents, in different places, show certain similarities which indicate that their causes were not independent of one another. We shall begin with Juba and Wau. A number of eye-witnesses and other contemporary reports have been published of the killings in Juba on July 8th and 9th.[225] Briefly it seems that at about 10.00 p.m. on July 8th, an army sergeant was either wounded or killed in an argument with a Southern hospital dresser over a transistor radio. At this, the soldiers in Juba took their rifles from the armoury and began systematically to burn the grass-thatched houses of the town and to shoot those who emerged. The actual killing is reported to have been done by a group of 70 soldiers, while the others cordoned off the five Southern sectors of the city. The population of Juba at the time was about 40,000, and many thousands took refuge in mosques and churches. On July 9th a Southern priest, Father Sylvester, prevented the destruction of the Roman Catholic cathedral by standing directly in front of a tank gun. At Juba hospital, troops broke in and asked for a Southerner named Dr. Clement. He and two other Southern doctors, who were about to perform an operation on an injured American teacher named Martin Daley, escaped by jumping through the window of the operating theatre,

---

225 See Kenya Weekly News, 30 July 1965, p. 17; The Reporter, Nairobi, 13 Aug. p. 15, and Oct. p. 19; The Observer, 25 July and 22 Aug.; Catholic Herald, 30 July and 3 Dec.; London Church Times, ……..; Target, Nairobi, October; Voice of Southern Sudan, Vol. 3, No. 2, October 1965, pp. 8-11; Mbali, op. cit., pp. 146-154 (report made by Clement Mboro and Gordon Mourtat of the Southern Front).

but the injured patient died. The total number of deaths is impossible to determine, but Southerners living in the town estimate it as over 1400. The official police figure was 116.[226] Although the immediate cause of the massacre was the fight over the transistor radio, there is evidence that the army fully intended to kill the Southern intellectuals of Juba in any case. This evidence is provided by a conversation on July 5th reportedly held between an army officer and a Southerner whom the officer mistook for a Northerner: the officer said that the army had received orders from HQ in Khartoum to kill educated Southerners beginning with officials of the Southern Front. Furthermore, the acting Governor, the Commandant of Police and an army officer are reported to have visited the hospital and cemeteries after the shooting with a list of names, instructing at each place whether the victims included certain Southern Front members.

The possibility that the Juba killings were not haphazard but in part deliberate is strengthened by the evidence from Wau three days later.[227] There the majority of educated Southerners living in the town were gathered at 8.30 p.m. on July 11th at the Wau Club and at a double wedding party in the house of Paulino Chier Rehan. Earlier in the day at Wau Cathedral, Ottavio Deng and Cipriano Chier had married two daughters of Chief Benjamin Lang Juk, and the wedding reception was being held in the home of the bridegrooms' uncle. At 8.30 p.m. units of the Sudan army arrived at the two places and without warning opened fire on the guests. 76 people were killed, including the two bridegrooms, 18 civil servants, doctor, 2 ex-M.P.'s, 4 hospital workers, 6 teachers, 6 students, the vice-chairman of the Bahr el Ghazal Province Council and 2 children. There seems little doubt that the occasion of the wedding feast was chosen by the government as a means of killing a large number of the Southern educated elite at one time.

In at least, two other places, Yei and Rumbek, there seems to have been a list of educated Southerners whom the government intended to kill. In Yei there were seven names, including prison officer Angelo

---

226 Daily Telegraph, 5 Dec. 1965, p. 5.

227 See the Kenya Weekly News, 30 July 1965, p. 17; the Reporter, Nairobi, 8 Oct. p. 17; Voice of Southern Sudan, Vol. 3, No. 2, Oct. 1965, pp. 12-14; A. Mbali, op. cit., pp. 154-156; Daily Telegraph, 5 Dec. 1965, p. 5. Information from Elisapana Kebi and Othwonh Dak.

Kenyi, police inspector Elijah Tor, A.D.C. Elisapana Kebi Mulla, Camilio Odonkis, Othwonh Dak, Filberto Lolik and Rudolf Gharib[228]. There was, however, a leak. The seven learned of the plan and advised the entire population of Yei to leave quietly. By the end of June, 2000 people had run away, and the town was practically deserted. The government departments vanished one by one first the medical department, then forestry, education, Public Works Department (P.W.D), and the police. When finally the postmaster departed the Governor sent orders for the A.D.C, and Mamor to be arrested, but on July, 14th they escaped into the bush just ahead of the army. Angelo Kenyi and Elijah Tor were less fortunate. The former had gone to Juba, was sent back to Yei and shot on July 17th. The latter was arrested and beaten; it is said he died later in hospital. In Rumbek, there was also a list, which reportedly had 65 names on it originally but later was reduced to 14[229]. It seems that some of the army officers there were on good terms with the Southerners and said that although they had had clear instructions to kill the leading people of Rumbek they could not bring themselves to do it. As it happened, the shooting on July 20th was sparked off by the arrival of a wounded officer from Mundri to be flown out for medical treatment, and amongst the dead were only 2 of the 14 on the list. One of these, Father Arkangelo Ali, who was taken from the mission to the army barracks and shot. The other was Paul Nul Bior, a prison officer who barricaded himself in his house and defended himself with his rifle before being killed by a grenade. The total number who died is uncertain: one estimate is 130.

In other incidents in Yambio, Maridi and Mundri there is no direct evidence of a list of names, but a relatively clear indication of the intention to kill educated Southerners. In Yambio on the evening of June 24th six teachers who were playing cards in the house of Oliver Kpakpuyo were arrested and taken to the army barracks.[230] The next morning Joseph Kisanga the police superintendent, acting for the D.C, who was in Juba at the time, went to the barracks to inquire about them. The officer

---

228 Eliaba Surur reports that altogether 23 people were killed in Yei
229 Information from a person whose name for the sake of his own safety cannot be
      disclosed. Information about the list is scanty, and needs additional confirmation.
      Another eye-witness report of the shooting may be found in Mbali, op. cit., pp. 156-159.
230 Information from Philip Nvue and Joseph Lokule.

in charge said that if Kisanga wanted to die in place of the six teachers he could; Kisanga replied that he was prepared to die provided justice was done. He was shot as he was getting into his car. His death was the signal for a mass exodus from Yambio and Nzara, some 5000 people running out of the town. Kisanga's Southern colleagues in the police were disarmed, and many are feared to have been killed.[231] In Maridi, the secretary of the Southern Front, the Mamur and the inspector of local schools were playing dominoes in the Mamur's house on July 5th at 5.30 p.m. when the army arrived and shot at the house without hitting anyone.[232] Later the D.C. arrived and apologized, saying that the soldiers had been supposed to go to the secretary's house. When they did arrive at his house later that night, he escaped for his life into the forest. A medical assistant and the assistant secretary of the Southern Front, Abel Kon, were however killed in Maridi about the same time. The belief is that the army was provoked by the Southern Front's reporting of military operations conducted against the villages around Maridi.[233] Finally, in Mundri on July 20th government troops surrounded the theological college at 3.30 a.m., the bursar's brother was shot, and Bishop Elinana Ngalamu escaped only by taking off his pyjamas and hiding in a hedge until morning.[234]

The account of what there seems little alternative but to describe as a governmental policy of genocide is long and cannot all be narrated here. But there are other killings during June and July which must be mentioned briefly. Kuku village, 1/2 mile south of Torit, was burned to ashes on July 4th with a loss of life estimated to be as much as 150.[235] On July 15th 86 people were reported to have been killed at Kapoeta.[236] And there are three

---

231 Again, information is scanty. There is a confused and rather misleading account in Mbali, op. cit., pp. 125-126.

232 Information from the Southern Front secretary, who believes that the soldiers aimed wide on purpose.

233 Richard Grey, in a letter to the Times of 16 Dec. 1966, says that he has seen a diary kept by a Southern priest at Maridi, in which the army's activities during this period are described.

234 See the Uganda Argus, 22 Oct. 1965, and Richard Gray in The Tablet, 13 Nov.

235 This figure is given by Joseph Oduho in The Observer of 17 Oct. 1965, but needs confirmation. It is of interest to note that the commanding officer in Torit at that time was Col. Jaafar Nimeiry, later President of the Sudan, and that he would presumably have ordered the operation.

236 The Observer, 17 Oct. 1965.

unconfirmed reports of killings at Chief Jambo's village at Mide on June 28th (400 deaths), at Yandoru in Yei district on late July (300 deaths) and at Lotole village near Kajo Kaji on Jane 30th.[237] It is true that further information is required about all these reported massacres, which apart from those at Juba and Wau have not been adequately described, before any firm conclusions can be drawn from them. But at the moment the acts available, inadequate and sketchy as they are, seem to indicate that in the latter part of June 1965 the newly-elected Sudan government decided to adopt a policy of attempting to crush the independence movement in the South by means of the deliberate killing of civilians. Khartoum continued to deny that government policy lay behind the massacres, and some quarters in the North considered the events of June and July (as has been suggested) a number of isolated instances of army indiscipline.[238]But the occurrence of so many killings, widely-spaced geographically, within such a limited space of time, is difficult to explain in this way, and the evidence seems to point to some degree of government coordination.

Let us now turn to the effect these massacres had upon the Southern liberation movement. Although the intention of Mahgoub's government was doubtless to weaken the will of the insurrectionists, and to show them that resistance was futile, the opposite effect seems to have been achieved. Particularly in Bahr el Ghazal, where during the easy days of the caretaker government Anya-Nya soldiers mingled freely with people in towns, and many forsook the hard life of the guerilla camp for the comfort of their own villages, the massacres hardened public opinion against Khartoum. The fact that some of the incidents were explicitly aimed at eliminating the Southern intellectual elite drove many educated people out of towns into the countryside, and a good proportion of the present Anya-Nya leadership derives from this source. Many more Southerners became refugees in neighboring countries. Exact figures are hard to obtain, but according to one set of estimates there were 10,000 Southern refugees in Uganda in February 1965, and anywhere

---

237 See the Uganda Argus.

238 This explanation is adumbrated in a letter from Peter Kilner in the Times, 27 Nov. 1965.

between 85,000 and 150,000 by December.[239] The significant increase in Anya-Nya military operations between June and December which, it is true, was as much due to the increased availability of arms from Congo as to the massacres, has been referred to earlier.[240] Generally speaking, the coming into power of Mahgoub's government reversed the movement of rapprochement between North and South that had been initiated by the caretaker government and drove the two sides back into extreme entrenched positions that have altered very little since. In the next chapter we shall describe some of the political changes undergone by the movement in exile from 1965 to 1967.

---

239 The first figure comes from the Times, 6 Feb. 1965, the second from the Observer, Foreign News Service release of 8 Dec. 1965 by Peter Kilner, and the third from Ian Colvin in the Sunday Telegraph, 28 Nov. 1965.

240 See for example page 71.

CHAPTER 15

SANU and the Azania Liberation Front

As mentioned above, the decisive break between the Sudan government and the Southern political movement in exile came when SANU's representative to the 12-man committee arrived from Kampala and was sent away.[241] This left Deng's wing of SANU, which had not returned to East Africa after the Round Table Conference but had remained in Khartoum, as the only party called "SANU" which was recognised by the Sudan government. SANU was effectively split, and the strain of there being two distinct groups with the same name proved to be too much for the party in exile, which as we shall see did not live past the end of the year.

---

241 See in addition to the references quotod in Chapter 13 the Uganda Argus, 23 June 1965 p. 5, where Peter Akol, SANU representative, says he was told in Khartoum that SANU working outside Sudan would not be acceptable to the 12-man committee. The reason given was that there existed a SANU group inside Sudan led by Mr. William Deng. Akol also reports Dr. Turabi, a spokesman of the Northern political parties, as saying that he would never again share the same table with the leaders of a resistance movement.

The middle of 1965, however, was a period of great activity for Jaden's SANU. The massacres of June and July brought about a hardening of attitude, and the party became more openly identified with the Anya-Nya. Jaden entered Sudan in June, and for almost two months toured parts of Central Equatoria with an Anya-Nya escort.[242] It was his intention to place the headquarters of the movement inside the country, and although subsequent events prevented this being done under SANU, the move was carried out by SANU's successor. Jaden conceived plans for organizing the various isolated elements of the Anya-Nya into a national army. The project envisaged an army of six battalions, each battalion comprising six companies of 150 men. Of these, four would be territorial companies, one would be battalion HQ and one would be mobile. This total army strength of 5,400 men is modest compared to an estimate of 11,200 actually serving at the time, though in another sense it is a more realistic figure when one considers that the same estimate provides the 11,200 men with only 1,789 rifes.[243]The commander-in-chief of the Anya- Nya was to be the president of SANU, thus, for the first time explicitly associating the party with the liberation army. Jaden furthermore envisaged the time when SANU would cease to exist as a party, giving way to a full-fledged provisional government of Southern Sudan.

These developments were not to come for some time, however. The rejection of SANU-in-exile's representative to tho 12-man committee gave the more militant Southern leaders in Kampala, who had all along been critical of holding negotiations with Khartoum, the chance to say "I told you so". In the last week of June 1965, Joseph Oduho and George Kwanai announced the formation of a new group, the Azania Liberation Front (ALF), dedicated to the principle of complete separation of the

---

242 Information from Jaden.

243 Document in the author's possession, dated 26 July 1965. This number increased greatly in the next few months, however, because of supplies from Simba.

South from the rest of Sudan.[244] Others supporting ALF were said to be Father Saturnino, Pancrasio Ochieng, Marko Rume nd Alexis Mbali. Of course, separation, was also SANU-in-exile's goal, and an announcement to that effect was made soon after the founding of ALF.[245] The division between the two was in fact less a matter of policies than of personalities, and what it came down to was that ALF attracted those who preferred the leadership of Joseph Oduho to that of Aggrey Jaden. In late August, an attempt was made to bring ALF and SANU together under the name of the Sudan African Liberation Front (SALF).[246]But, as Albino remarks, the marriage was premature, and SALF proved to be nothing else than the new name for Jaden's SANU until a more genuine reconciliation was achieved in December.

The merging of ALF and SALF came about on December 19th. It resulted from the work of a reconciliation committee under the chairmanship of Dr. Justo Muludiang.[247]The new name ALF was retained, and Oduho was made president and Jaden vice-president. The constitution of the new ALF is an interesting document. It begins:

> We the African people, owners and masters of the country presently known as the "Southern Sudan", victimized by the perpetuation of political, cultural and economic domination and oppression, and all

---

244 See Uganda Argus, 28 June 1965, p. 5; the Reporter, Nairobi, 2 July 1965, p. 15; Kenya Weekly News, 9 July, p. 17; Albino, p. 59. The choice of "Azania" may strike the reader as surprising, considering that it is the name by which the eastern coasts of Africa were known in the Graeco-Roman world, and that the Southern Sudan lies considerably inland. The name however was not new to the movement. Document 2M/219 of the Southern Sudan archive states that in 1961, before the founding of SANU, the leaders in exile adopted "Azania" as a possible name of their future independent state. Jean Zeigler reports that one of the early names for the freedom fighters was the "Azania Secret Army" (Le Monde, 22 July 1966, p. 5), and the name also occurs in the Black Book documents referred to earlier. Later, "Azania" was also adopted by the South African freedom movement as the name of their projected future state, although Basil Daviidson for one considered the Southern Sudanese nationalists to have a stronger claim to the name than their South African cunterparts (See Document 1E/256, p. 10, of Southern Sudan archive).

245 Uganda Argus, 14 July 1965, p. 5

246 Uganda Argus, 2 Sept, 1965, p. 3; Albino, p. 60,

247 see the Daily Nation, Nairobi, 24 Dec. 1965, p. 1; Uganda Argus, 30 Dec. p. 4; the Reporter, Nairobi, 31 Dec. p. 13. Other members of the committee, which had been formed on October 30th, were Othwonh Dak, Paul Achire, Stephen Lam, Serafino Swaka, and Abdel Rahman Sule.

forms of colonial policies and practices which have been rejected by the African continent....have therefore formulated and bound ourselves to this constitution for the sole aim of liberating the Southern Sudan and establishing a free and independent African nation so that the black man in this part of the continent may realize security, justice, welfare and his hitherto lost human rights and dignity"[248].

Besides the people of the three provinces of Bahr el Ghazal, Equatoria and Upper Nile, the constitution provided also for the liberation of the Ngok Dinka of Kordofan province. The supreme authority of ALF was vested in an 11-man National Executive Council, and it was specified that the headquarters of the movement should be in the Southern Sudan. A significant feature of the constitution was that it made no provision for changes in the executive council by democratic process. Dr Muludiang, commenting on this, spoke of such processes as normally being followed only "in peace-time conditions"[249].

In accordance with the constitutional stipulation that the headquarters should be located in the Southern Sudan, Joseph Oduho made a 450- mile trek in Eastern Equatoria from January to March 1966, and several ALF meetings were held in the area of Lobone in the East during May, June and July. The exact dates, locations, and persons attending the latter are not known, except that it seems the first formal executive meeting was held in Father Saturnino's headquarters at Tul July 8th -22nd, and that at least 7 executive members attended[250]. The meetings seem to have been complicated by the fact that Fr. Saturnino, who did not belong to the executive

---

248　Southern Sudan Archive, document 1C/1205. This document should be compared with 1C which seems to be an earlier version entitled "The Constitution of the Azania Liberation Movement".

249　The Daily Nation, Nairobi, 24 Dec. 1965, p. 1.

250　See document 2C/30 of the Southern Sudan archive, p. 6. Jaden was not there: he had been dismissed in April following his signing of a joint statement with William Deng which said that ALF had agreed to accept the decisions of the 12-man committee (Uganda Argus, 4 Feb. 1966; the Reporter, Nairobi, 8 April). The ALF executive at the time of the July meeting was composed of Joseph Oduho, President; Elia Lupe, Vice-President and Secretaries for: Defence, International Affairs, Home Affairs, Finance, Information, Education, Legal Affairs, Refugees and Community development and Organization and Coordination.

council, had more power and influence than any of its members[251]. They were also marked by the emergence of the new Secretary for Defence, Ezbon Mondiri, as the most dynamic member of the government. Mondiri appears to have been responsible for the most original idea to come out of ALF. This was the replacement of the old colonial division of the South into 3 provinces and 21 districts by a new division into 8 regions, a region being smaller than a province but more extensive than a district. The purpose of this division was to facilitate adminintration in a country which was immense enough in the days of the British, but which had been made many times more immenee by the breakdown of all forms of communication except travel on foot. In such conditions the effective administration of an area the size of a province was impossible. Mondiri's idea of dividing the country into regions proved a popular one, and has been adopted in one form or other by the various provisional governments that have existed since[252].

Following their meetings in July, the executive of ALF scattered and never assembled again. Oduho went to Kampala, having disagreed with Father Saturnino over the matter of aid from foreign sympathizers. It seems that Oduho had been promised some aid, but when it arrived, it went to Fr. Saturnino instead of to him as president of ALF. In consequence, Oduho's authority was undermined (an example of the counterproductivity of certain types of foreign aid). Fr. Saturnino remained in the HQ at Tul. Mondiri embarked on a lengthy tour of the South, which we shall briefly describe.

As was remarked before, Mondiri was a man of great energy and determination. Without him, ALF would have remained a small East bank organization of little importance. Mondiri's tour gave ALF a nationnl image and did something to convince different parts of the country that they were fighting for the same cause. Accompanied by Severino Fuli, he

---

251 Jean Ziegler reports that Oduho's title was "President of the Morement", while Fr. Saturnino's was "Chairman of the National Movement" (Le Monde, 22 July 1966, p. 5).

252 The originol plan is to be found in document 2E/1041 of the Southern Sudan archive, dated July 1966. Under the SSPG the number of regions was increased from 8 to 9 (3 per province), and the system of administration by regions underwent considerable development. Even in Joseph Lagu's organizntion, where the civil government has reverted to the old system of administration by districts, the military organization retained the system of 9 regions.

wan escorted to the west bank of the Nile by Joseph Lagu and travelled through the areas of Kajo- Kaji, Yei and Aba. He then went north-west to Maridi[253]. At each of the many Anya-Nya camps and headquarters at which he stopped, he explained the new policies and regulations of ALF to the soldiers. After leaving Maridi in October, he went to the new Anya-Nya headquarters at Lomilingwa, which Mondiri had ordered to be built so as to remove it from its former possibly dangerous location near the Congo border. The headquarters of ALF were thus split, the military command being at Lomilingwa, and the political HQ east of the Nile. In January Mondiri made a tour of Anya-Nya camps in the vicinity of Rumbek where as noted earlier he appointed Philip Nanga as commander for Bahr el Ghazal and also recruited a number of Dinka soldiers for Lomilingwa. Mondiri returned to his HQ early in February, and as we shall see had his work interrupted by an attempted *coup d'état* later that month.

Mondiri's tour (even the mere fact that such an extensive trip was possible) provided a certain amount of information about conditions in the South in 1966/67. Four other accounts from about the same time, written by European newspapermen, also throw light on the matter, and these we shall briefly consider. Two of them visited the South as guests of the Anya-Nya, and two as guests of the Sudan government, so they provide a good cross-section of opinion.

The first account was written by Anthony Carthew, who travelled to Lazzaro Mutek's camp in the Dongotono Mountains in January 1966[254]. Carthew describes his walk of 70 miles through parched scrub-land and forest, encountering every few miles a burned-out village, to the abandoned Roman Catholic mission station of Isoke. Situated in a green mountain valley, Isoke and the higher and more inaccessible retreat at Dito were estimated by Carthew to contain 1,000 soldiers armed with 100 rifles. His articles provide a slightly sensationalized account of a white man's impressions of an African guerilla camp, including a striking

---

253 See document 2C/30 of the Southern Sudan archive. As reported above, Mondiri's delegation met the eastern edge of the newly- formed Zande administration at Maridi, with the not very happy result that Simon Mohandes was dismissed as D.C. and re-appointed as ALF political officer.

254 The Daily Mail, 31 Jan., and 2 Feb. 1966.

portrait of the half-mad Mutek, who greeted Carthew with two shots fired into the dust at his feet. But with the exception of one or two brief observations ("Here a race war of immense ferocity is being fought.... The African is killing the Arab because he is an Arab. The Arab is killing the African because he is an African"), Carthew's articles are devoid of thought or reflection upon the nature of the conflict he was witnessing. The same cannot be said of the two contributions of the journalists Jean-Francois Chauvel and Jean Ziegler, which in the best tradition of French journalism are full of philosophical digressions on the history, motives and passions that lie behind what they saw.

Chauvel entered Sudan the day after Christmas 1965 near Nimule, and proceeded via Loa and Opari up to Magwi[255]. He was accompanied by Severino Fuli and Nathaniel Oyet, an MP who had formerly represented Kapoeta and who at the time of Chauvel's tour was commander of D Company based at Kilira. Chauvel was confronted with exactly the same combination of waterless bush and burned-out villages as Carthew. Arriving at the former mission station of Loa in Madi country, he learned of the series of attacks and counter- attacks which had resulted in the total destruction of the few small inhabited centres of the area. On the 8th of August 1965, a group of Anya-Nya under command of Arkangelo Loku had waited in ambush at the river where the Northern soldiers of Opari went to draw water. The Northerners were warned by a Southern spy, but ignored the warning and went anyway. In the ambush, 15 soldiers were killed and their water-truck fell into the river. The remaining Northerners, furious that their spies had not reported that the Anya-Nya were armed, returned to Opari and murdered sub-chief Rafaele Abuni, his wife and children, and some other Southerners who were living near the post. On Auguet 17th it was the turn of Loa, when following an attack led by Paulino Munyoro the Northern garrison withdrew to Nimule, taking the Madi chief with them. The Anya-Nya burned the empty buildings that the army had used; a few days later, the army returned and destroyed the mission station. As Chauvel remarks, "Ainsi vont les choses au Soudan", meaning "this is how things are in Sudan"

From Loa, Chauvel travelled up to Magwi and met Taffeng. On the

---

255 Le Figaro, 24, 25, 29, 30 March 1966. Chauvel's account of the trip may be compared witb Severino Fuli's in Document 1C/287 of the Southern Sudan archive.

way he took part in a village dance to celebrate the end of the rains and translated the dancers' song:

You scorn the Anya-Nya as if they were wet hens
But they will cut you in pieces.

You call them bow and arrow people
But they will kill you like chickens.

Do not speak evil of the Anya-Nya
They have pointed ears and will cut you in pieces.

Do not tell where they are hiding
They will cut you in pieces.

Do not deceive the Anya-Nya
They are your army and will cut you in pieces.

At Magwi, Chauvel persuaded Taffeng to mount an attack on the army post, in order to show the fighting abilities of the Anya-Nya. This was done, with Chauvel hiding behind an ant-hill some 200 yards from the post. The engagement took place early in the morning and lasted about six minutes before the Anya-Nya withdrew. Fuli (a little, hesitantly) judged the operation to be successful "because the Anya-Nya sustained no loss". Chauvel was more dubious, though he did point out that it was the first time in those parts that a post had been attacked in broad daylight with the help of a machine gun[256]. Although he said, he would not be surprised if Magwi were eventually evacuated like many other posts in the area, at the time of writing the Northern army was still there and shows even less likelihood of being dislodged than in Chauvel's day. Up to now, the last word is still Carthew's:

"This, then, is the Anya-Nya. It would be absurd to suggest that they can ever win the disastrous way they have embarked on. But to the refugees who are crowded into this mission (Isoke), and to those others I have seen in the forests and hills, the Anya-Nya offers some kind of protection, if not hope."

---

256 Chauvel's account is not unlike David Robin son's report of an unsuccesful attack 4½ years later on Kajo-Kaji. See The Observer Magazine. In both cases, the Anya-Nya were late in arriving at their attacking stations.

We now turn to the long article of Ziegler in Le Monde[257], in which the author sketches the historical background and the political dimensions of the Southern problem with great skill. The scale and nature of the conflict are indicated by Ziegler as follows:

"The war has claimed, since the 1955 mutiny, about 500,000 victims. This is the figure which a foreign observer arrives at by correlating information provided by the government, statements by ALF, and estimates made by the representatives of certain international organizations based in Kampala. The medical, economic and administrative infrastructure of a region the size of France has been almost entirely destroyed. There exits no front, no line of fire. Hundreds, perhaps thousands, of villages have been abandoned. Entire communities have disappeared into the forest. A whole people appears to have returned to the neolithic age, abandoning the hard-won conquests of a rudimentary civilization. Along the roads - frequently pitted with holes dug by the guerillas- exist villages burned, empty, and in ruins. Deep in the woods, invisible beneath the green forest roof, other villages have been built. These are unhealthy and devoid of the most elementary amenities, but often provided with a church and a small school."

Of considerable interent is Ziegler's description of his visit to Juba and the mood of the people he encountered there, both Southerners and Northerners. Juba struck him as nightmarish, a town beset by spirits. His Sudan Airways plane extinguished its lights on beginning to descend: the stewardess explained this as a temporary electrical fault, but the British pilot admitted later that the Anya- Nya had recently shot down an airplane. The town of 60,000 inhabitants was guarded by 5,000 troops. This number was in addition to the unarmed Southern policemen whose task of maintaining order was made simple by what Ziegler described as a lack of animation in the streets. In fact, he found that since the events of July 1965 people did not linger outside their houses without good reason. The impression was of a city under siege, not only from without but from within.

Talking in the hotel bar to Major-General Ahmed al-Sharif, the army

---

257 21 and 22 July, 1966.

commander in the South, Ziegler learned that 18,000 troops, or about two-thirds of the Sudan army, were at his disposal. These were at the moment occupying, according to the General, about 20 Southern towns and villages where permanent army installations were to be found and which the General described as impregnable[258]. Surprisingly, the General believed that no lasting military solution was possible and that political negotiations were a necessity. Negotiations, on what basis? Possibly on the basis of according some degree of autonomy to the South. But independence? No, that was not negotiable. Ziegler tried to probe beneath the surface and discover what exactly it was that made the idea of independence unthinkable to the military officers in the South. His conclusion was that it was not merely the desire to maintain the integrity of the Sudan's national territory. Instead, he discovered, the officers believed that they were defending the frontiers of the Arab world. It is this "supplementary vocation", as Ziegler puts it,

> "in which they seem to believe with impressive fervour that explains their frequently accusing the civil government of 'laxity' and 'irresponsibility'. It is for the sake of this vocation that they are willing to accept heavy sacrifices: to fight in a climate and in conditions often inhuman; to run the daily risk of murderous ambushes without ever being able to confront the enemy; to see the endless war consume every yenr 12 to 14 million Sudanese pounds out of a total government budget of little more than 60 million."

This then was Juba in 1966; a town which a frightened civil population "defended" against their own countrymen by an army which believes its mission in to protect the Arab world. A city of paradoxes, indeed. one of the more encouraging features of Ziegler's report, the fact that the Northern army commander believed in the necessity of a negotiated settlement, was confirmed by another foreign reporter who visited the South as a guest of Khartoum. "There has got to be a political solution", Keith Kyle was told by Ahmed al-Sharif, months before Ziegler's visit, "it cannot be settled by

---

258 This number would be in addition to the numerous small posts also occupied by the army.

the military."[259] Although Kyle's reports are not as full as Ziegler's, they are of interest in that he was able to visit Maridi, one of the largest army posts in the South. Kyle found that road transport to Maridi was next to impossible due to the fact that not only was a heavy escort required, but also, because all the bridges had been dynamited, convoys had to carry bridging equipment which they put across each river and then pulled up again to be used for the next river. By dint of keeping a daily plane running to Juba, the army had succeeded in re-staffing the Maridi administrative HQ, supplying the garrison, and resettling civilians within the town. But Kyle remarks that the life was entirely artificial. Those resettled civilians had to cultivate their gardens within the confines of a narrow military cordon, schools were still closed, and the town depended wholly on its air link with Juba.

Returning now to events in the countryside, we shall describe the attempted coup d' etat against ALF of February 20th 1967, which eventually led to the downfall of Mondiri. ALF itself did not have long to live, and in August of the same year was replaced by the Southern Sudan Provisional Government.

The precise motives of those who rebelled against Mondiri in February 1967 are not clear[260]. Some say that the coup was instigated by the Roman Catholic missionaries, who disliked Mondiri for his alleged communist connexions, and who with the death of Fr. Saturnino a month earlier had lost their principal spokesman in the movement[261]. Others say that it represented merely a desire on the part of certain Anya-Nya officers to get rid of the civilian politicians above them. In any case the principal military participants appear to have been Ferdinand Goi, Camillo Odongi and Repent Sunday who persuaded Paul Ai Gbatala, the senior officer in Angudri, to sign a declaration stating that the army had taken

---

259 Two of Kyle's reports appear as a release of the Observer Foreign News Service, 24 March 1966, and in the Sunday Nation, Nairobi, 27 March 1966, pp. 9 - 10.

260 Most of the author's information comes from Documents of the Southern Sudan archive, and from Elisapana Kebi, Francis Wajo, Ezbon Jodi and Gordon Muortat.

261 Fr. Saturnino was killed on January 22nd 1967 near Lokung in Northern Uganda after being arrested by the Uganda Army. According to an eye-witness account in the Reporter of 10 March 1967, he became convinced that he was going to be shot, and was killed when he tried to overpower his guards. For a slightly different report, together with a short account of his life, see (documents of the Southern Sudan archive). A eulogy of Fr. Saturnino appeare in The Vigilant, 7 Feb. 1967.

over the government from ALF. No sooner had the document been signed, however, than confusion set in. Goi was chosen to take the declaration to Mondiri in Lomilingwa, but according to one story met two Dinka friends of Mondiri on tho way who persuaded the other Dinka soldiers with Goi not to proceed any further. Goi became sick, and after being carried back to Angudri was arrested by Gbatala. Gbatala, it seems, had been informed by Mondiri's friends that Goi was planning to overthrow him. Meanwhile, Mondiri had heard the news and hastened to Angudri with William Hassan, the ALF chief of staff. On arrival there, he was arrested but soon released by the Dinkas, who had told Gbatala they would not take part in the conspiracy. Mondiri declared the coup ended and returned to Lomilingwa to prepare for an Anya-Nya convention he had summoned. But unfortunately, the sequence of events did not end there. What had been up to that point a comedy of plots and counter-plots ended tragically with the death of many people. Some of those who had been arrested by Mondiri for conspiring against him escaped, and went to the Moru HQ at Ngiri. From there a large force of Moru set out for Lomilingwa, and fought the battles referred to above, Mondiri escaped, Lomilingwa was destroyed, and with it ended the power of ALF to the west of the Nile. Four months later, the Southern Sudan Provisional Government was formed.

CHAPTER 16

The Southern Sudan Provisional Government

At a large convention held at Angudri in August 1967 the formation of a new national body was announced, the Southern Sudan Provisional Government. The calling of the convention seems to have been largely the work of Aggrey Jaden, who though dismissed as vice-president of ALF in March 1966, continued to be active as chairman of the defence council of Central Equatoria region. In early 1967 Jaden went on a lengthy tour of his region, proceeding as far north as Amadi, and talked to among others 9 government-appointed chiefs with complete authority in their areas.[262] Four of these chiefs were in Yei district, 3 in Juba district, and 2 in Amadi sub-district. All were reportedly unanimous in their rejection of the Khartoum government, and in their desire to fight to a finish. His resolve strengthened by this knowledge, as well as by the pleas of those who had learned of the destruction of Lomilingwa and sought for recon-

---

262 Information from Jaden. It seems to have been around this time that Jaden attempted to form a political organization known as "Home Front," doubtless intended as a rival of ALF. The attempt, however, met with no success.

ciliation between the two factions of Morus. Jaden proceeded to Aba and summoned the convention with the help of Elia Lupe and of an *ad hoc* organization committee under the chairmanship of Camillo Dhol.

The Angudri convention, attended by some 300 people who had come either by invitation or for arms purchasing, opened at 10 a.m. on August 19[263]. Jaden, in his opening address, sketched the history of the struggle and condemned the many causes of disunity such as personal ambition, desire for gain, tribalism and politicking. What he proposed was not another party or front, but a government in which all the elements of Southern leadership would be united. By a vote of 30 to 2 among the official voting delegates, all of whom were civilians, not Anya-Nya, the name "Southern Sudan Negro Provisional Government" was adopted. (The word "Negro" was dropped in January 1968). After this, Jaden was elected president and Camillo Dhol vice-president by 20 and 18 votes, respectively. During the following days, while Jaden and Dhol were forming their cabinet and secretariat, the convention proceeded to study the relationship between the political and the military sides of the movement in the three provinces, to adopt a draft constitution and a national flag, and to resolve to merge all the various guerilla camps into a national army entitled ANAF (Anya-Nya National Armed Forces). Having accomplished its work, and according to one source having surprised itself by the degree of unity achieved, the convention was dissolved on August 28th.

Why was Angudri successful? For various reasons, perhaps the most significant of which was that for the first time a large-scale convention was held inside Southern Sudan, in the presence of the military men and political officers who had been doing the basic grass roots "work" of the movement, and whose efforts may have shamed the politicians into uniting. Secondly, those among the politicians who held strong views and had proved difficult to work with in the past vere absent. Father Saturnino was dead, Joseph Oduho was in the east, and Ezbon Mondiri

---

263   A brief account of the convention appears in Sudan Informazioni 5/6, 20 Nov. 1967,
      p. 8. Additional information from Aggrey Jaden, Gordon Muortat, Lawrence Wol
      Wol, Kuaclieth Banak and Simon Mohandes. Although the convention began on the
      19th, the official date of opening was given out as August 18th, in memory of the 1955
      mutiny. The name "Angudri" is that of a man who was a refugee from the 1955 mutiny
      and who became a sub-chief in the area which now bears his name.

was arrested at the convention under the pretext of being a communist (he was alleged to have been in possession of a document offering help from the Chinese, which in the light of the latter's proven expertise in guerilla fighting might have benefitted the Southerners but which doubtless went against their mission-influenced background and ideology). Finally, a major factor in bringing unity was the strict observance of equal representation of all parts of the South in the composition of the cabinet. As we shall see, this matter of equal representation is a double- edged sword, and in the end, may have proved as much a weakness as a strength to the SSPG. There was a tendency for ministers to regard themselves quasi-permanent representatives of their home areas and hence as immune to dismissal - this led to inactivity and in some cases non-participation. But at the same time, the knowledge that all regions were represented in the government doubtless contributed to a genuine national sentiment.

The method of selecting the cabinet was as follows. Five cabinet posts were allotted to each province, making fifteen in all. In order to ensure that the most important posts were fairly distributed, each province was given certain specified ministries. Thus for example, Upper Nile got Defence, Information and Cabinet Affairs, Bahr el Ghazal the Vice-Presidency, Foreign Affairs and Justice, Equatoria the Presidency, Interior and Finance. Even the twelve posts of deputy ministers were distributed on a geographical basis. At the convention, each province had its own meeting to decide which individuals would fill the positions allotted it. It then passed its list of names through a steering committee, composed of two members from each province, to Jaden and Dhol. As it turned out, the steering committee's recommendations were adhered to in almost all appointments made[264]:

1   President: Aggrey Jaden
2   Vice President: Camillo Dhol
3   Minister for Defence: Akuot Atem
    Deputy: Arkangelo Wanji Ella

---

264   This list is taken from The Southern Sudanese Gazette No. 1, March 1st, 1968, (Document 1E/5 of the Southern Sudan archive) and represents certain changes from the original one of August 1967. Even so, it includes appointments of at least five (Dak, Wol Wol, Oduho, Lam and Koak) who never took up their posts.

4   Minister for Interior: Elia Lupe
    Deputy: Solomon Anyang
5   Minister for Foreign Affairs: Gordon Muortat
    Deputy: Clement Moses
6   Minister for Education: Othwonh Dak
    Deputy: Rudolf Kwot
7   Minister for Finance: Tadeo Bidai
    Deputy: Daniel Kot
8   Minister for Justice: Gabriel Kau
    Deputy: Vacant
9   Minister for Information: George Kwanai
    Deputy: Andrew Achijok
10 Minister for Health: Michael Ngamunde
    Deputy; Lazarus Latjor
11 Minister for Agriculture: Lawrence Wol Wol
    Deputy: Marko Rume
12 Minister for Cabinet Affairs: Kuaclieth Banak
13 Minister for Communications: Joseph Oduho
    Deputy: Stephen Lam
14 Minister for Animal Resources: Elia Duang
    Deputy: Simon Mohandes
15 Minister for Social and Refugees Affairs: David Koak
    Deputy: Amadeo Awad.

The first cabinet meeting took place in January 1968 in Bungu, the headquarters to which the government moved after 3 or 4 months at Angudri. The Public resolutions of this meeting are embodied in the first issue of the Southern Sudanese Gazette, dated March 1st 1968, and include the following items. First, Bungu is proclaimed to be the 'Provisional Capital of the Liberated Southern Sudan'. (To put people off the scent, Bungu was advertised in the Gazette as being 25 miles from Juba on the Juba-Yei road. In reality, Bungu was located in dense forest a few miles south of Yei. Next, following the list of cabinet ministers given above, the division of the country into 9 administrative regions was announced:

REGION comprising DISTRICTS AND SUB-DISTRICTS

1	Eastern Region	Kapoeta and Torit
2	Central Region	Juba, Yei and Amadi[265]
3	Western Region	Yambio and Maridi
4	Aweil- Raga Region	Aweil and Raga[266]
5	Jur River Region	Wau and Gogrial
6	Lakes Region	Rumbek and Tonj
7	Nile Basin Region	Bor, Fangak and Bentiu
8	Sobat Valley Region	Nasir, Akobo and Pibor
9	Northern Region	Malakal, Kodok and Renk.

The next items in the Gazette are policy statements concerning (i) Khartoum, (ii) the rest of Africa. Under (i), the SSPG expresses unqualified opposition to the proposed holding of elections in the Southern Sudan in April 1968[267]. It asserts that a state of war exists between South and North, and that election might lead to the imposition of a solution acceptable only to the Northerners. The SSPG also condemns the Sudan government's attempts to draft a constitution, saying that the present Southern MPs have no mandate from their people to adopt any constitution. Finally, the SSPG calls on the Southern political parties operating in Khartoum to dissolve themselves and join the liberation movement. Under (ii), the SSPG pledges itself to work with the other liberation movements in Africa for the abolition of colonialism, imperialism, communism(!), and all forms of national and racial oppression. Concerning the refusal of the OAU to discuss the Southern problem on the grounds that it is an internal matter relating to the Sudan alone, the SSPG says that "the negative policy practised by the OAU will not in any way destroy our hope that the Organization will soon rise to her full responsibility." The SSPG, "while supporting true African unity, shall relentlessly resist with all means at her disposal the Arab Colonialism in the Southern Sudan until full independence and human dignity is achieved by the Southern people."

---

265 The inclusion of the Morus in Central Region was a contentious issue. See below.

266 The division of Bahr el Ghazal into the regions given here also raised questions. Those such as Elia Duang who had gone to a lot of trouble in bringing Aweil and Tonj together were distressed at the thought of their separating again.

267 For these elections, and the attempt to draft a constitution, see below.

The remainder of the first issue of the <u>Gazette</u> is devoted to immigration regulations, establishing that no one may enter Southern Sudan without a permit, and to the regulation and licensing of the numerous traders who enter the territory of the SSPG carrying goods for sale in markets. It ends with an order to all Southerners in other countries, who are out of touch with the people and the present political leadership, to stop presenting their personal views as the views of the movement. Better still, they should return home, since "to continue living abroad at this time, while extensive parts of the country have been liberated and a government formed, is a waste of time."

The second issue of the Gazette, published May 1st 1968, continues in the same vein, with the announcement of the new government's Judiciary structure, regulations for magistrates, a set of "mixed guides" dealing with relations between the army, police, civil administrators and the public, and a game and fisheries act[268]. Reading the two numbers of the National Field Day, a mimeographed review edited by George Kwanai that also dates from the first half of 1968[269], gives one a good idea of the vitality and wealth of ideas which the SSPG was able to draw upon. But this creative period, in which it seemed possible that the movement might be able to formulate its aims and ideology, and evolve its own mode of government, was of extremely brief duration. Internal stresses within the SSPG brought its administrative machinery to a halt before the end of 1968, and the two issues of the Gazette and of the Field Day were all that were ever published.

The question must now be asked, how far did the arm of the SSPG reach? In how many areas of the South was its administrative presence felt?

---

268   Document 1E/6 of the Southern Sudan archive, reproduced in Sudan Informazioni 42, 25 May 1969. The "mixed guides" are of interest in that, not dealing with situations within the ken either of the former British administration in the Sudan or of the Islamic sharia law, they have had to be evolved from scratch. An example:
Section 8B. WHEN LOOTING IS NOT A CRIME
1. The act of looting is not a crime when the property confiscated is that of an enemy (Arabs) betrayer or traitor, provided such confiscated properties are surrendered to the government property and no individual ownership or such property is allowed whatsoever, unless there was an order to distribute such properties.
2. It is also not a crime when in certain areas, and under certain hard circumstances, the armed force is being chased by an enemy and cutting normal daily contact of the army with the citizens for the free supply of ration at times, under such circumstances can the armed force unblameably loot whatever quantity of food or goats or any other food stuffs for their feeding hurriedly under such conditions. This means that if after contact there was no free will to supply them.
269   Documents 1E/25a and 1E/256.

The answer is that its arm was long but its grasp unsteady, and there were certain important regions into which it did not penetrate. Eastern Equatoria for example never participated, and following a meeting held in March 1968, at which a resolution was passed that the people of Eastern Equatoria did not recognize the government and leadership of Jaden, the regional commissioner appointed by the SSPG for that region wrote declining the appointment[270]. In Bahr el Ghazal, as was mentioned above, Jur River, Aweil, and a section of Western District had by dint of considerable effort been welded into a fairly smoothly functioning administrative unit by the beginning of 1968. In no way did this unit fit into the SSPG division into regions. Hence although the province was willing to cooperate with the SSPG, the latter's system of administration was not well adapted to local conditions there. In Upper Nile, it is safe to say that up until the time of the demise of the SSPG; its civil administration had had no appreciable influence on the administrative structure and system of tax-collection that had prevailed in the rural areas of the province since 1965. In Bahr el Ghazal and Upper Nile, the SSPG was, in a sense just beginning its work when it died. More serious, however, was its failure to bring either Zande or Moru-land within its orbit.

Zande-land had sent delegates to the Angudri convention, and in Tadeo Bidai, Michael Ngamunde and Simon Mohandes had three members of the cabinet who were either Azande or belonged to the group of small partially Zande-ized tribes around Maridi. Bidai and Ngamunde attended cabinet meetings in January 1968, at which they presented certain conditions which had to be met if Zande-land were to participate in the new government. Chief among these was the demand that military leadership at the national level should be in the hands of those who had been trained as officers in the Sudan Defence Force, namely, Abujohn, Lagu and

---

270 The meeting was held just at the time that Lagu and Oduho were laying the foundations of the so-called "Anya-Nya National Organization" in the East, and this fact doubtless had a lot to do with the refusal.

Magot[271]. But the Commander in Chief of the ANAF was Taffeng, with Paul Ali Gbatala and Paul Awel as his deputies, and Jaden's government was not prepared to revoke these appointments, so Bidai and Ngamunde returned to Zande-land. There two large meetings were held in March, and May 1968 at which only Habbakuk spoke in favor of continuing to support the Provisional Government, and in June Zande region formally withdrew from the SSPG. As mentioned above, these meetings also saw the replacement of Habbakuk by Abujohn as Zande military leader.

The case of Moru-land was somewhat more complicated. At the Angudrí convention, the Zande delegates maintained that the territory covered by the whole of Yambio and Maridi districts was too large to be encompassed within a single administrative region, and it was therefore decided thac Amadi sub-district would be transferred from Western to Central Equatoria. But when this news reached Moru-land it was not well received. The Morus argued that since the coming of the British, they had been linked administratively with the people of Maridi, and that according to the proposed transfer, they themselves would be divided between two different regions. In January 1968 a Moru delegation under the leadership of Elisapana Kabi[272] went to Bungu to present the Moru objections to splitting their territory in this way, and also to request that Mondiri and three of his former supporters be handed over for trial in connection with the Lomilingwa affair. The reply of the SSPG was that these requests required more careful study before any action could be taken; that in particular concrete evidence would have to be presented of crimes allegedly

---

271 Frederick Brian Magot attended Loka Intermediate School and Nabumali High School in Uganda, where he was a contemporary of Ezbon Mondiri. After doing a course in veterinary science at Khartoum he joined the army in 1954, receiving his commission on August 1st 1955. Magot left the army in 1960 during the turmoil caused by Brig Shenan's attempted take-over, and became a trader on the Tembura-Wau road. He escaped into the forest just before the army burned his shops in July 1965, and in 1967 joined the Anya-Nya, being appointed Chief of Staff by the SSPG when Lagu turned down the post in 1968. Magot became a member of the Revolutionary Council of Anyidi, and in 1970 was absorbed into Lagu's organization, undertaking a mission to the United Nations on behalf of the SSLM in November of that year.

272 Elisapana Kabi Mulla, born about 1927, qualified as a clerk in 1950 and joined the civil administration. At the time of the troubles in July 1965, he was acting district commissioner in Yei, and following his escape into the bush he did political and administrative work for the movement and for the Moru people. In 1968 he became actively associated with Lagu'group, and early in 1971 was appointed Province Commissioner for Equatoria in the civil admintration of the SSLM.

committed by Mondiri; and in the meantime could some Moru soldiers be sent to Bungu to be integrated into the ANAF? This reply did not satisfy the Morus, and from Bungu they went to Zande-land, where in the meeting of March 1968 they agreed to cooperate with the Azande in military (though not in civil) matters and accepted Abujohn as supreme commander. As a result, no Moru forces served under the SSPG except for 30-40 sent by Jackson, the Kediru leaders, and Moru-land remained outside the Provisional Government's system of regional administration. In September 1968 a commission under Marko Rume was sent to investigate whether the Mundu, Baka, Avukaya and Makaraka people around Maridi wished to be associated with Central or Western Equatoria for administrative purposes, but the results were inconclusive. Before a more thorough study could be made of the situation, the life of the SSPG came to an end. No doubt, given time and patience, these problems could have been solved. But time was precisely what the Provisional Government lacked, and although it accomplished some small miracles, the bulk of its ambitious administrative programme remained unimplemented.

Military Organization

Turning now to the SSPG's military organization, the Commander-in-Chief of the ANAF was Taffeng. Taffeng himself was not at the Angudri convention, but arrived shortly afterwards, having been sent by ALF to investigate the Lomilingwa affair. It is said that he was persuaded to accept the job by Lazarro Mutek, who happened to be buying arms at Angudri at the time of the convention. As Commander-in-Chief, Taffeng inherited a rather unenviable military position. The Anya-Nya were for the most part divided into small armed bands organized on a tribal or clan basis; Mondiri's failure and the sacking of the national HQ at Lomilingwa, together with Goi's attempted coup, had had a devastating effect on morale; and the amount of territory controlled by the

Anya-Nya had shrunk steadily since the end of 1965[273].

Considering what it began with, it is surprising that the Provisional Government was able to accomplish as much as it did. The key to the SSPG's military policy was: integration and nationalization of all forces. First, instead of the Anya-Nya being a many-headed monster, there was to be a unique chain of command stretching from top to bottom of the ANAF[274]. Second, officers and ranks were to be rotated out of their home areas and sent to serve in other districts and provinces (ideally, only one-third of the forces of anyone province would be local troops. Although this ideal was never fully achieved either by the SSPG or its successors, one authority estimates that, out of a total of about 6,000 Anya-Nya, 4,000 went from their own province to another one between April and August 1968). Third, arms-buying was not to be done by individual commanders of territorial units, for use by these units, but all arms money was to be funnelled through the SSPG ministry of defence. This last regulation led to considerable friction. For example, when a Chollo contingent arrived in early August in 1968 to buy arms, the Minister of Defence Akuot Atem ordered that the money they carried (estimates range from £500 to £6,000) should be passed through him. Eventually, it is said (though this story requires additional confirmation) the Chollos went home with neither arms nor money. This was an instance of implementing a policy which, though fundamentally correct as seen through the eyes of a newly-formed national government, was nevertheless dangerous in being open to serious abuse.

Three major efforts were made by the SSPG to carry out their military programme of integration and nationalisation. These took

---

273 See the map in the New York Times, 15 April 1968, p. 16, which gives a fairly accurate picture of the situation as of April 1968. A short description of 25 separate engagements between the ANAF and the Sudan Defence Force between February and August 1968 is contained in South Sudan Dialogue with President Nyerere, a pamphlet issued by the SSPG.

274 It is an interesting point whether in fact this is the best way for a guerilla army to be organized, or whether clusters of small autonomous forces are not more effective. Certainly the latter are more resilient in that they cannot be paralysed by lack of communication or by a break-down in overall leaderahip. On the other hand, if the small autonomous forces are in the habit of attacking each other as often as the common enemy (and instances of this are far from unknown in the Southern Sudan) then doubtless an overall chain of command is a good thing.

the form of three major expeditions, one to Bahr el Ghazal, one to Bor, and one to Eastern Equatoria. The expedition to Bahr el Ghazal was under the military command of Simoni Jada, and included Simon Mohandes as political commissioner. The expedition, named the "Lol crack force," comprised 140 soldiers with 80 arms and left in August 1968. Its purpose was to unite the three different military areas of the province, which had been operating independently of each other for years, and also to bring back soldiers from Bahr el Ghazal for further integration. The first stop on its itinerary was Rumbek, where in conjunction with local troops it fought some large-scale engagements with the Sudan army. But before its mission to Rumbek is discussed, the death of the military leader of that area must be described.

Each political movement or front in Southern Sudan has its own *cause celebre*: ALF's was Lomilingwa, and the SSPG's was the execution of Philip Nanga[275]. As mentioned earlier, Nanga had been associated with ALF and had kept Lakes District separate from Jur River/ Aweil, operating out of his own base camp in the Redstone hills south of Mvolo. Although he was a brave soldier, there were complaints against him on other grounds, and on two different occasions, he was put under arrest by his own junior officers. In late 1967 or early 1968, having been appointed SSPG commander for Bahr el Ghazal, he made the mistake of arresting two ministers, Gabriel Kau and Andrew Achijok, at Angudri. (Kau was from Rumbek, and "arrest" was occasionally used as a means of settling old scores.) Achijok eventually escaped to Bungu, and when Nanga arrived there, he was in turn arrested, a government soldier being shot by Nanga's bodyguard when Nanga resisted. Nanga's case was heard in full court-martial, with three officers and two civilians sitting on the board. After five days' deliberation, Nanga was found guilty of armed rebellion and sentenced to death. (The civilians held that the sentence should be life imprisonment, but the officers argued that the SSPG had no way of enforcing such a sentence.) He was sent to Morta, and was

---

275 Information from Gordon Muortat, Elia Duang, Simon Mohandes, Arkangelo Wanji, and Eliaba Surur.

in prison there along with 70 other prisoners[276] when the Sudan army attacked the camp on June 29th 1968. Nanga could easily have escaped, but instead, put himself in charge of the prisoners and led them to a safe place. When the attack was over he led them back again, and despite the fact that the Northern soldiers had burned down the prison[277] he told his fellow prisoners that they must all be loyal and await the verdict of their government. Shortly afterwards he was executed by Michael Lorwe, the commander of No. 3 Company based at Morta. At that, his death was probably due to misunderstanding, for Lorwe was unaware of the fact that death sentences had to be confirmed by the President, and Jaden had not confirmed Nanga's.

It is difficult to say what effect Nanga's death had on the success of the Lol crack force's mission to Rumbek and to the rest of Bahr el Ghazal. The force succeeded in doing what had never been done before, namely uniting all the Bahr el Ghazal Anya-Nya under one organization. This was accomplished by its combined military and political leadership: Simon Mohandes developed filariasis in Rumbek and had to return to Bungu, but his deputy Amadeo Awad carried on in his place. He and Simoni Jada together visited Teetadol, Gogrial, Aweil and finally Goi's camp south of Wau, where no doubt the fact that Awad was a Bellanda travelling with a force composed largely of Baris helped to convince the Anya-Nya of the region that in accepting integration they would not be handing themselves over to domination by the Dinkas. Jada's force returned to Bungu in about May 1969, bringing with it money, large number of Bahr el Ghazal soldiers, and considerable prestige.

The second expedition, to Bor, was less successful than the first, but nevertheless had a considerable impact on at least part of Upper Nile Province. Known as the "Sobat Crack Force," the expedition under the command of James Loro left headquarters around August 1968 and took with it Akuot Atem as its political commissioner. On its way, the force overran a police post at Anyidi near Bor, and in October launched a big

---

276 Mostly women. Although the existence of large numbers of women prisoners may be due to the fact that, in times of stress and social upheaval, the number of cases of suspected poisoning increases, it may also be due to the fact that male criminals find it easy to run away and either go into a town or join the Anya-Nya in some other area.

277 On that particular attack, the soldiers burned the regional commissioner's office, the dispensary, the rest house, etc., everything in fact except the ANAF headquarters.

attack on Bor town, using Blackseed recoilless guns with a range of six to eight miles. It is said that the Sudanese Prime Minister, Mohammed Ahmed Mahgoub, was visiting Bor at the time and was evacuated by aeroplane[278]. Although the attack appears to have been successful, the aftermath was not. Akuot's force met a contingent of Nuer soldiers at Bor under the command of Samuel Gai Tut, and although the latter seems to have been perfectly willing to be integrated into the SSPG command some disagreement arose between them[279]. A fight ensued, in which Gai's soldiers attacked Akuot's headquarters and several people were killed. Most of the arms of the Sobat Crack Force were taken either by the Nuers or the local Dinka Anya-Nya of Bor, and it is a relatively small and demoralized force that returned to Bungu early in 1969.

The third expedition, led by Sapana Pekki and named the "Nile Crack Force", had more modest aims than either of the other two. It was sent to integrate the Anya- Nya of Eastern Equatoria, and though it failed in this task it did succeed in retaining its arms and keeping its forces intact. This was no mean feat, for in late 1968 and early 1969 Taffeng was on leave in his village in Horiok country and seems to have made attempts to involve Sapana's force in various Eastern region intrigues[280]. But Phillip Angutwa was sent twice from Bungu to make sure that the force restricted itself to such targets as the police post at Katire, and in April 1969 it arrived safely back in Central region. The unfortunate thing was, that some months before Sapana's force and the others from Bahr el Ghazal and Upper Nile returned, the Provisional government had ceased to exist.

---

278 Information from Eliaba Surur.

279 No one the author has talked to was clear about the nature of the disagreement. One or two have suggested that whereas Akuot wished to integrate them on the spot, the Upper Nile soldiers wished to go to Bungu for integration. Another said that Gai was angry about Akuot's confiscation of the Chollo arms money (see above).

280 For example, there seems to have been little love lost between Taffeng and Lagu. At one point in November 1966 Lagu attacked Taffeng's headquarters at Lorifa, and Taffeng doubtless would have been glad to use the SSPG force to settle this and other scores.

The Death of the SSPG

The death of the SSPG dates from the sudden and mysterious departure of its president in September 1968, although the machinery of government continued to funation until early 1969. Why did Jaden leave? The reason most often cited is that he wanted to reshuffle his cabinet but that certain ministers objected, saying that ministerial posts had been allotted on the principle of equal representation to provinces. If Jaden wished to reallocate them, he would have to call a new convention and seek its authorization. Now it had been resolved at Angudri that a new convention should be summoned in a year's time in any case, so there was good reason for Jaden to adopt this course of action, but for some reason, he was opposed to it. It may be significant that Jaden left just after a cabinet meeting at which it was resolved to hold a new convention[281]. Without telling anyone where he was going, he simply called his bodyguard and walked away. Various people, including Gordon Mourtat, visited him in East Africa during the following months and asked him to come back, but Jaden would not. The reason that he himself gave to the author for his departure was that he was discouraged - that he had hoped for greater military success but eventually came to perceive that this was impossible given the lack of trained manpower in ANAF. To this must be added the usual Equatoria/ Nilotic rivalries. Many Equatorians were alarmed at the prospect of losing a large proportion of their arms if the principle of equal sharing among provinces were to be established, and Jaden was doubtless no exception. Nor were these fears entirely groundless, as the fate of the Sobat Crack Force demonstrated. Nevertheless, if the tribal emotions and preju-dices that underlay so many events of 1963-72 were ever to be overcome, it would be through organizations like the SSPG that attempted to be truly national in character, and for this reason Jaden's departure though understandable was regrettable.

To sum up, during its brief period of life the SSPG laid down policies and a programme which, on paper at least, offered a better chance of generating a sense of national identity and purpose than the policies of any previous administration. Given time, the governnent might have

---

281 Information from Kuaclieth Banak.

aucceeded in establishing an administration in which all elements of the South could have worked together in harmony and mutual respect. But the harsh realities of tribal politics, personal weakness, and warfare fought under the most desperate conditions eventually proved too much for the Provisional Government, and within a year and a half of the Angudri convention, it was no more. What carried on its work were its successors: the Nile Provisional Government, Anyidi, and Joseph Lagu's organization.

CHAPTER 17

Politics in Khartoum, 1965 – 1969

While Southerners in the forests of the South and in exile had been building their own political organizations and actively resisting the Sudan government, other Southerners had remained in Khartoum and were attempting to express their African political consciousness and ideals in a variety of different ways. Although their activities produced no large-scale triumphs, and in some cases would doubtless have been regarded by the Anya-Nya as betrayal of the Southern cause, they did succeed in retaining some small voice in the government for the South. In addition, the debates in which Southerners participated concerning the Sudan's constitution and national goals continued to be of interest and significance. For this reason, if for no other, events taking place in the political arena of Khartoum during the parliamentary period, 1965-69 must be considered an integral part of the history of the South.

The Southern Parties

Emerging from the Round Table Conference in March 1965, the Southern Front and William Deng's SANU established themselves as the only Southern political parties of any importance based in Khartoum. The Southern Front was registered as a political party in June, its President being Clement Mboro, Vice-President Gordon Muortat, and Secretary-General Hilary Paul Logali. It published The Vigilant, which, as mentioned earlier, was banned for six months for its reporting of the Juba and Wau massacres and was not reinstated until after court judgment which completely vindicated the newspaper.[282] SANU was publicly launched as a nationwide party at a rally of some 2,000 Southerners on April 11th 1965 in Omdurman. It operated under the personal leadership of William Deng until an internal split developed in 1967. In addition to SANU and the Southern Front, two smaller parties were the old Liberal Party, revised under the leadership of Stanislaus Paysama and Buth Diu, and the Sudan Unity Party, founded in January 1965 by Santino Deng.[283] Although the political effectiveness of these two parties was insignificant, the Sudan Unity Party made an evil name for itself in the South by its association with NOUS (National Organization for the Unity of the Sudan) and with a strong-arm terrorist group known as the "harass el watan" (National Guard).

At the Round Table Conference, the two main Southern parties adopted different policies for the settlement of the Southern problem. The Southern Front held to the principle of self-determination, maintaining that whatever constitutional proposals were made in Khartoum, the Southern people had the right to accept or reject them in a plebiscite. SANU, on the other hand, took the view that at the time of independence in 1956 the South had in effect committed itself to being part and parcel of the nation, and hence the only question remaining was what form their

---

282   See Malwal, Bona, "Sudan and South Sudan", op.cit, p. 113. In giving its verdict, the judge said: "the government of Sudan had been proven in the court of law, to have committed atrocities against its own citizens.".

283   Albino, p. 57. The effective strength of each of these parties was no more than two men, Santino Deng being joined in Sudan Unity Party by Philemon Majok. (The latter succeeded Luigi Adwok as Southern representative on the Supreme Council in June 1965.)

participation in a united Sudan would take.[284] The solution proposed by SANU was a federal system of government. As time progressed, and it became apparent that neither self-determination nor federation was acceptable to the Northern parties, SANU and the Southern Front gradually reduced their initial demands. They eventually came to a level where, if the parliamentary period had extended for another year or two after 1969; it was probable that they would have agreed on a compromise constitution and passed it in the Constituent Assembly. However, this process whereby the Southern politicians in Khartoum slowly retreated from their original positions was interrupted by General Nimeiri's coup in May 1969, and so we cannot be sure what the outcome would have been. This chapter will indicate some of the milestones of the long, hard, and discouraging path trodden by the Southern politicians in that period.

Al-Sadiq al- Mhadi's Premiership

The cabinet of Mohammed Ahmed Mahgoub in June 1965 had origi-nally included two SANU ministers, Andrew Wieu and Alfred Wol. They, however, resigned following the Juba and Wau massacres, leaving Buth Diu as the sole Southern representative in the cabinet. This state of affairs continued until July 1966, when Mahgoub's government was defeated in parliament, and a new Umma/NUP coalition was formed under Sadiq al-Mahdi, the great-grandson of Mohammed Ahmed.[285] At the time of his accession, there were hopes that Sadiq, who was only 30 years old and had read at Oxford, would be able to break away from the entrenched positions of the past and begin to explore new solutions for the South. Buth Diu, who had largely lost the confidence of Southerners, was replaced by two civil servants, Jervase Yak and Arop Yor. But Sadiq's actions soon convinced Southerners that, if indeed he was the man to solve the problem of the South, the only solution acceptable to him would be on the North's terms. This fact comes out clearly in his attitude toward

---

284 These policy differences between SANU and the Southern Front are clearly stated by Isaiah Majok in The Vigilant, 9 February 1969.

285 For an account of the internal division within the Umma Party which produced this change, see Africa Confidential, September 1966, pp. 5-6.

the 12-man committee's report.

The 12-man committee submitted its report on September 26th 1966, and produced a set of constitutional proposals which though falling short of federalism nevertheless went a certain way towards meeting Southern demands. The system proposed was a regional one, with the following main features.[286] Each region would have its own legislative and executive, the head of the executive being appointed through a joint process in which both the region and the centre participated. Administrative powers were to be divided between the regions and the central government, the general pattern being that the centre would lay down policy, although each region would have its own local police. As to the geographical boundaries of the regions, there was disagreement, the Southern members of the committee holding that the South should be one region while the rest of the country should constitute either three or six more. The Northern members, on the other hand, maintained that the present division of the country into nine provinces would suffice for the division into regions, and that if the South were made into a single region this would perpetuate the sense of confrontation between South and North. The report acknowledged that "both sides maintain their stands on this point". In his speech submitting the report, Yousif Mohammed Ali, the chairman of the 12-man committee, summed up its basic conclusions as follows:

> The Sudanese political parties participating in the Round Table Conference were unanimous in their judgment that the present status quo - centralized unitary government- can no longer serve our national interest. It was evidently incapable of surmounting challenges which face developing countries like ours, where political independence has preceded nation-building, and where the national ethnical composition is diverse, and where geographical, cultural, historical and economic factors breed separatist attitudes[287].

On submission of the report, the logical thing for the government to do

---

286 The text of the proposal is to be found in Appendix 3 and in Albino, pp. 123-130. The system is not too different from the one eventually embodied in the 1972 Addis Ababa Agreement.

287 The Vigilant, 27 September 1966; Appendix 3.

would have been to re-convene the Round Table Conference, to which the 12-man committee was supposed to report. But Sadiq effectively ruled out any such action, saying that when the Round Table Conference was originally called a political vacuum existed. This vacuum was now filled by a constituent assembly and political parties, whose job it was to discuss and resolve national issues.[288] Instead, therefore, of recalling the Round Table Conference, Sadiq summoned first a Political Parties conference and then a Constitutional Draft committee. These groups discussed the 12-man committee report but ended up by rejecting its proposals and replacing them by the draft of a unitary Islamic constitution. As will be seen shortly, this constitution came within a hair's breadth of being adopted early in 1968. But let us return for the time being to Sadiq, and the growing sense of disillusionment with his policies on the part of the South.

In October and November 1966 Sadiq made a tour of the Southern provinces, and reports of his speeches there give a fairly good indication of his approach to the Southern problem. For one thing, he seems to have spoken only in Arabic, and to have provided no translation into any local languages for the benefit of non-Arabic-speakers.[289] In Wau in early November the Prime Minister said that a new treason law was being drafted which would consider as crimes any call for a plebiscite, self-determination, or separation for the South.[290]During a short break in his tour to attend the OAU summit conference in Addis Ababa, Sadiq remarked at a press conference that there are major tribal groups as well as small ones; if we grant them the right to self-determination, nothing would be left to us.[291]

This statement was taken up the next day in an editorial in The Vigilant, in which the author inquires who the "we" are that the Prime Minister is referring to. He answers his own question in this way:

These are the few riverain Arabs who had benefitted in the Sudan from British imperialism and got educated and sent to colonialist British's universities. They are the ones who think that a person called a Sudanese

---

288 Ibid.

289 The Vigilant, 20 November 1966.

290 Ibid., 4 November 1966.

291 Ibid., 13 November 1966. See also, Africa Confidential, 26 December 1966, p. 5.

is none other than themselves and that they own, as a right of succession to British imperialism, the rest of the tribes in the Sudan.[292]

Sadiq ended his tour with a visit to Malakal, in which he is reported to have told a meeting of chiefs and notables that it was the educated Southerners rather than the villagers who were responsible for the Southern problem.[293] In various other speeches in Upper Nile Sadiq (i) praised the army and told them to finish with the remaining pockets of rebels; (ii) refused to condemn the activities of the "harass el watan"; and (iii) stressed the importance of elections in the South so that permanent constitution could be passed in the Constituent assembly. This matter of elections was an extremely controversial one, and as we shall see Sadiq probably alienated a fair proportion of his fellow-countrymen, both in the South and in the North, by insisting that they take place.

The elections of April 1965, as noted above, were confined to the Northern Sudan. But unfortunately, 21 candidates had already registered for Southern constituencies by the time this was announced, and they eventually won their case in the courts to be seated as "unopposed" members of parliament[294]. Since they were all political unknowns and in fact included 14 Northern merchants living in the South, they could hardly be said to represent Southern opinion. Nevertheless, Sadiq wished not to dismiss them and have entirely new elections in the South, but simply to go ahead with the remaining 39 of the 60 Southern constituencies. Even under normal conditions, this would scarcely have been a policy calculated to assure Southerners that their democratic rights were being observed. Furthermore, conditions in the South were far from normal, and the assassination of William Nhial is only one of many examples that could be chosen to show this.

William Nhial was the SANU representative in Aweil, having been sent there from Khartoum by William Deng, specifically to prepare for the forthcoming elections. SANU, unlike the Southern Front, did not lay down as a condition for participating in the elections the lifting of the state of emergency, or the removal of the "unopposed" members.

---

292 Ibid., 14 November 1966. The tone of the passage indicates that bias and intolerance were not the monopoly of the North in the Sudan.

293 Ibid., 20 November 1966.

294 Albino, p. 58.

According to newspaper reports, on September 24th 1966 Nhial was killed by the harass el watan or National Guards belonging to NOUS[295]. Valentino Akol, another SANU representative in Bahr el Ghazal, said that Nhial's death together with that of five other Southern officials in Aweil had been preceded by threats from local harass el watan. The latter, who though provided with arms by the government received no salaries, and were alleged to have lived off property confiscated from Southerners suspected of supporting the Anya-Nya, seem to have had at least the tacit support of government security forces. Thus when two other SANU officials, Ezekiel Kodi and Alfred Ulodo, wrote to the authorities in Bahr el Ghazal to say that they knew of witnesses who could give evidence concerning Nhial's murder, they were promptly arrested[296]. Concerning NOUS in general, one of the most serious revelations of the whole affair was that the organization was controlled by none other than the speaker of the constituent assembly, Mubarak El Fadil Shaddad[297]. The fact that this man who, if anyone, should have been politically neutral, was the sponsor of an organization which engaged in political murder, indicates more clearly than anything the extent to which democratic institutions at that time in the Sudan were a facade behind which power, privilege and prejudice operated.

In such circumstances, it was hardly surprising that many people should say that the elections organized by Sadiq were a sham, or that a PDP delegation should find "sufficient evidence to convince the public that elections in the South are not possible under the present situation."[298] Nevertheless, Sadiq persevered, and elections were held on March 8th

---

295 The Vigilant, 3, 4, 5, 6, 10 October 1966. Although the Khartoum Morning News merely reports that Nhial "disappeared" there seems little doubt that The Vigilant's is the correct one. Additional corroboration is provided by an article in the Sudan Unit Party's newspaper in October 8th entitled "The end of William Nhial", in which it is said that Nhial was killed because he was "training Anya-Nya". (The Vigilant, 11 October 1966).

296 The Vigilant, 17 October 1966.

297 This piece of information was provided by Philemon Majok, in the course of an attack on Santino Deng. See The Vigilant, 2, 11and 12 October 1966. Deng was the principal Southerner supporting NOUS, and on return from a tour of the South in September 1966 claimed to have registered the names of 540 "rebels" and persuaded their relatives to hand them over to the security forces. (Africa Confidential, 25 September 1966, p. 6).

298 The Vigilant, 7 February 1967. The PDP found that even inside Wau government authorities had to move with a military escort, and that football matches were played under the protection of the tanks.

1967. The following were the results:

Party	Seats won
Umma	15
SANU	10
NUP	5
Independents	3
Sudan Unity Party	2
Liberal Party	1
Total	**36**

No voting was held in three constituencies – Maridi North, Jur and Amadi; Yei-Kaya, and Yei-Kajo Kaji - because of rebel activity. The Southern Front boycotted the elections, although one of their members, Luigi Adwok, defected and was elected as an independent in Upper Nile. The popularity of the elections may be judged by the fact that out of the PDP's estimate of 50,599 people in Juba, 5,620 registered to vote and 1,775 voted, of whom 1,200 were Northerners[299].

Once the membership of the constituent assembly had been completed, it was Sadiq's intention that a constitution should be approved. But in May Sadiq's uncle, the Imam al-Hadi al-Mahdi, withdrew his support from the government and Sadiq was defeated in a vote of confidence. The rivalry between the two members of the Mahdi family proved deeply injurious to the Umma party, and from then on it was split into two wings. Interestingly enough, the split in Umma also produced a division in SANU, for when Mahgoub was once again elected Prime Minister, and Sadiq went into opposition, Alfred Wol and two other SANU MPs refused to join Sadiq's "Congress of New Forces."[300]Instead Wol accepted a ministerial position in Mahgoub's cabinet, as did Buth Diu.-

The Islamic constitution was only prevented from passing at the eleventh hour by a peculiar combination of chance and circumstance, as will be seen below.

How did the demand for an Islamic constitution arise? Its main

---

299 Ibid., 7 February and 20 March 1967. The NUP also acknowledged that most of the voters were Northern merchants, officials and soldiers. (The Vigilant, 26 March)

300 Ibid., 25 and 30 May, 5 June 1967

proponents were the Muslim brotherhood, who created a political body known as the Islamic Charter Front to organize support for it. The Umma party also, in keeping with its Mahdist traditions, favoured such a constitution, although Sadiq and the younger intellectuals of the party are said to have maintained that the Islamic conception of the state was entirely compatible with modern democratic government[301]. Finally, the influence of Islamic and Pan-Arab revivalist ideas, which tend to view post-colonial Africa as a sphere of possible Islamic expansion, cannot be ignored in any discussion of Islamic institutions in the Sudan. Such ideas are reported to have been expressed by the Imam, speaking to King Faisal in Saudi Arabia in 1965:

> The Sudan is, in its majority, an Islamic Arab country. It constitutes the Islamic Arab spearhead in Africa and peaceful invading vanguard in the unexplored areas of Africa.[302]

Whatever their reasons for adopting it, the idea of having an Islamic constitution appears to have been supported by a good proportion of Northern Sudanese politicians during the period 1965-69. In October 1966, when the Political Parties Conference was about to open, and the Constitutional Draft committee was being discussed, both the Umma party and the NUP renewed an earlier pledge they had made for an Islamic constitution[303]. From then until May 1969, the idea of such a constitution was the subject of prolonged debate on the part of Northerners and Southerners alike. An understanding of the issues involved, and the fears and emotions they engendered, is essential for any study of North-South relations in the Sudan.

The Political Parties Conference opened on October 17th 1966, and took up the discussion where it had been left by the 12-man committee. In searching for a system of government acceptable to both North and South,

---

301 Africa Confidential, 8 April 1966, p. 3. This view is probably quite consistent with another one reportedly held by the Imam, to the effect that religious and political leadership are indistinguishable.

302 Africa Confidential, 13 August 1965, p. 6. The Imam is also reported to have told King Faisal that the Sudan "can supply you with all your basic requirements – livestock and human labour".

303 The Vigilant, 2 October 1966. The idea was not new, having been debated in the constitutional committee of 1956-58.

the 12-man committee had settled on a type of regional government, but had left unresolved two major points of disagreement. These were, the method of selecting the head of the regional government, and the question whether the South should be one region or three[304]. Neither of these points was settled in the Political Parties conference, and the disagreements were passed on to the Constitutional Draft committee, which began its deliberations on February 19th 1967. In this committee, however, larger issues soon took the place of the ones referred to above. The Islamic Charter Front, which had boycotted the Political Parties conference on the grounds that the type of regionalism being discussed would inevitably lead to separatism[305], joined the Constitutional Draft committee and argued for a system of government that would be Islamic and centralized. Despite the opposition of the tiny Southern minority on the committee, the idea of having an Islamic constitution was endorsed[306]. Two weeks later, against strong Southern protests, the committee accepted a proposal to change from a parliamentary to a presidential system, in which all executive powers would be vested in a directly-elected president, and the powers of regions to run their own affairs would be greatly diluted. This was the constitution which was presented to the Constituent Assembly in January 1968, and which was later re-discussed in committee from October 1968 to May 1969[307]. Its main features and the issues surrounding it will be considered under the following headings.

(i) Islam as an established religion

Article one of the constitution reads "The Sudan is a Democratic Socialist Republic founded on Islamic faith." Article three says that "Islam is the official religion of the state and the Arabic language is its official

---

304 Africa Confidential, 28 April 1967, pp. 7-8.

305 The Vigilant, 11 November 1966.

306 Ibid,. 29 April 1967. At the decisive meeting there were 3 Islamic Charter Front representatives, 7 NUP, 7 Umma, 4 Independents, 1 Nuba, 1 SANU and 1 Southern Front.

307 For the text of the 1967 constitution see The Vigilant, 16 and 23 January 1968, and for that of the apparently identical 1968 version, The Vigilant, 25 November 1968; the Morning News, 4, 5, 8, 9, 10, 11, 12 December 1968; and the Sudan Echo, 3, 4, 5, 6, 8 December 1968. The various 1968 texts are collated in Sudan Informazioni 34/35, 10 February 1969, pp. 18-41.

language." So many attempts were made by Southerners of all parties to delete or amend these clauses that one can only conclude that their aversion to them was extremely deep-seated. Arguments against them generally went as follows. To introduce religion into politics is to confuse two quite different things. Religion is a private affair of the individual and his God, while the state is for everybody. The people in the South are not opposed to religion, but they feel that the best way to avoid religious intolerance, animosity and contempt is to adopt a secular constitution. If a religious constitution were adopted, would men of evil intentions not be given an opportunity to use religion as a slogan behind which to hide, and as a means of justifying discrimination?[308] Arguments such as these were common. But underlying them ran a deeper fear and a deeper emotion, which few Southerners managed to put in writing but which many of them doubtless felt. This was the fear that with the coming of Islam, they would lose their identity as Africans. That the possibility of this happening was as much the hope of Pan-Arabists as it was the fear of Africans, and yet that the hope and the fear together rested on a mistaken premise, is well expressed in a Vigilant editorial:

It is not, however, Islam as a religion and Arabic as a language which the Islamic Charter Front wants. Nobody is against anyone embracing any religion he wants, or learning that fancies him. It is the replacement of Western European religions, languages and cultures which the ICF advocates in Africa. This springs from a premise that Africa is a void, or that the African has no soul of his own, no culture of his own and no originality peculiarly his own. Since Western Europe is apparently on the decline in Africa, Arabism must step in. These two are historical anatagonist which once clashed for many years in Europe and Palestine during the Middle Ages. The next field of battle is therefore supposed to be Africa which is cultureless and possessing no heritage. We do not want to antagonize anyone just as much as we ourselves do not wish anyone to antagonize us. The Western imperialists, the Arab imperialists and the communist imperialists will find that Africa has its own. Whether it is written or not, it is there in the soul of every African that he possesses his own identity. This is not usually aggressive as history has shown through

308 See The Vigilant, 16 January 1968, p. 4; 17 November 1968, p. 3; 15 December 1968, p. 1.

African receptiveness of all foreigners, but when these foreigners try to downgrade it, it can raise its head[309].

This mistaken assumption to which the writer alludes, which we call the "African culture void" assumption, was a fairly common one in former times, but is encountered only rarely nowadays. Surprisingly enough, one finds it reflected in an article on the Sudan published as recently as 1969. The author summarizes the contents of Sadiq al- Mahdi's pamphlet on the Southern question[310], describing it as "possibly the most constructive example of Sudanese Moslem thinking about the relation of Islam to Christianity in Africa":

> He [Sadiq] argues that only the revealed religions can supply the deficiencies in the beliefs and morals of the tribal organs... The best environment for spread of Islam, he believes, is toleration, which imperialism denied to it. With the disappearance of imperialism, this knot is untied, and no national government in Africa can rightly go back on this. Among the reasons he gives for expecting the spread of Islam in free conditions is that the bitterness aroused by past Moslem slavers is alight compared with the deeper and more active bitterness of the African for the white man.[311]

It would be an interesting exercise to compare the passage about supplying the deficiencies in the beliefs and morals of the tribal pagans with 19th century views such as Livingstone's:

> The population is sunk into the very lowest state of both mental and moral degradation, so much so indeed it must be difficult or rather impossible for Christians at home to realize anything like an accurate notion of the grossness of the darkness which shrouds their minds[312].

---

309 Ibid., 19 October 1966. The writer was Bona Ring.

310 The Question of the Southern Sudan, in Arabic, Khartoum 1964. The author knows of no English translation.

311 Norman Daniel, "The Sudan", in Islam in Africa, Kritseck and Lewis (eds.), New York 1969, pp. 201-211.

312 Livingstone's Missionary Correspondence, 1841 – 1856, London 1961, p. 18. The letter was written from Bechuana-land.

(ii) **rights of non-Moslems**

A more practical objection to the Islamic constitution was that it would relegate non-Moslems to the status of second-class citizens. Thus in a panel discussion with Dr. Hassan al-Turabi, secretary-general of the Islamic Charter Front, Abel Alier pointed out that in history during the Islamic ascendency the highest office held by a non-Moslem was that held by a Greek accountant. Dr. Turabi replied that the Moslems in the Sudan were in a majority anyway and that in such a situation a Southerner should not pretend to aspire to hold the highest office of state.[313] The question of whether the 1967/68 Islamic constitution would actually prohibit a non-Moslem from becoming president is unclear. Article 28 states that citizens are equal in rights and duties without discrimination based on race, sex, or religion. However, article 113 says that Islamic <u>sharia</u> shall be the main source of laws in the Sudan, and article 142 that judges must follow the general principles of <u>sharia</u> where no specific legislation exists on the point at issue. It follows, according to <u>The Vigilant</u>, that judges who are bound to apply <u>sharia</u> must, if called to give their opinion on the point, rule that <u>sharia</u> law prohibits a non-Moslem from leading Moslems.[314] Whether a Sudanese court would actually have ruled in this way if the Islamic constitution had been adopted is difficult to predict.

(iii) **Sharia law**

Under this heading, Southerners objected that adherence to sharia has turned out to be more of a hindrance than a help in solving problems of modern development. In coping with these problems, many Arab governments have introduced reforms which could not, by any degree of rationalization, be regarded as in conformity with <u>sharia</u> law[315]. And yet, under the Islamic constitution it was reported that no legislation contrary to the <u>sharia</u> would have the force of law, and that all previous

---

313 The Vigilant, 16 October 1966; Albino, p. 65.

314 Ibid., 16 January 1968, p. 4.

315 The Vigilant, 7 April 1967.

legislation contrary to the <u>sharia</u> would be repealed and replaced.[316]This programme, if carried through, would have had a devastating effect both on the civil courts, which in the Sudan are distinct from the <u>sharia</u> courts, and on customary law. Concerning the latter, Francis Deng observes that although it is an integral feature of tribal life in the South, its status in the Sudan suffers from a peculiar ambiguity. It is employed by over 80% of the people, yet there is a general feeling that customary law is inferior and something to be ashamed of[317].

However, Deng also notes that in other African countries the downgrading of customary law, fashionable in the colonial period, has been reversed in post-colonial times, so that its popularity among educated people in the Sudan may now be due to increase. Finally, concerning the civil courts, a speech by President Azhari in December 1968, in which he pledged himself to work for the establishment of the <u>sharia</u> rather than the civil court as the main court in the land,[318]indicated that even before the adoption of the Islamic constitution the government was moving toward the implementation of some of its provisions.

(iv) Education

Should the state guarantee the right of religious minorities to run their own schools? This has been a contentious issue in the Sudan since 1957, when all mission and private schools in the South were nationalized and the people were forbidden to open new ones. (in the North, were and still are allowed.) Southerners were fearful that under the Islamic consti-tution the right to open schools with a religious orientation would be denied them, but although at one point it appeared that this might be so,[319] articles 19 and 32 of the final 1967 draft do grant this right.

---

316   Ibid., 28 April 1967.

317   Francis Deng, Tradition and Modernization, A Challenge for Law among the Dinka of the Sudan, New Haven 1971, p. 376.

318   The Vigilant, 29 December 1968.

319   The Vigilant, 17 July 1967, p. 3.

(v) **Language**

Strictly speaking, language issues are distinct from religious ones. But because of the intimate relationship between Islam and Arabic the two can hardly be discussed separately. A brief history of Arabic in Southern schools, as given by Ware Lolomode in The Vigilant[320], reveals the highly charged and emotional character of the language question.

According to Lolomode, Arabic was first introduced into Southern schools in 1952. The next step came shortly after independence, when the teaching of local languages such as Bari and Dinka using Arabic script was introduced. These languages had been taught successfully for many years using the Roman alphabet – so successfully in fact that according to Lolomode the highest literacy rate in the Sudan was to be found in Yei district, where in 1957 a survey revealed that 97% of the adult population could read and write. But the experiment using Arabic script proved to be a failure, and it was abandoned. In March 1967 it was announced that henceforth the medium of instruction in all elementary schools would be Arabic. Lolomode sharply criticizes this decision, pointing out that ever since Arabic was made a compulsory subject for the intermediate entrance examinations, the results of these examinations had been "painful." Those who passed were either Northerners or the small minority of Southerners brought up in an Arabic milieu; these were taken to academic interme- diate schools while the remainder were sent to Islamic <u>mahads,</u> institutions designed to produce religious teachers. Similar problems are said to have existed at a secondary level. On reading Lolomode's article, it is difficult to avoid the conclusion that the enforced introduction of Arabic into Southern schools produced strong resentment on the part of many Southerners.

The same emotional reaction was evoked when in September 1966 it was announced that promotions in the civil service would be denied those who did not know how to read and write Arabic[321]. Southerners immedi- ately protested that the government's policy was in direct contravention of the resolution of the Round Table Conference on equality of opportunity for employment, to the effect that "there will be no discrimination by reason only

---

320   Ibid., 30 April 1967.
321   Ibid., 5 September 1966. The Ministry of Interior's circular to this effect is printed in the issue of 13 September.

of religious beliefs or language or race."[322] They do not however appear to have been successful either in changing the government's policy or in incorporating the reference to language into the resolution on equality of opportunity in the draft constitution[323]. Nor did they succeed in obtaining the recognition of English as a second official language[324]. On these issues the Northern stand seems to have been unyielding, although there can have been no doubt in anybody's mind as to the importance attached to them and to related constitutional issues by Southerners. As one contributor to The Vigilant put it:

> Deprive a person of his language, his culture and his political rights, and you will have deprived him of his dignity. The Islamic Constitution is intended to do just that and Southerners ought to realize and appreciate what this means for them[325].

Enough has now been said about the Islamic constitution and the emotional atmosphere surrounding it. Its fate in the Constituent Assembly in January 1968 formed part of a political crisis of major proportions. Although the details of what went on are not precise, it seems that the draft constitution passed its second reading by a vote of 168 to 4, with SANU members absenting themselves during the vote[326]. However, crucial delays had been introduced in the discussion of the draft by those who were opposed to its Islamic clauses, with the result that it became apparent that not enough time was available for its third and final reading before the elections which the government had scheduled for April. When it became apparent that Sadiq, who favored passing the constitution and postponing elections for another year, might be able to obtain enough votes to defeat the government on a motion of no-confidence, the Prime Minister and his supporters took the unusual step of resigning *en masse* from the Constituent Assembly[327].

---

322 Ibid., 6 September 1966, p. 3.

323 See Article 28.

324 The Vigilant, 29 December 1968, p. 5. It is significant that the Addis Ababa agreement recognizes Arabic as the official language and English as the principal language of the South.

325 Ibid., 3o April 1967, p. 4,

326 Ibid., 30 January 1968. The Vigilant reports however that eight Southerners, including Luigi Adwok, voted for the constitution.

327 Ibid., 13 February 1968. The rationale behind this step was that a Constituent Assembly with membership less than two-thirds cannot pass a Permanent Constitution. The resignation would serve that purpose.

Faced with the resignation of 104 out of 220 members, the Supreme Council dissolved the Assembly on February 7th and ordered elections. Although Sadiq and his group, furious at this stratagem, tried to force their way into parliament and eventually held an "under the tree Assembly" outside and raised a constitutional suit they did not wait for the verdict of the court as they went and joined the elections process. Thus, they were unable to have the dissolution revoked. In this way, through a combination of extraordinary circumstances, the Islamic constitution failed to become law.

The 1968 Elections

Elections were held as planned starting on April 18th, the party obtaining the most votes being the Democratic Unionist Party (DUP) formed in late 1967 by a merger between the NUP and the PDP. The results were as follows:

Party	Seats won
DUP	101
Umma / Sadiq	36
Umma / Imam	30
SANU	15
Southern Front	10
Independents	9
Umma independents	6
Islamic Charter Front	3
Beja Congress	3
Nubas (GUN)	2
Communists / Socialists	2
Nile Party	1
Total	218

One or two points need to be made concerning these elections. First, it is doubtful whether the security situation in the South was much better in April 1968 than it was in March 1967. It was in any case far from normal, as may be seen from the fact that the highest number of recorded votes was only 4,910 in Tonj Central for William Deng, while the winning candidates in Kajo Kaji and one of the Torit constituencies received a total of 95 and 30 votes, respectively[328]. The prevailing insecurity situation in the South provided opportunity to the security organs to create obstructions against candidates of the Southern Front and SANU. This is particularly reflected in the fact that the Southern Front which enjoys support in the three Southern provinces got less seats than SANU which draws its support from only Bahr el Ghazal Province. The insecurity situation made it easy for political opportunists from other parties to get elected. The resulting group of members from the 60 Southern seats could not by any stretch of the imagination be said to be representative of Southern opinion[329]. Secondly, it will be noted that the two main Southern parties, Southern Front and SANU, managed to elect altogether only 25 out of a total of 60 Southern MPs. Why did so many Southern constituencies elect members of Northern parties? Apart from insecurity, part of the answer lies in the inadequate funds and resources which the Southern Parties had at their disposal – resources without which it was impossible to pay the deposits of candidates, travel, holding rallies, etc. Clement Mboro, for example, is said to have personally borrowed £500 on security of his house at Port Sudan in order to pay the campaign expenses of the Southern Front.[330]

Immediately after the election, an event occurred which shocked many people, but which if one knew all the events from 1955 to 1972 would probably not appear out of keeping with them. This was the assassination of William Deng. Deng had driven on the morning of May 5th from Tonj to Rumbek, arriving at 12 noon[331]. He spoke briefly to the SANU district branch about the current political situation, and also reported to Rumbek police station, where he was warned against travelling without an army escort. (Deng preferred to travel alone because he feared army "protection" more than what he was supposedly being protected against.) At 2:30 p.m. Deng and six travelling companions set out to return to Tonj. He was in a hurry because a Northern Sudanese army officer

---

328 Albino, p. 72. A number of voting irregularities are reported on pp. 72-74.

329 In this respect, the situation is to be connected with that of 1958: see above.

330 Information from Bona Malwal Madut Ring.

331 Information from an article in the second issue of the National Field Day, reprinted in Sudan Informazioni 31/32, 10 December 1968. The article summarizes a SANU circular on the subject. Additional information from Peter Nyot and Philip Abbas.

had told him that he also was going to Tonj, and would await Deng's party on the way so that his army unit could provide an escort. Deng and his companions were never seen again. Four days later, on May 9th, the Rumbek police informed the local branch of SANU that their bodies and bullet-riddled car had been found at Gurmar River, 15 miles along the Tonj road. On the following day, Samuel Aru, the secretary-general of SANU, drove to Gurmat River and transported Deng's body to Tonj. There seems little doubt that Deng had been killed by the army. There are said to exist witnesses of the shooting, and a pile of used cartridges, of the G3 type used by the Sudan army, was discovered nearby.

Although a full commission of inquiry was promised, nothing was ever done, and when it was reported that the government was considering offering Deng's widow £3,000 compensation, she wrote to the newspapers declining the gift unless the guilty parties were brought to trial[332]. Like so many cases of disappearance and death in the South, the incident simply faded from public notice and was forgotten.[333]

Not much remains to be said about the remaining months before the parliamentary period came to an end in May 1969. The government resulting from the 1968 elections was a coalition of the DUP, Umma/Imam and the Southern Front, Clement Mboro and Hilary Logali serving as cabinet ministers. Debate on the Islamic constitution was resumed in committee in October, and by May the government was saying that it would be presented to the Constituent Assembly in July. If no definite decision were reached on it then, they threatened to present its principal clauses to the public in a referendum[334]. Once again the Southern politicians prepared themselves for a struggle. But once again the Islamic constitution was a victim of events, this time in the shape of the coup d'etat of Major-General Nimeiri.

---

332 The Morning News, Khartoum, 15 September 1968.

333 According to Philip Abbas, it was Azhari who ordered Deng's assassination. Sadiq had been defeated in the elections, and Deng was the logical successor as leader of the opposition. Abbas reports that his name had already been announced on the radio. Note the timing of the assassination: before the election results were made public on May 6th but after they had presumably become known in Khartoum. Nyot also reports that when Deng reported to Rumbek police they informed Wau, and that a message came back shortly after, in code, to army headquarters at Rumbek.

334 The Vigilant, 11 May 1969.

The 25 May 1969 Coup d'etat

Major-General Jaafar Mohammed Nimeiri came to power on May 25th 1969 in a *coup d'état* organized by a group of young army officers known as the Free Officers Movement. Before the events leading up to the coup are described, something must be said about another group of people in the North, who as it turns out had been planning a different coup on the very same day as Nimeiri's. These were the various underground organizations of non-Arab peoples of Northern Sudan, represented mainly by the Fur, the Nuba, the Funj and Beja tribes.

Although discussion of the growth of political consciousness among non-Arab Northern Sudanese lies outside the scope of this book, a brief outline will be helpful here. The earliest political group was Dr Adam Adham's Black Block, founded in 1938. Although the Black Block could have served as a powerful voice for non-Arab Sudanese, it was deprived of all political effectiveness by the British, who refused to license it as a political party following complaints by the Ashiqqa and the Umma that it was racist in outlook[335]. After the demise of the Black Block, some of its members founded social organizations on a regional basis, such as the General Union of the Nuba Mountains (GUN, founded in 1954) and the Beja Congress[336]. Their members agitated for decentralization of governmental powers in 1958 parliament.

During Abboud's regime, these regional political movements went underground, GUN organizing cooperative shops in the Nuba Mountains and encouraging people not to pay poll tax as a means of demonstrating their dislike of the "Arabs" in Khartoum.[337] After the downfall of Abboud in 1964 the organization came out into the open once more, and at a general meeting of GUN in El Obeid in late 1964 a constitution was drawn up. In February 1965, at the time of Queen Elizabeth's planned visit to El Obeid, a second meeting was held which was attended

---

335 See for example a letter by Tia Gitta Tutu in The Economist, 29 August 1970, p. 4, and Tutu's paper "Black Power in the Sudan", New Middle East No. 34, July 1971, pp. 21-25.

336 A similar Fur organization, Jebhat Nahdhat Darfur (Darfur Awakening Front), was started later, about 1963 or 1964, by Ibrahim Dereg.

337 For the reason why resistance to poll-tax symbolized this dislike, see footnote 18 of Appendix 2.

by no fewer than 71 sultans, nozars and meks from western Sudan.[338] At this meeting, the GUN constitution was read and warmly supported: it was resolved that henceforth only western Sudanese should represent the people of Kordofan and Darfur in Parliament. Although Ibrahim Dereg was not present, exposure to the new ideas of GUN influenced the meks and sultans of Darfur favourably towards the political organization, *Jebehat Nahdhat Darfur*, that he had established in Khartoum. However, there was disagreement over whether candidates for election could run as members of one of the big national parties. The Darfur leaders maintained that there was no objection to candidates being sponsored and supported in this way, the Nuba leaders supported GUN in believing that their representatives should be politically and financially independent. In the 1965 elections, 8 GUN members were elected, the majority of the remainder from western Sudan being Umma.

In the Constituent Assembly, the 8 GUN members joined 11 Beja Congress in opposing the government's policy on the South and its foreign policy. Philip Abbas,[339] who was the leader of the group, spoke frequently on the theme that the interests of the African people of the country were being neglected at the expense of those in the Khartoum/Wad Medani area. At one point he tabled a motion that Sudan should withdraw from the Arab League, seek friends in Western rather than in Eastern Europe, and establish close ties with Black African states. Naturally enough, such views did not endear GUN and the Beja Congress to the government, with the result that little expenditure for development was allocated to their areas. In the elections of 1968, their strength was reduced from 8 and 11 to 2 and 3 respectively.

Frustrated in their attempts to achieve political recognition by legitimate means, the indigenous Northern Sudanese channelled their nationalist

---

338 Information from Philip Abbas. Nozars and maks are western tribal chiefs.

339 The Rev. Phillip Abbas Ghaboush was born in 1925 in Hagar Sultan, Nuba Mountain. He learned Arabic in a Qoranic Khalwa near Dilling, and did his theological training at Mundri Theological College and in Khartoum, becoming ordained Anglican priest in 1958. From 1961 to 1964 he worked in the Nuba Mountains, until after the fall of Abboud he was asked to organize GUN as a political party. Abbas resigned from active church work and was elected to the Constituent Assembly in 1965 and again in 1968. Despite offers of a cabinet seat in various coalition governments, he remained steadfastly in opposition and spoke eloquently on the rights of the indigenous peoples of the Sudan. Following USALF's attempted coup in May 1969, Abbas left the country.

sentiment into underground organizations. Five of these bodies – a Nuba group, the Negro Organization, Suni, the Free Negroes Organization, and the Sudanese Inland Organization—came together in April 1969 to form the United Sudanese African Liberation Front (USALF). Their aim was to overthrow the government and install a Black African-dominated one which would stop the war in the South and create a federal state. As many of USALF's members were in the army, plans for a *coup d'état* progressed rapidly, and the date was set for May 25th. However, some last-minute delays caused the date to be postponed to May 29th, and by that time it was too late, Nimeiri's group having forestalled them. Although it seems that Sadiq el- Mahdi was also at that time making plans to seize power, the rumour that Sadiq's and USALF's coups were one and the same appears to be untrue[340]. The anti-Arab character of USALF was such that any alliance with Sadiq would have been highly unlikely. Following the failure of USALF's attempted coup, and learning that he was about to be arrested, Philip Abbas escaped in June to Ethiopia and sought help in promoting the cause of Black Northerners from exile.

On May 25th, Major-General Jaafar al-Nimeiri came to power.[341] Few Southerners appear to have mourned the passing of Mahgoub's government, whose only new initiative toward solving the Southern problem had been to ratify a military agreement under which the Soviet Union would supply some £40 million of equipment.[342] Furthermore, one of Nimeiri's first acts was to promise that the South would be granted regional autonomy, and to announce that a new Ministry of Southern Affairs would be created[343] and headed by Joseph Garang, a Southerner. The story of how Nimeiri kept his promise, and the signing of the Addis Ababa Agreement, is beyond the scope of this book.

---

340   The rumour was based on the discovery among Sadiq's papers of a list of the cabinet posts he would distribute, in which Philip Abbas' name appears as Minister of the Interior.

341   For Nimeiri's coup and the background to it, see Ruth First, The Barrel of a Gun, pp. 271-277, and the article on Sudan in Legum and Drysdale, eds., Africa Contemporary record, 3rd edition 1971.

342   A Soviet military delegation visited Sudan in September 1967, and the agreement was concluded in July 1968. By September, arms had started to arrive Port Sudan, and it was reported that 50 Russian instructors had been sent to advise in the conversion from British weaponry (African Report, news summary, 1968).

343   See Appendix 4.

CHAPTER 18

Southern Sudan Liberation Movement

The resistance to the Sudanese regimes grew up as localized fighting groups that lacked any coordination, let alone a central command. With the inception of the Anya-Nya movement in Equatoria and the necessity to purchase arms in the Congo, armed groups from Upper Nile and Bahr el Ghazal began to interact with their brethren in Equatoria and the Southern politicians that fled the country in the early 1960s. Attempts at national organization as we have seen were faced with lack of a unified leadership and the absence of an external support to the cause of the struggle.

Things began to change in early 1969 with the changed geopolitical situation in the region and the Middle East. Following the Arab-Israeli six-day war in June 1967, Sudan had declared itself a frontline state in the fight against Israel and deployed troops in the front line between Egypt and Israel in Sinai. Also, the same period saw the growth of the Anya-Nya movement, albeit with a divided leadership.

In early 1969, Joseph Lagu resumed contacts on his own with the Israeli

Embassy in Kampala. He was familiar to them as he was introduced to the embassy by Joseph Oduho some years earlier[344]. Within the same year, General Joseph Lagu was invited by the Israeli government to visit Tel Aviv. For sure, it must have been at the back of the minds of their leaders that a strengthened Anya-Nya will no doubt force Sudan to pay more attention to its defence than fighting in Sinai. The choice of Lagu could not have been by chance. In the Anya-Nya, one government after another has come and gone without delivering tangible military support to the fighters to wage war. Joseph Lagu, a trained Sudan army military officer, who joined the movement in May 1963 as a 1st Lt, was unhappy with the way the Anya-Nya was being managed by the politicians and General Taffeng.

Shuttling between the Israeli embassies in Kampala and Nairobi, he was able to travel to Israel through Kinshasa where he spent more than two weeks of interviews, military lectures and ground appreciation as well as touring the battlefields of the six-day war.

At the end of Lagu's programme in Tel Aviv, the Israeli Government agreed to assist the Anya-nya militarily and financially and to send a team to Southern Sudan after Lagu's return there to assess the situation on the ground. The trip eventually took place in May 1969[345] and airdrops were made at Owiny-ki-Bul in Eastern Equatoria under the supervision of an Israeli military team that had arrived there in June. According to Lagu, flights delivered various types of arms, mainly old infantry weapons, mark 4 rifles, Bren light machine guns, Sten submachine guns, 2 inch mortars, etc., as well as food provisions[346]. The Israeli team continued thereafter to assist in training Anya-nya officers and men. Some officers were sent for training in Israel and Ethiopia[347].

Having secured military support, Lagu started contacts with field commanders to come under his leadership. The first to join him was Brigadier Joseph Oteo Akuon who brought Upper Nile under Lagu's leadership and became his second-in-command. Then Lagu invited Col Samuel Abujohn, commander of the Western Equatoria Region and

---

344 Lagu, Joseph, Sudan: Odyssey Through A State From Ruin to Hope, MOB Centre for Sudanese Studies, Omdurman Ahlia University, 2006, 195.

345 Magaya, M.A., op.cit., p. 67.

346 Lagu, Odyssey, p. 213.

347 Ibid., p. 23. Officers were trained in Ethiopia. Only a few were taken to Israel for training mainly in signals.

they met in Kampala at the end of April 1969[348]. They had discussions on the future of the Anya-Nya movement after which Abujohn pledged his support and that of the Western Equatoria Region to Lagu. He was promoted to the rank of Brigadier and became the third in command of the Anya-Nya under Joseph Lagu[349].

By early 1970, Central Equatoria under the command of Col. James Loro joined the united command under Joseph Lagu. After undergoing training at Owiny-ki-Bul, he was confirmed the commander of the infantry battalion at Morta located between Kaya and Kajo-Kaji. In the same year, the Anya-Nya forces in Bahr el Ghazal under Col. Emmanuel Abur joined Joseph Lagu. With him were a good number of officers including Albino Akol Akol, Joseph Kuol Amoum and Andrew Makur. Thus, by the end of 1970, the unity of all the Anya-nya forces in Southern Sudan has been completed under one Commander-in- Chief, Major-General Joseph Lagu[350].

In 1970 Lagu announced the establishment of the "Southern Sudan Liberation Movement" (SSLM). This comprised the Anya-Nya High Command, with him at the top, the head of the police force, some public service officials, and two representatives to foreign countries, namely, Mr. Angelo Voga Morgan, in Kampala, Uganda and Mr. Enoch Mading de Garang, for London and Europe, also Managing Director of the Grass Curtain newspaper[351]. Grass Curtain was a quarterly journal published by the "Southern Sudan Association" in London between May 1970 and May 1972. Enoch Mading de Garang was co-founder and editor-in-chief. The Grass Curtain was successor to "Voice of Southern Sudan". The last edition of the Grass Curtain published the full text of the Addis Ababa Agreement.[352]

---

348 Magaya, op. cit., p. 66.

349 Ibid., p. 68. This information is contradicted by Ga'le,(see below), pp. 358-9, who in the lineup of Lagu's administration puts Abujohn as Lagu's Deputy (second in command) and Brigadier Joseph Akuon as the commander of Upper Nile Brigade (No. 5 in seniority). Officers were trained in Ethiopia. Only a few were taken to Israel for training mainly in signals.

350 Magaya, op.cit. p. 75

351 Ga'le, S.F.B.T., Shaping a Free Southern Sudan, Nairobi: Paulines Africa, 2002, p. 358-59.

352 Ahmed, Abdel Ghaffar Mohammed, "Sudan Peace Agreements: Current Challenges and Future Prospects", Sudan Working Paper, SWP 2010:1, footnote 11, p. 6

Curiously but unsurprisingly, no political executive set-up was established; Lagu loathed the politicians for their lack of unity. General Lagu decentralized the administration and organized the Anya-nya as territorial guerrilla forces with three Brigades one each in Equatoria, Upper Nile and Bahr el Ghazal. However, many politicians joined the SSLM.

The assumption of power in Uganda by Brigadier General Idi Amin Dada on 25 January 1971, witnessed an open support to the Any-nya by the Ugandan Government. This was also the period when relations were established with Israel following Joseph Lagu's visit to Tel Aviv in 1969 referred to earlier. This window of opportunity lasted for just under two years as the strain in the relations between Idi Amin's Uganda and Israel led to the closure of the Israeli embassy in early 1972. This blow to the Anya-Nya was not compensated for by Amin's sympathetic attitude towards the Southern Sudanese struggle.

Training of Officers

As soon as the military logistics started to be air-dropped at the newly established HQ at Owiny-ki-Bul, it was decided to start training the Anya-Nya officers so as to raise their capacity and capability. Ethiopia was chosen as the venue to conduct a six-month intensive officers' training course, which was run by Israeli instructors. The subjects covered in the basic training were: drills, weaponry, demolition, command and control, tactics, basic administration, etc. The first batch comprised fifteen officers, all of whom, save one, came from Eastern Equatoria and Upper Nile. They included Edward Peter, William Alira, John Okwahi, Peter Marcello, Kamilo Odongi, Amos Agok, Mabil Riak, Stephen Ogut and Matthew Pagan. The only officer from Western Equatoria was Major Alison Magaya[353].

The second batch was composed of officers from the same areas but with more from Western Equatoria. These included Dominic Kassiano, Severino Morris, Michael Saiba, Felix Peter, Richard Babiro, John Maluk and Arnold de Mabior.

---

353 Magaya, p. 75

The officers from Bahr el Ghazal and Central Equatoria attended the third batch together with others from Eastern and Western Equatoria and Upper Nile. Some officers of the first batch were trained at the same time with the third batch, but the fourth batch was the last conducted abroad. Subsequently, officers were trained at an officers' training school which the Anya-Nya leadership had established at its HQ, Owiny-ki-Bul.

The Anya-Nya suffered a big blow when in early 1971, Owiny-ki-Bul was attacked and overrun by an enemy force from both Obo and Nimule (i.e. north and west). This forced the Anya-Nya to move its headquarters to Labone, where it remained until the end of the war in 1972[354].

Improved Capacity of the Anya-Nya

The training of the officers and the provision of logistics tremendously enhanced the capability of the Anya-Nya forces to prosecute the war more effectively. The fighting was all over Southern Sudan with the enemy sustaining heavy casualties and the balance of forces changing considerably in favour of the Anya-Nya.

It was this growing strength of the Anya-Nya as well as political developments in the country following the abortive communist-inspired coup in 1971 that concentrated the minds of Nimeiri and his colleagues in the May regime to take the course of a peaceful resolution of the conflict more seriously than before.

Contacts between the Sudan Government and the SSLM representatives abroad started through intermediaries in 1971. Despite the ups and downs, these contacts led eventually to holding peace talks in Addis Ababa in November the same year culminating in the Addis Ababa Agreement which was concluded towards the end of February 1972.

---

354 Ga'le, op.cit., p. 358-61. Magaya, op.cit., p. 79, claims that Awingbul (Owiny-ki-Bul) was not overrun by the enemy and that the move to Labone was due to its better suitability as HQ because of its mountainous terrain.

Chapter 19

Conclusion

The previous chapters were an attempt to trace the origin of the Anya-Nya, its development and the struggle it waged against the governments that came and went in Khartoum. The work is by no means exhaustive but highlights important phases in the armed struggle. It begins with the events that led to the Torit mutiny. But was Torit incident on 18 August 1955 the revolution that was transformed into the Anya-Nya? The answer is a 'yes' or 'no' depending on which vantage point one tackles the matter from.

In 1955 the Southern Sudanese had many grievances against the North for not heeding to the special safeguards they demanded in the Juba Conference as a condition for the two parts of the country to get independence as a united sovereign state. The clearest proof of that was the Political Parties Agreement signed in Cairo in 1953 between the Northern parties on the one hand and Egypt on the other to move quickly towards self-determination of Sudan. The Southerners were not represented in that meeting on the flimsy excuse that there was no Southern political party at that time. Afterwards, Prime Minister Ismail Al Azhari whose party, the NUP, had been advocating union with Egypt fell into disfavour with the two Sayyeds (Ali El Mirghani and Abd al Rahman al Mahdi of the *Khatimiyya* and *Ansar* sects, respectively) turned into an advocate of the independence of Sudan so as to pull the rug from under their feet. He thus began to move quickly to take the necessary steps towards independence. This move won him the favour of the British who loathed any association of Sudan with Egypt. As we have seen, it is these moves of Prime Minister al Azhari that triggered the mutiny in Torit. No doubt there was pent-up anger among the Southern Sudanese but there was no political planning of or political leadership to the actions that took place in Torit on the morning of 18 August 1955. The soldiers were angry and did not want to be transferred to the North and therefore took the law into their own hands. Apart from targeting their Northern officers, there was indiscriminate killing of unarmed Northerners. Then heeding to a misplaced faith in the British, who promised them fair trials if they surrendered, the leaders of the mutiny obliged. The consequences were disastrous: the military tribunals set up by Khartoum tried them in the last week of October 1955, and in a few days the sentences were handed down; all the leaders and most of the soldiers were sentenced to death and executed by fire squads. There was no coordination with Malakal or Wau where Companies 3 and 4 of the Equatoria Corps were stationed. Significantly, the leadership of the Bahr el Ghazal province in Wau had remained in the hands of Southerners when the Northern Governor escaped on hearing about the mutiny in Torit and the killing of Northerners. If there were a political leadership such a situation would have been a great advantage to the rebels. By September, the rebellion has been practically crushed and a few individuals remained with guns here and there in the mountains of Eastern Equatoria. A few of them survived to witness the formation of the Anya-Nya in 1963. Thus, there was no continuity between the Torit mutiny and the Anya-Nya except in relation to a few officers who had run for their lives (Gbatala, David Dada, etc.) or who were jailed before the mutiny (Taffeng). In this sense, it is hard to term the action that took place in Torit on 18 August 1955 of and by itself a revolution. However, it was the first action taken by organized armed Southerners against Khartoum and served as an important and significant contribution to the political awakening of the Southern Sudanese and sharpened their resolve to take up arms. It was the most single action that contributed to the objective and subjective conditions necessary for the Southern revolution. Therefore, it is an occasion to celebrate.

Another milestone in the political consciousness of the South Sudanese was the political unrest that took place in Nzara and Yambio in 1955 well before the Torit Mutiny. The kind of slogans raised and actions taken showed political maturity that could have been harnessed and turned into positive opposition of the regime in Khartoum if there was a political leadership to the opposition.

It is extremely doubtful whether the Southern politicians intended from the beginning to join armed struggle. It was not until General Ibrahim Abboud assumed power, dissolved Parliament in 1958 and started to crack down on the Southern politicians that the largest group crossed the border to Uganda at the end of 1960 and were joined by William Deng in February 1961. There they formed the SCDNU which did not mention armed action as one of its means of the struggle. The same was the case when the name morphed into SANU not long after. Even after the formation of the Anya-Nya where these leaders were in the driving seat, they continued to deny any relationship with the armed struggle. Yet, this tactics did not pull wool over the eyes of the host countries and Joseph Oduho, the President, escaped arrest narrowly in Congo and was later arrested in Uganda, convicted and served 9 months in prison for "managing an unlawful society and raising an army" (p. 32). So, what was the point?

Except for Eastern Equatoria, the political leadership of the armed struggle never had close contact with the fighting men on the ground. This was a great disadvantage but in a way was a blessing in disguise. No armed movement can succeed to achieve its objectives without a committed political leadership with a clear programme that guides the struggle and to which the army is answerable. As we have seen, the political leaders of the Anya-Nya under various names and labels held an ill-defined chain of command with the soldiers. Therefore, their effect on the operations in the battle fields was minimal. That nebulous relationship was in a way a blessing in that had it been so strong the continuous bickering and divisions among the politicians that were the hallmark at that time would have resulted in dangerous divisions among the troops. Such divisions were witnessed here and there but this was the exception rather than the rule.

It cannot be denied that some of the many governments and Movements that sprang up during the struggle of the Anya-Nya did really try their best to work out a programme for the struggle. They enunciated objectives to be achieved, worked out structures of governance and laws to govern the South under their administration, etc. They even set up media organs to report on what was taking place from their perspective. An example here is the SSPG programme. However, this serious attempt was cut short by a number of challenges including the desertion of the President who chose to live in exile.

The Achille's heal in the whole political work of the Anya-Nya was its failure to make use of the Cold War rivalry by then to its favour. For no good reason one government after the other were condemning communism at par with colonialism and imperialism. For instance, in the Angudri Convention that gave birth to the SSPG, Ezbon Mondiri was arrested for having been a communist and in possession of a document offering help from the Chinese (p. 130)! Thereafter, the policy statement pronounced that "the SSPG pledges itself to work ...for the abolition of colonialism, imperialism , communism, and all forms of national and racial oppression" (p. 132)! Whereas colonialism and imperialism were for real where was that communism to be abolished in Sudan or Africa for that matter? This uncalled for anti-communism rhetoric did great disservice to the armed struggle. In view of the mission- influenced Southern leaders this may come as no surprise, even though Fr. Saturnino, himself a Catholic priest, did recognize the need for extending cooperation beyond the borders. He made an attempt to win over the Simba but that was unsuccessful as the Simbas proved to be unfriendly for they were being supplied arms through Juba by Egypt and Algeria on ideological grounds. Avoiding to identify with the most likely pole to assist, the Anya-Nya remained without a country supporting them militarily, benefitting only from windfalls of unplanned events: first, the collapse of the Simba rebellion and, second, the six-day war between the Arabs and the Israelis in 1967. In the first case they had to buy the guns of the fleeing Simbas and in the second they were given used captured weapons by the Israelis. True, the Israelis trained the Anya-Nya and gave them some support but this came late in the day (late 1969) to change the military balance drastically in their favour. They should have grasped the truism that political and military support will only be delivered not for altruistic reasons but for an interest.

For one reason or the other, Southern politicians and military officers alike have somehow led themselves into believing that in their struggle with the North the British would stand with them. The politicians learned it the hard way when the agreement that was worked out by the Northern parties and Egypt in 1953 that did away with the 'Southern safeguards" was fully endorsed by the British. Little did they realise that British interests in Egypt and in Sudan were paramount to any other sentimental feeling. The soldiers in the Torit mutiny requested help from British forces in East Africa (p. 8). Not only did such help fail to materialize but they were advised to surrender. They did not live to regret their big error of judgement.

What are the lessons to be learnt in the struggle of the Anya-Nya?

First, Self-reliance, a cardinal requirement of a successful guerrilla warfare has been one of the strong points of the Freedom Fighters which later became the Anya-Nya. They were able to establish a network of supporters and scouts all over the South especially in towns. These supporters collected resources which were used to buy arms and ammunition to wage the armed struggle. In this endeavour, it was supported by the Southern Front. Second, waging a people's war, the Anya-Nya relied on the support of the civil population and won them to its side, even establishing civil administration in the liberated areas. It goes without saying that it also dealt ruthlessly with the enemy agents among the population. Third, the Movement was not led by a political group that had formulated a programme or ideology for the armed struggle, call it a vanguard if you may. It was the military that took the lead followed by the politicians. Therefore, the failures that were associated with forging a strong relationship between the politicians and the military where the former must lead were to be expected. Fourth, the political leadership was divided all through and when Joseph Lagu united the fighting men in 1970 he swung to the other extreme by forming a military leadership under him with no structured political leadership. Yes, there was a political body called the Southern Sudan Liberation Movement (SSLM) but it was just in name without structure. Ezbon Mundiri who led the SSLM delegation to the Addis Ababa talks with the Government in 1971 had no known specific position in the Movement, and so was Joseph Oduho that Joseph Lagu took with him for the ratification of the Addis Ababa Agreement in 1972 after having dismissed his entire negotiating team. The only exception to this was the editor of the newspaper, Grass Curtain, which was the mouthpiece of the SSLM. Fifth, the Anya-Nya failed to make a proper appraisal of the prevailing international situation by then. At a time when the Cold War was at its peak, it continued to be openly anti-communist without discernible reason. The Socialist camp was most likely to help as it did to the other African liberation movements at the time. That the Anya-Nya was a separatist movement would not have stood against that assistance as long as the country/entity providing assistance sees an interest to be served by that struggle. Next door, the Katanga and South Kasai separatists in Congo were supported by Belgium against the Prime Minister Patrice Lumumba on ideological grounds. Ezbon Mondiri was far ahead of his peers not only in seeing this point but also in forging the unity of the Anya-Nya by deeds, not just words. Last but not least, the Anya-Nya fighters fought gallantly and valiantly enduring very adverse conditions in the pursuit of their struggle. They used machetes, bows and arrows, spears, muzzle loaders and terrified the enemy. When conditions improved, several people followed one gun and they were indefatigable. It was only in the last year or two that having one's own gun became common.

APPENDIX 1

Resolutions of the Round Table Conference on the South, Khartoum, March 16-29, 1965.

We the delegates of the following Political Parties and Organizations:
1. Islamic Charter Front
2. National Unionist Party
3. People's Democratic Party
4. Professional Front
5. Sudanese African National Union (SANU)
6. Sudan Communist Party
7. Southern Front
8. Umma Party

attending the Round Table Conference on the South meeting in Khartoum at the House of parliament from March 16-29, 1965, having considered all aspects of the Southern Question, are convinced:
1. that national conciliation was imperative, and
2. that the differences in views are not beyond solution, and
3. that only through peaceful means can these differences be settled, and do hereby resolve:

1   That the following steps be taken by the Government in order to normalize the situation in the South:

i) The implementation of the agreement between the governments of Uganda and the Sudan concerning refugees and thereby resettling them.

ii) Approaching the governments of other neighbouring countries with a view of reaching similar agreements over the refugees.

iii) Resettlement of those inside the country whose homes and property have been destroyed.

iv) To request the government

    a) To alleviate famine in those parts of the South affected thereby;

    b) To investigate the inherent cause of famine and floods in the South and take the necessary steps.

v) Retransfer of all Southern schools from the North to the South.

2   That the following lines of policy be adopted:

i) Selection of more Southerners for training as:

    a) Police and Prison Officers;

    b) Administrators;

    c) Military Officers;

    d) Public Health officers and Medical Assistants;

    e) Forest Officers;

    f) Game and Fisheries Officers.

ii) The Southernization of Administration, Police, Prisons and Information Service whenever qualified Southerners are available. Where they are not available steps should be taken to accelerate their training and promotion.

iii) Equality of opportunities for employment and equality of wages. There will be no discrimination by reason only of religious beliefs or language or race.

iv) Freedom of Religion and freedom of Missionary activity within the laws of the land.

v) Allowing of private persons or bodies to open schools as long as these persons and bodies conform to the law of the land.

vi) Freedom of movement.

vii) Establishment of a University in the South.

viii) Opening Girls' Secondary Schools and an Agricultural School in Malakal.

ix) Re-establishment of Yambio Agricultural School, Juba Training Centre and Malakal Veterinary Centre.

x) All Southern schools to be headed by qualified Southerners. Ignorance of Arabic language shall not bar promotion to the post of headmaster.

xi) Finding jobs for the unemployed.

xii) The establishment of national economic Council for Economic Development with a subsidiary agency for economic development in the South. This will consider the detailed schemes presented by the team of investigation of 1954 and any other schemes in all aspects of development and plan their implementation. The government should also consider the revival of the Azande Scheme.

xiii Giving priority and facilities to the local population in the exploitation of land.

3   That the delegates who participated in the conference are determined on the rectification of these grievances and the execution of these policies and that they are prepared to go into a peace campaign to tour the South, to pacify and normalize and see to it that they will employ all their resources to end all hostilities in two months' time.

4   i) That the conference considered some patterns of government for the Sudan and could not reach a unanimous resolution as required by the rules of the conference.

ii) We have, therefore, appointed a twelve-man committee to dwell on the issue of the constitutional and administrative set-up which will protect the special interest of the South as well as the general interest of the Sudan. The committee shall in addition have the following terms of reference:

    a) to act as a watch-committee on the implementation of the steps and policies agreed upon.

    b) To plan the normalization of conditions in the South, and consider steps for the lifting of the state of emergency and the establishment of law and order.

iii) The findings of the committee shall be presented to the conference which shall be called by the government within three months.

5   We consider that in addition to these achievements the conference was successful in:
i) Affording an opportunity to political leaders from the North and South, for the first time in six years, to meet in an amicable atmosphere and exchange views on the Southern problem.
ii) Affording an opportunity to the sister African countries invited to the conference to acquaint themselves with the problem and enlisting their sympathy and support for its solution.
iii) Allaying the doubts and suspicions between political leaders of North and South and establishing a firm basis for understanding and co-operation.
iv) Providing an opportunity for our people in the South and the North to know the facts and thus appreciate the problem and see it in its true perspective.
We believe that only through such an appreciation can our people forge ahead and utilize their energies and resources in building the future; only through this can our great ideals of peace, love and confidence be a reality.

6   We express deep gratitude :
i) To the Chairman of the Conference for all the skill and impartiality with which he conducted the meetings of the Conference, thus contributing to its success.
ii) To the Observers, their Governments and peoples for taking great interest in the affairs of the Sudan and for their ceaseless efforts to see that National conciliation be realized; and for their invaluable contribution to the ultimate success of the Conference.
iii) To the Secretary General and Secretariat for the devoted and tireless efforts exerted by them before and during the Conference and thus making it a success.
iv) To the Sudan Government for taking the initiative and adopting a forward policy that resulted in the holding of the Conference and for the support, moral and material, which it generously extended.

Selections from nine articles written by a Northern Sudanese Journalist on the Round Table Conference.

The articles appeared under the name of "Observer" in El Ayam newspaper, Khartoum, during the month of April 1965. Translation of them, from which the following selections have been taken, appeared in The Vigilant, Khartoum, 5 May – 19 June 1965. These translations, in turn, have been reproduced in Round-Table Conference on the Southern Sudan, a booklet issued by the Sudan Informazioni News Agency in 1970.

I am not an advocate of war, but I welcome war in the cause of justice. I said in my previous article that the government did not stick to its neutral stand, though that stand was harmful to the country, but instead took several measures which strengthened the position of the outlaws. What were these measures?

The declaration of the general amnesty, [which] during the Military Regime and the present regime released from prison the most dangerous anti – North persons. During the Military Regime the declaration of amnesty led to the release of all soldiers of the Southern command, policemen and warders who actually committed murders during the 1955 mutiny. Those are the ones who make up the Anya-Nya movement. The general amnesty by the October government[355] filled the towns with people of the most vile intentions. As the general amnesty was accompanied by granting public liberties, those released took over leadership of the political movement in the towns and directed it against Northerners. They began to collect "compulsory" contributions publicly and send them to the Anya-Nya gang in the form of supplies...

The second measure taken by the government was the Southernization of posts in the South. . . .[This] was not done at the will of the government. It has been carried out at the wish and will of the Southern Front. In Yambio the secretary of the Minister of the Interior southernized all the posts including that of the Inspector of Local Government. As to the teachers and headmaster of the religious institute[356] he said he had no Southerners, to replace them so he told them to pack and leave the town. They did so. In Maridi, Yei, Torit and every place the Southern Front submitted notes requesting that Southerners should replace Northerners.

The third of these measures . . . was the removal from the Round Table

---

355   . i.e., Sirr el-Khatim's government.

356   Presumably an Islamic one

Conference of the Southern parties which are demanding and sticking to unity.[357] The presence of the pro-unity parties would have meant in its simplest form, that not all the South is against unity and that the conflict is not only between Northerners and Southerners. It would have meant that the conflict is between Northerners and some Southerners on one hand and some Southerners and others on the other. Even for propaganda purposes, it would have been better to broadcast along with the point of view of the Southern separatists the point of view of the Southern unionists. This would have been the most effective answer to the separation movement.[358]

"Giving priority to local residents to utilize the land."[359]

Comment. This is a ridiculous resolution if we do not read viciousness in it. The land is more than the needs of the local citizens, even if their number is increased by tenfold. There are millions of feddans of virgin land left fallow. It did not and will not happen that land will be taken away from a citizen to be given to another.[360] Then, what is the purpose of this resolution?

I can sense in it a reference to the land given to some Northerners for establishing coffee plantations. What the conferees missed is that what the natives need is the incentive to work and not the land. The resolution turned out to be ridiculous and malicious, because it indicates to the foreign reader and to African countries that Southern citizens are not given priority in distribution of the land. There is no doubt that countries like Uganda and Kenya and others in East Africa will not understand this resolution as the Northern conferees understand it, because these countries were plagued by the problem of settlers who took for themselves the best African lands and exploited them. This was one of the reasons behind the African revolution. This resolution means to those Africans that the Southern revolt is similar to their revolution.

This resolution and other resolutions mentioned above- such as equality in job opportunities; equality in wages; preventing discrimination on religious, racial or language grounds; freedom of religion; freedom of propagation of faith; allowing organizations and individuals to open schools; freedom of movement - all these resolutions have been adopted behind the back of the Northern negotiator with the aid of his good-heart-

---

357 e.g., the Sudan Unity Party.

358 From the third of the articles in El Ayam, translated in The Vigilant of 29 May 1965, reprinted in the Sudan Informazioni booklet, pp. 90-92.

359 From the resolutions of the Round Table Conference, Section 4, paragraph 13. See above.

360 There is evidence which contradicts this statement. In his opening speech at the Malakal conference of February 1965, the chairman of the Wad medani branch of the Southern Front said that "In 1956 the land on both banks of the White Nile between Kaka and Malakal was distributed to Northern landlords, and when the Dinka from Renk refused to surrender their land, force was used to eject them. All the efforts made by the Dinkas to regain their land through legal proceedings were of no avail. Similar hard conditions were also laid down for possession of rice cultivation land in Aweil". (Southern Sudan Archive, Document1B/1109. Also in 1960, according to Elia Lupe, the D.C. of Yei gave away Southerners' land near Yei to Northerners for coffee plantations.

edness. He considered them to be a matter of course. All these resolutions, in spite of being a "matter of course", are intended by the Southern negotiator (and this is what actually happened) to appear to the foreign reader, especially in the African countries where Southern propaganda has stressed that the Arabs ore colonizing them, as demands which will be carried out. These resolutions will be understood and will appear similar to the demand of Negroes in America, Southern Rhodesia and South Africa. Such understanding by Africans is our condemnation as colonialists who impose discrimination on religious, language and racial grounds.[361]

Let us find a way out and convert the elements of defeat we faced in the Round Table Conference, to lead us to victory that would keep the country united.

Our first mistake is our good-heartedness, that drove us Dervishes to take hold of childish assumption, and thus we lost sight of the true dimensions of the problem. This good-heartedness made us assume good intentions in the counter party, and for this reason we retracted and retracted without any response from that party which was, and still is, very cautious and very suspicious.

This good-heartedness has prevented us from taking advantage of the split in SANU. We believed that William's[362] wing was siding with us, but it appears that he is still loyal to his organization, and he is working here inside as an agent, and that is why we failed to strengthen him, and raise him so as to blow hard on the other party...

We failed not only in deepening the split within SANU, but also made it possible for the other party[363] to disperse our lines and make us dispute among ourselves. They voted in the Supreme Council of State on the side of elections[364], but later on, they stood against it, supporting P.D.P. in boycott of elections. Furthermore, they asked for guarantees for the South[365].

Our good-heartedness made us overlook the true dimensions of the problem and limit our attention to the Round Table Conference. We could not realize the fact that neither SANU nor terrorist Anya-Nya are holding themselves up. But according to Uganda's Minister of Interior all these are tools in the hands of foreigners..... We all know that imperialism and Zionism are behind them. The Zionist star on a cartridge, left behind after attacking Tonj and killing nine policemen and prison warders[366], this star betrayed the part Zionism is playing now. The Catholic Church also smuggled weapons inside cases marked church items so as to escape inspection. These weapons were handed to the terrorist Anya-Nya. The scene of weapons at Gulu Church in Uganda is still alive in mind.[367]

This good-heartedness made us disappoint the Sudan Unity Party and freeze their activities. We have abandoned elements pro-unity, and obliged them to hide themselves by

---

361 From the seventh of the articles in El Ayam, translated in The Vigilant of 16 June 1965, reprinted in the Sudan Informazioni booklet p. 104.

362 Deng's

363 The Southern Front

364 See p. 107

365 The reference may be to the guarantees Southern Sudanese demanded from the British in the Juba Conference in 1947 and subsequently in the early 1950s.

366 Presumably, the attack referred to on p. 87.

367 The author has been unable to discover what is being referred to here.

growing beards and wearing watches on the right hand (the two distinctive symbols of the rebels)[368]. The beards are grown after that of Lumumba to idolize him, but it is strange that these beards are now turned against his principles.

To win the coming round, we should not be good-hearted men, we should assume ill-intentions, cunningness in the other party, and behave according to these assumptions.

1　First, to refuse the guarantees they are now asking for. They aim at (a) paralyzing the prospective Constituent Assembly, (b) weakening the government authority and limiting it to the North only, (c) we should be aware of the idea that says that the Assembly has no power over the South until by- elections are carried out in the South under a weak government. Insecurity will continue. In fact by saying so we give them a strong card to play.

2　Second, despite all sayings that were said against elections we can convert the matter to act rightly an follows:

a)The new government should practise her authority over the South and North, and hit hard on outlaws so as to disperse them.

b) Portfolios for Ministries of Local Government, Interior and Defense should not be entrusted to a Southerner. No Southerner who is a member of either SANU or the Southern Front would act against the interest of his group.

Southern unionists can benefit us greatly. They should be appointed ministers, and no heed should be given to SANU or Southern Front regarding the appointment of ministers[369]. We should not lean on Equatoria in this respect. The Dinkas and Nuers were very angry for there was not a Dinka in the cabinet.[370] I still recall the discontent that overtook the Dinkas when Sayed Ambrose Wol was turned out.[371] Again, when William Deng decided to come home, the Dinkas reacted against the dissenting factions by saying that they had become toys, in the hands of "Fertit", meaning tribes of Equatoria province.

c) We should get benefit out of tribal conflicts. I do not mean "Divide and Rule", but I mean that the present terrorism is not in the interest of all Southern tribes. We must explain to them the disadvantage of mutiny. The Toposa tribe, who grasped this wisdom, is an example. This tribe alone defeated the mutineers, because she regarded rebellion as a source of instability through which her animal wealth would be lost.[372] Bitter enmity comes from poor tribes.

3　Third, the government has adopted the resolutions of the Round Table Conference. In previous articles I have mentioned that implementation of any item of these resolutions would turn out to be our defeat. If it becomes necessary, then implementation should be carried out under these conditions:

368　Southerners living under the government wear watches on the left wrist, Anya-Nya on the right.

369　The writer of the article seems to have been quite prescient here. See p. 145.

370　Note however that Gordon Mourtat replaced Ezbon Mondiri in March 1965.

371　Ambrose Wol Dhal was appointed a minister in the caretaker government before the Southern Front's list of names was received. He was then dropped in favour of Mondiri.

372　See p. 64.

a) To cease violence and terrorism in the South.

b) To hand arms over to the government.

These two conditions are the least we could expect in response to the conference resolutions…

4 Fourth, in spite of the fact that the rainy season does not create suitable circumstances for military action, there is a chance to crush the rebels and destroy their camps before they develop into a real danger to us. This will be in September when weeds and grass rise up high providing facilities for their hiding.

5 Fifth, military action will not only weaken and disperse the outlaws, but it will also render it impossible for them to cultivate their lands and stock foods for further needs. It is necessary to control food supplies, distribute them to loyal tribes and individuals. It is childish to supply food to those who face us with enmity and rebellion. Such action is essential so as to lead to weakening the position of the outlaws.

6 Sixth, we should not fail or fall short in assisting the Congolese rebels. They did what we could not do. They secured our frontiers (Sudan-Congo frontiers), The Zande region, adjacent to Tshombe's frontiers, has developed into a very dangerous strategy.[373] Let us be certain that the Congolese rebels will win at last. We should mobilize all our resources (we can even send volunteer warriors), because their failure means that the South will separate forever. Cooperation between outlaws and Tshombe is well known to all and is not a secret.

Cutting rebels' nails is bound by the success and victory that Congolese rebels will attain. Let us abandon hesitation. Let us discard good-heartedness. Time is not in our favour. We are in need of action, of placing a direct hit that might weigh the balances in our favour.[374]

---

373 What is presumably implied here is that where the Simbas are in control in Congo, they prevent supplies reaching the Anya-Nya.

374 From the ninth of the articles in El Ayam, translated in The Vigilant of 5 May 1965, reprinted in the Sudan Informazioni booklet pp. 82-84.

APPENDIX 3

Recommendations of the 12-man Committee to the Chairman of the Round Table Conference On the South, June 1966

His Excellency,
The Prime Minister

On the 29th of March, 1965 the Round Table Conference on the South resolved to that the findings of the 12-Man Committee which was to dwell on the Constitutional and Administrative Set-Up, "shall be presented to the Conference which shall be called by the Government within three months".
On the 30th of March, 1965 Sayed Sirr El Khatim El Khalifa the then Prime Minister announced to the conference that the Government was pleased to adopt these resolutions and do everything necessary for its success.
The Committee was set up nearly 2 months after the Conference, and for this as well as other good reasons it was not possible to finish the work within the specified period.
When your government took office, we had the pleasure of meeting you on the 22nd of July, 1965, and you informed us that irrespective of whether we came to an agreement or not you will call for the reconvening of the Conference in November, 1965.
On the 15th of January, 1966 we met again together and after expressing your gratitude and appreciation for the stage which the Committee had covered you called upon us to finish the remaining items and declared: "once you come to some conclusions, we can fix a date for the Conference."
We now have the pleasure to inform your good self that we have come to the conclusions which we submit herewith, so that you may fix a date and kindly pass our report and minutes to the Chairman of the Conference.

With best wishes,
Yours sincerely,
Yousif Mohd Ali
CHAIRMAN
12- MAN COMMITTEE
Khartoum,
26th June, 1966.

Report of the Twelve-man Committee to the Chairman of the Round Table Conference on the South.

Dear Sir,

1   On the 29th of March, 1965 the conference resolved to set up this Committee,
a) "To dwell on the issue of the Constitutional and Administrative set-up which will protect the Special Interest of the South as well as the General Interest of the Sudan." Also
b) "To act as a watch committee on the implementation of the steps and policies agreed upon."
c) "To plan the normalization of conditions in the South, and consider steps for the lifting of the state of emergency and the establishment of law and order."

2   A Special Minute of the Conference dated 29th March 1965 stated:
"After discussing the terms of reference of the Committee which shall dwell on the Constitutional and Administrative Set-Up of the Sudan, it was agreed on the statement as drafted but with this clear understanding by all delegates:"
The terms of reference of the said Committee do not include the consideration of the two extremes – that is to say: Separation and the Present Status Quo."

3   We now have the honour to submit our Report.

4   The Committee held its first meeting on the 27th of May, 1965. This was nearly two months after the Conference, and was due to the occupation of the Government and Political Parties in the General Elections.
We held a total of 48 meetings and heard expert witnesses on some subjects.

Chapter I
Implementation of Resolutions and Normalization of Conditions

5   The first tasks which the Committee undertook were under its second and third terms of reference.
Thus in its second meeting it decided to ask the Prime Minister to submit to the Committee a report on the state of security in the South and the execution of the Round Table Resolutions. Also it moved that acts of violence being committed in the South be condemned.

6   On the 9th of June, 1965 P.M. Sir El Khatim El Khalifa attended the meeting of the Committee and presented a report on the state of security and the implementation of the Round Table Conference Resolutions:
The outlines of the report were:
That a Ministerial Committee had been set up to plan and supervise the implementation,
That it had already considered several reports from the concerned ministries on implementation,

That some resolutions were in fact long term policies and were not meant to be carried out immediately,
That the increase in the incidents of violence after the conference was obstructing the implementation of other resolutions,

7   Again on the 22nd of July the present Prime Minister, Sayed Mohammed Ahmed Mahgoub who had then taken office attended the Committee meeting on its invitation. His stand was that the government did start the implementation by transferring Southern Officials to the South but those officials regrettably began to instigate the policemen and prison warders against the Government and to assist the mutineers. The situation deteriorated and schools and hospitals had to be closed. Implementation could only be resumed when law and order were established. The members of the Committee conveyed to the Prime Minister their views on this stand.

8   On the 15th of January, 1966 the Prime Minister attended the Committee's meeting again and reiterated his stand on this point.

9   The normalization of the situation in the South meant in the first place the re-establishment of law and order. If a peaceful solution was to be attained acts of violence had to cease.
But the two approaches to the question of establishment of law and order which could not be reconciled during the long discussions of the Conference reasserted themselves again on the Committee: Is the establishment of law and order a pre-requisite for the implementation of the Resolutions – in whole or part?- or is it rather that only through implementation of the Resolutions can law and order be established in fact? The Northern members adopted the first approach and the Southern members the second.

10   There was also a difference of stand on the condemnation of acts of violence. The Round Table Conference declared the conviction that only through peaceful means can the differences be settled. The members of the Committee were, therefore, unanimous in condemning acts of violence.
But who were the culprits?
Two answers were submitted.
The Northern members submitted that acts of violence by the terrorist organization, the Anya Nya, should be condemned.
The Southern members submitted that violence was being committed not by the Anya Nya alone but by the Government's security forces as well. Both were to be condemned.
Although the two submissions were discussed seriously and in detail no common answer could be agreed upon in the end.

11   But the whole experience had its instructive side as well.
However different the approaches may be, security which was the real basis for the normalization of the situation in the South was primarily the responsibility of the

Government and it was now evident that unless the Government adopted an attitude of utmost cooperation it was unlikely that any efforts by the Committee in this respect could bear fruit. And the circumstances were not the most favourable for such an attitude. The Committee, therefore, turned its attention to its first and main term of reference.

Chapter II
The Constitutional & Administrative Set-up

12 Although the Round Table Conference could not reach a unanimous resolution on the pattern of Government which should be adopted it did resolve that two forms of solution:
Separation and Present Status Quo (centralized Unitary government) should not be considered by the Committee.
The members were asked to submit to the Committee their proposals on the Constitutional and Administrative Set-Up, and four Schemes were submitted on behalf of the following four:
1 SANU)
2 Islamic Charter Front) Appendix A (1 to 4)
3 Southern Front)
4 National Unionist Party)
The Umma Party decided to adopt the principles in the National Unionist Party Scheme.

13 Two schemes were challenged in the Committee as being outside its terms of reference. The Southern Front's Scheme and the Islamic Charter Front Scheme. It was submitted that the first was a separatist scheme and the latter no more than the present status quo.
The Chairman after considering the submissions entertained both applications and set aside the schemes. The submissions and rulings are given in Appendix B (1 to 4). Thereafter, the ICF adopted the principles of the NUP Scheme and the SF adopted the stand explained in its memorandum dated 26th September, 1966 (Appendix C).

14 The Committee found that the Constitutional and Administrative formula which it was trying to work out was of two main parts: the Distribution of Powers between the Centre and the Region and the Relationship between the two and further that its objective would be facilitated if the Distribution of Powers was considered first.
Therefore, lists containing the powers proposed to remain in the Centre and those proposed to be transferred to the Region were worked out from the Schemes accepted by the Committee, and the study began.

15 The result was that the Committee were agreed that the following powers shall be exercised by the Central Government:
1. National Defence
2. External Affairs
3. Currency

4. Communications and Tele-Communications
5. Foreign Trade
6. Nationality
7. Customs
8. Inter-Regional Trade.

Concurrent Powers:
The following powers were to be concurrent between the Centre and the Region in the following manner:

16 Security Forces:
1 The National Legislature shall by enactment, organize the security forces. This will include:
a Recruitment and Use of the National Police Force which carries out the functions assigned to such forces.
b The Recruitment and Use of Local Police Forces.
2 The Head National Executive shall be the ultimate authority as regards the security forces and can in certain circumstances place any of these forces under his direct command.
Subject to (1) and (2) above, the Region shall recruit and use the local police force.

17 Education:
1 The policy of education shall be National and in the hands of the Centre. Policy has been defined to include at least the following:
Syllabuses, National Planning of Education,
Definition of Standards and Qualifications.
2 The Administration of education up to the intermediate level should be the responsibility of the Region.
3 And that it should be concurrent in the secondary stage so that the Centre and the Region may each establish such schools and administer them.
4 That Higher Education (post secondary) should be in the hands of the Centre.

18 Public Health:
The Centre should retain:
1. The General Policy and Planning
2. Education and training of doctors, the registration of doctors and all other professions attached to the medical profession.
3. Control and supervision of assisted projects.
4. National Policy for Nutrition.
5. Control over drugs and poisons.
6. Medical research and control of epidemics.
7. Registration of births and deaths.
8. Hospitals. The licensing and the supervision for maintenance of the standards is the province of the Centre – but the administration is concurrent, so that the Centre and the Region may each administer the hospitals established by it.
And the following to be transferred to the Region:

1. Control of Endemic diseases.
2. Environmental Health Services.
3. School Health Services.
4. Health Education.
5. Maternity and Child-Welfare Services.
6. Supervision of Markets.
7. Training of Village Midwives.
8. Training of Medical Assistants and opening of Dispensaries.

19 Antiquities:
Both the Centre and the Region may carry out excavations.

20 Labour:
1 The Centre shall lay down the Policy
2 The execution of the policy as laid in the legislations should be by the Region.

Regional Powers
1. Regional and Local Government Administration.
2. Regional Public Information.
3. Promotion of Tourism.
4. Museums and Zoos.
5. Exhibitions.
6. Projects: Establishment of Local Roads, Maintenance of Main Roads – Town and Village Planning.
7. Protection of Forests, crops and pastures – according to national legislation.
8. Protection and Development of Animal Resources – according to national legislation.
9. Land Utilization and Agricultural Development in accordance with the national plan for development.
10. The study and development of languages and local culture.
11. Commerce and Industry: Local Industries, organization of markets, trade licenses, formation of cooperative societies.

The Government of the Region

22 The Legislative Machinery:
Each Region shall have its legislative body in the form of an assembly elected directly on the same conditions as to qualification as that applied to the Central Parliament. This assembly exercises its right of enacting Regional Law and supervising the local executive machinery as well as setting down the policy for it.
The constitution defines the power granted to the Regional Legislative Assembly as agreed on.
23 The Executive Machinery:
1. The Legislative Assembly elects the members of the executive Council for the Region.

2 These are responsible to the Legislative Council which can dismiss them.

It was agreed that the Head Executive should be from amongst the inhabitants of the Region and that he should be responsible for the Central Agencies and units in the Region by Delegation from the centre as well as for the Regional Executive Machinery. This is to guarantee coordination and unity of leadership.

It was also agreed that this necessitates that he should be appointed through a joint process. But there was difference over the exact procedure to be followed.

There is a view that the Regional Assembly should offer two candidates and the Central Government should choose from between them.

The Relationship Between the Central and Regional Authorities

23 We had to consider here how to strike a balance between preserving the Sovereignty of the National Parliament to protect the vital interest of the Nation and at the same time securing the autonomy of the Regions and protecting them against any persistent and unwarranted interference by the centre in their spheres of power. We would like to clarify that when our agreed system of government is adopted as part of the constitution, there can be no withdrawal of the regional Powers except by a constitutional amendment with a two thirds majority. Further it is conceded that the Central Parliament being sovereign – subject to the constitution – may overrule any Regional legislation or take the initiative in legislating within the sphere of the Regional Powers. But in order to protect the Regions against any unwarranted encroachments by the Centre we recommend that:

a) A declaration be written into the constitution to the effect that this sovereignty is granted to parliament:

    1 To protect the vital interest of the country, and

    2 To guarantee the co-ordination of Regional Legislations and provide leadership and initiative.

b) Before any such legislation is passed by parliament there must be full consultations with the Regions concerned.

The Southern Front representative associated himself with the supremacy of the central parliament provided his proposal on the geographical division was accepted, (for this view please see Paragraph 26(3)(c) infra).

25 Emergency:

1. We were agreed that in the case of a public security emergency occasioned by an external or internal threat the Centre may either suspend any of the Regional Powers or dissolve the Regional Assembly provided that in the latter case elections must take place within one month after the emergency and

2. A declaration of emergency has to be approved by a resolution of parliament within two weeks of its announcement.

26 The Regional Geography:

After it has finished with the distribution of powers and the relationship between the Centre and the Region, the Committee went on to consider the geographical location of the Regions.

1   The Southern members suggested dividing the country into 4 regions:
a) South (constituting the present Southern provinces);
b) East (constituting Blue Nile and Kassala);
c) West (constituting Kordofan and Darfur):
d) North (constituting Khartoum and Northern Province);

Or

To adopt the present division in the Northern Provinces making six Regions out of them and making the three Southern Provinces into one Region.

2   The Northern members suggested adopting the present administrative boundaries for the Provinces creating nine Regions out of them.

3   Southern members gave the following reasons:
a) Any division must start by the North and the South as the two units because of the differences between them in Culture, Religion, Language and Race.

b) The South considers itself as a unit and the Southern citizens have expressed their wish to remain as a unit and there is nothing in this demand that is detrimental to the public interest. Also our basic duty is to solve the Southern problem and this necessitates giving this fact due consideration and not treating the South as the other parts of the country where no such problem has arisen or not to the extent of the Southern problem.

c) The guarantees agreed upon for the protection of the autonomy of the Regions will not be sufficient unless we enlarge the Regions geographically so that the public opinion in them will carry such political weight that the Centre shall have to pay that fact due consideration.

In fact this was put as a condition by the representative of the Southern Front for his agreement to the relationship between the Centre and the Region agreed in Paragraph 24.

d) The present administrative divisions are inherited from the Colonial Administration and are based on the tribal system and our duty is to adopt a system that weakens tribalism and so help Sudanese nation-building.

5   The Northern members based their view on the following:
a) It is preferable to begin by the present administration divisions. This facilitates administrative activities as the main advantage of Regional Government is that it limits administrative units to smaller areas thus avoiding administering large units from a far Centre. The South from the administrative aspect is too large to be administered from the Regional Capital.

b) It is true that we are primarily interested in the solution of the Southern problem but we must take note of the repercussions of any solution that we propose. In view of existing claims for regional autonomy any scheme that we develop is bound to serve as an example.

c) In substance the demand of the Southern parties has been for a constitutional set-up that would enable local initiative for the advancement of their Region. This, it is submitted, is satisfied whether the 3 Southern Provinces are united or separate.

d) If the South is made into one Region this will perpetuate the sense of confrontation between North and South which we are trying to end through these efforts.

As there may be some sentimental feeling that urges this demand, and as sentimental feelings can be legitimate and beneficial it may be met in this case by allowing any number of Regions to pool any of their services.

e There is no objection to any adjustment of Regional boundaries later on if experience indicates such change.

Both sides maintain their stand on this point.

Chapter III: miscellaneous

27 Representation of SANU:
When the 12-man Committee was set up, the Secretariat contacted the parties which were represented in the Conference, Sayed William Deng was contacted on behalf of SANU and a delegation of three members was formed. When they came to sit on the Committee a problem immediately arose. The Southern Front submitted a telegram from "SANU" in East Africa dismissing William Deng from the party and authorizing the SF to represent them in the Committee. Sayed William Deng and his supporters on the other hand maintained that they were the legitimate representatives of SANU which since the Round Table Conference has been exclusively functioning inside the Country; there was no other SANU in fact.
The question was which of the two SANUs (inside or outside the Country) was entitled to sit on the Committee.

28 After long discussions a representative of SANU (Outside) – Mr Peter Akol – flew in from East Africa and appeared before the Committee.
After hearing his case the Committee decided to recognize SANU (Inside) as the legitimate party entitled to representation in the Committee. The Southern Front recorded its objection.

Boycott by Some members:
29 On the 22nd of July, 1965 the People's Democratic Party communicated to the Committee its decision to withdraw from it. The grounds for the decision are given in their memorandum (Appendix D).
30 And on the 19th of August, 1965, the Sudan Communist party decided to withdraw from the Committee and demanded the freezing of its activities. The grounds are given in their memorandum (Appendix E).
31 The Committee issued a statement commenting on the withdrawals (Appendix F).

Finance and Development
32 The Committee had the benefit of expert opinion on Finance and Development from Senior Officials in the Ministry of Finance and Economics. The financial arrangements between the Central and Local Government under the Provincial Administration Act 1962 and the Local Government Ordinance were considered.
We recommend That:
1 A Committee of Experts be set up to study and recommend the financial arrangements which shall be adopted under our proposed system of Government.

2 A Central Development Commission be set up with Regional Sub-Commissions and with a proportional representation of Regions in the Commission.
The memorandums exchanged between the members of the Committee are provided in Appendix G (1-3).

Educational Policy

33 The representative of the Southern Front expressed his stand in the following terms: " I agree that educational policy be national, but there are regional peculiarities that reflect on education. So it is necessary to give the Region the opportunity to plan this side of the policy of education."

Cultural Relations with Other Countries:

34 The representative of the Southern Front proposed that the Region should have The right to establish cultural relations with other countries independently from the Central Government.
The Northern Parties rejected the proposal.

Home Guard (Militia)

35 The representative of the Southern Front maintains that each Region should have the right to establish a Home Guard (Militia) to assist the security forces.
The Northern Parties rejected the proposal.

Acknowledgment:

We wish to place on record our appreciation of the invaluable assistance which we have received from the Secretariat of the Committee, and from members of the Civil Service whose expert opinion on some subjects greatly facilitated our work.

Khartoum the 26th June, 1966

Chairman: Yousif Mohammed Ali
Islamic Charter Front: Dr Hassan El Turabi
National Unionist Party: Abdel Latif El Khalifa
People's Democratic Party (Withdrew: 20-7-1965)
Professional Front: Sayed Abdalla El Sayed
SANU : William Deng
Andrew Wieu
Ambrose Wol
Sudan Communist Party (Withdrew: 19-8-1965)
Southern Front: Hilary P. logali
Abel Alier
Lobari Ramba
Umma Party: Mohammed Dawood El Khalifa.

APPENDIX 4

Policy Statement on the Southern Question, 9 June 1969

Delivered by Major General Jaafar Mohammed Nimeiri,
Chairman of the Revolutionary Command Council.

Dear Countrymen,

Warm congratulations and greetings to you on this historic occasion of your revolution.

No doubt you have heard of the broad aims of the revolution outlined in my speech and in that of the Prime Minister which was broadcast on 25 May. Our revolution is the continuation of the October 21 popular revolution. It works for the regeneration of life in our country, for social progress and the raising of the standard of living of the masses of our people throughout the country. It stands against imperialism, colonialism and wholeheartedly supports the liberation movements of the African and Arab peoples as well as other peoples throughout the world.

A Historical Background

Dear Countrymen,

The revolutionary Government is fully aware of the magnitude of the Southern problem and is determined to arrive at a lasting solution.

This problem has deep-going historical roots dating back to the last century. It is the result of the policies of British Colonialism which left the legacy of uneven development between the Northern and Southern parts of the country, with the result that on the advent of independence Southerners found themselves in an unequal position with their Northern brethren in every field.

The traditional circles and parties that have held the reins of power in our country since independence have utterly failed to solve the Southern question. They have exploited state power for self-enrichment and for serving narrow partisan interests without caring about the interests of the masses of our people whether in the North or in the South.

It is important to realise also that most of the Southern leaders contributed a great deal of the present deterioration of the state of affairs in that part of our beloved country. Over the years, since 1950 to the present day they have sought alliances with the Northern reactionary circles and with imperialism whether from inside or outside the borders. Personal gain was the mainspring of their actions.

Dear Countrymen,

The enemies of the North are also the enemies of the South. The common enemy is imperialism and neo-colonialism, which is oppressing and exploiting the African and Arab peoples, and standing in the way of their advance. Internally, our common enemies are the reactionary forces of counter-revolution. The 25 May Revolution is not the same as the *coup d'etat* of November 1958. That was a reactionary move staged by the imperialists in alliance with local reaction in and outside of the army. It was made to silence the demands of the masses of our people both in the North and the South for social change and genuine democracy.

The Revolution of May 25 is the very opposite of the coup *d'etat* of 1958. Our revolution is, we repeat, directed against imperialism, the reactionary circles and corrupt parties that destroyed the October Revolution and were aiming at finally liquidating any progressive movement and installing a reactionary dictatorship.

Dear Countrymen,

The revolutionary Government is confident and competent enough to face existing realities. It recognizes the historical and cultural differences between the North and South and firmly believes that the unity of our country must be built upon these objective realities. The Southern people have the right to develop their respective cultures and traditions within a united Socialist Sudan.

In furtherance of these objectives the Revolutionary Council and the Council of Ministers held joint meetings and after a full discussion of the matter resolved to recognize the right of the Southern people to Regional Autonomy within a united Sudan.

Regional Autonomy Programme

You will realise that the building of a broad socialist-oriented democratic movement in the South, forming part of the revolutionary structure in the North and capable of assuming the reins of power in that region and rebuffing imperialist penetration and infiltration from the rear, is an essential pre-requisite for the practical and healthy application of Regional Autonomy.

Within this framework and in order to prepare for that day when this right can be exercised, the Revolutionary Government is drawing up the following programme:

1.   The continuation and further extension of the Amnesty Law;
2.   Economic, social and cultural development of the South;
3.   The appointment of a Minister for Southern Affairs;
4.   The training of personnel.

The Government will create a special economic planning board for the South and will prepare a special budget for the South, which aims at the development of the Southern provinces at the shortest possible time.

Dear Southern Countrymen,

In order that we may be able to carry out this programme it is of the utmost importance that peace and security should prevail in the South and that life returns to normal. It is primarily the responsibility of you all whether you be in the bush or at home to maintain peace and stability. The way is open for those abroad to return home and co-operate with us in building a prosperous Sudan, united and democratic.

Bibliography

Abd al-Rahim, M., *Imperialism and Nationalism in the Sudan: A study in Constitutional and Political Development, 1899 - 1956*, Oxford: Clarendon, 1969.

Akol, Lam, *South Sudan: From Colonial Neglect to National Misrule,* London: Gilgamesh, 2009.

Albino B. Oliver, *The Sudan: a Southern Viewpoint,* London: oxford University Press, 1970.

Alier, Abel, *Too Many Agreements Dishonoured: Southern Sudan*, Khartoum: Abel Alier, 2nd reprint, 2003.

Beshir, M.O., *The Southern Sudan, Background to Conflict*, London: Praeger, 1968.

Deng, Francis Mading, *Tradition and Modernization, A Challenge for Law among the Dinka of the Sudan*, New Haven: Yale University Press, 1971.

Ga'le, S.F.B.T., *Shaping a Free Southern Sudan*, Nairobi: Paulines Africa, 2002.

Henderson, K.D.D., *Sudan Republic*, London: Ernest Benn, 1965.

Holt, P.M., *A Modern History of the Sudan*, London: Weidenfeld and Nicolson, 1963.

Lagu, Joseph, *Sudan: Odyssey Through A State From Ruin to Hope*, MOB Centre for Sudanese Studies, Omdurman Ahlia University, 2006.

Magaya, M.A., *The Anyanya Movement in South Sudan, 1962-1972*, Kisubi: Marianum Press, 2014.

Malwal, Bona, *Sudan and South Sudan: From One to Two*, Basingstoke: Palgrave Macmillan, 2015.

Mbali, Alexis, *The Nile Turns Red*, New York, 1967.

Norman, Daniel, "The Sudan", in *Islam in Africa*, Kritseck and Lewis (eds.), New York 1969.

Oduho, J. and W. Deng, *The Problem of the Southern Sudan*, London: Oxford University Press, 1963.

Poggo, Scopas S., *The First Sudanese Civil War: African, Arabs and Israelis in the Southern Sudan, 1955 – 1972*, New York: Palgrave Macmillan, 2009.

Shibeika, M., *The Independent Sudan*, New York 1959.

Report of the Commission of Inquiry .into the Disturbances in the Southern Sudan during August, 1955, Khartoum 1956.

Index